IGOR REN1
A Town Called

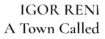

Igor Rendić
A Town Called River

Book one of A Town Called River

Edited by
Antonija Mežnarić and Vesna Kurilić

Cover by
Korina Hunjak

Paperback typesetting by
Tamara Crnković

Copyright ©2021 by Igor Rendić
This edition copyright ©2021 by Shtriga

ISBN
ebook 9789538360145
paperback 9789538360169

shtriga.com
shtrigabooks@gmail.com

Rijeka, 2021.

The publication of this book has been funded by the City of Rijeka.

 Grad Rijeka

Igor Rendić

A TOWN CALLED RIVER

Rijeka, 2021.

TABLE OF CONTENTS

Dedicated to my nona.
She wasn't a krsnik, but she didn't need magic to be awesome.

STEP BEHIND
A CURTAIN...

Rijeka literally means 'river' in everyday Croatian. Growing up, it never seemed strange to me—only after we moved, and I was surrounded by other languages on a daily basis, did I realize it was like naming a town Forest or Hill without using an old-timey word to do it.

But it doesn't stop there. Rijeka is called that because one of its main geographical features is, you guessed it, a river that runs through it. They named it Rječina, which is, I am dead serious, an augmentative form of 'river' in Croatian. So you have a town called River and the Big River river passing through it.

And the river isn't even that big...

I stood waiting in front of my grandma's apartment, and also hoping the damn headache would finally go away. It had been following me for the last two days, an occasional dull stab in my temples and behind my eyes, more annoying than genuinely painful. Sometimes it would be accompanied by lights suddenly being too bright and sounds too loud.

The lawyer's email had said Mrs. Kovač, my nona's next door neighbor, would be bringing the key. I could vaguely recall Mrs. Kovač's face and voice, a dim memory from childhood that was more an impression than a clear image. But there was a bit that wasn't dim at all: every time I'd pass by her door when I was a kid, it always smelled like freshly baked cakes inside. There was no smell coming from behind that door now, just like there was no faint scent of lavender seeping from under grandma's.

I kept wondering what the apartment would look like, what had changed during the past two decades.

There was that pang in my gut again. Guilt.

But there's nothing to be done about that, I thought. My mind went to my checklist: go to the apartment. Meet Mrs. Kovač. Get the key. Visit the grave. Meet the lawyer in two days; find out what grandma's last will and testament is. Sort things out if needed. Go back home.

I knocked on Mrs. Kovač's door again. As I did, my left ear popped and there was a squealing, hissing sound that made me close my eyes in pain as the headache stabbed at my temples again.

"Fucking hell," I growled.

A deep breath or two later both the pain and the sound faded away. I was grateful that, when my right ear had popped almost immediately after coming off the plane at the Krk airport, there was no pain.

I shook my head to clear it. The email had said noon, so I guessed she went out and got held up. Or maybe she'd forgotten?

Footsteps echoed up the stairwell. Stone steps well over a century old, just like the building itself. I leaned over the iron-and-wood railing and—it wasn't Mrs. Kovač. This was a woman around my age. She looked up at me as she was climbing the stairs and after a moment's silence she smiled. "I wondered if I'd recognize you."

I blinked. "I'm sorry, I—"

She ran up the final few steps, stopped in front of me, and shook my hand. "*Pavle, zaboravio si me?*" she asked.

I looked at her: she was shorter than me by half a head, maybe, with dark blonde hair in a messy bun at the back of her head, one of those hair chopstick thingies sticking out of it. Did I forget her? I wondered how she knew me, how she knew my old name—that is, the Croatian version of my name, Paul. And then there she was, only now a child, with much shorter hair, several gaps in her smile and a lankier build.

"Katrina?"

She nodded, her brown eyes glowing with delight at my words. Katrina Kovač, whom I used to play with in the courtyard while staying at grandma's on the weekends. Whom I'd gotten into more than one fight with—literally, punching and wrestling and cursing and bruising and scratching. And whom I also enjoyed hanging around with a lot so, so long ago.

"Wow," she said, sizing me up. "You've grown." She smiled wistfully. "I remember when I was taller than you."

"That was by a centimeter, maybe," I said, suddenly and vividly recalling the two of us and a couple of other kids from the building marking our height against an old wooden plank we'd found in the courtyard and placed up against a wall.

"Yeah, my glory days, apparently," she said. "What are you, one ninety?"

I shook my head. "Good god, no. You're off by ten."

"*Znaš još uvijek hrvatski?*" she asked then. I was expecting it. I was anxious about it. *Can you still speak Croatian?*

I grinned uncomfortably. "I can still understand most of it when spoken or read. Well, spoken slowly and clearly. But I—I haven't spoken it regularly for... a long time." A very long time.

"So you'd rather not try?" she asked, grinning and teasing. "*Daj, koliko loše može biti?*"

How bad could it be? I was thinking it could be really bad.

"*Jako loše, mislim. Znam riječi ali se bojim se gramatika i sintaksa i sve ostalo su jako loše.*"

She blinked. "Wow, that wasn't nearly as bad as I'd expected," she said. "You used all the right words in almost all the right ways. Your accent is wonky but that's okay, I guess."

"Points for trying?"

She made a face but then grinned wryly. Some things obviously didn't change despite decades passing; her character, for example. "So you go by Paul now?"

I nodded. "Yes, it was easier to use that version of the name."

"See, my mom and dad were smart, gave me an internationally pronounceable name right from the start."

Then her face fell because we both remembered why we were here.

"I'm very sorry for your loss," Katrina said, smiling kindly and sadly. She reached out and touched me on the forearm gently, with just a hint of awkwardness.

"Thank you," I said, echoing the awkwardness of her touch. I am *not* good at small talk or at talking when I'm uncomfortable, and uncomfortable I definitely was.

The silence lasted probably only for a couple of seconds, instead of what felt like an hour before she said, "I've got the keys." She dug them out of her pocket and offered them to me.

I took them, unlocked the door, feeling awkward because muscle memory took over but at the same time I was way taller now than when I used to unlock it on my own regularly.

My head was pulsing, somewhere in the back. I ignored it.

And then we were inside, and I was reaching for the switch on the wall to the left that was still there. The light revealed the same hallway and doors of the same color and the stone floor still dark. But it felt empty and my throat tightened as something gently squeezed my temples for a moment or two and then let go.

"Hey, you okay?" Katrina asked, her hand on my shoulder.

I turned and nodded. "Yes, I—I'll be fine." I looked at the door at the end of the hallway. "I need to use the toilet."

"Sure," she said. "Do you—do you want me to leave? Or wait outside?"

I turned. "No," I said. "I—I'd like to see her grave. I can come back here later. Is that okay? I mean, I know where the graveyard is, but if you could take me to the grave because I think I've forgotten where it is?"

She nodded, smiling. "Of course. I'll wait for you outside."

She left me alone in the hallway. It was just as I remembered it from... too long ago. My gut clenched, my mouth suddenly dry. My heart pulsed, almost synced up with the dull headache at the back of my skull.

I was in the L-shaped hallway that all the various rooms of the apartment opened onto. Each door was just as I remembered, the cold stone floor was as I remembered—but nothing smelled like it should. There was no smell of cooking, no scent of fresh bread or baked potatoes or pizza right out the oven. Just still, empty air.

I stood there for just a moment, thinking tears might come—but they didn't. I walked to the tiny toilet at the very end of the longer section of the hallway, did my business there, washed my hands in the much larger bathroom next to it and left the apartment, imagining check marks.

We left Croatia almost immediately after the war ended. Rijeka had been lucky in the early 90s. Yugoslavia falling apart meant a lot of suffering and fear and death for many. I'd had several refugee kids in my class in elementary school, some from Croatia, some from Bosnia. For the most part, they fit in, as much as they could. I'd made friends with several. Some of them stayed for years, others would be here today and gone the next day, to relatives and family friends outside Croatia, sometimes with their parents, sometimes not. The internet and cell phones were the stuff of American movies and having pen pals was something that my generation had never really gotten into. It was an early life lesson: people come into each other's lives, people leave; people move on.

I stood under the warm sun, looking at my grandparents' grave. The photo they'd used for the headstone was of a woman older than I remembered but still healthy-looking. Heart attack, they'd said; in her sleep. She hadn't suffered. It was a mercy for which I was grateful.

Below her image and name were those of my grandfather. The raised letters of his name were weathered, in stark contrast with my grandmother's. Decades that separated their deaths were obvious even without looking at the dates.

He'd passed away in the early nineties, during the only summer I ever went to a language school instead of spending the summer break at my grandparents'. By the time I'd returned to Rijeka, they had already buried him.

His photo was of the man I still remembered him as: warm eyes; slim, angular face with the square jaw of a film star. In another stark contrast, the face in nona's photo was so much older than the image of her in my mind. And yet, it was still undeniably her: the bright eyes, corners of lips always hinting at a smile. In my memories she was always smiling, even when she was cross with me—sometimes especially then. I'd sometimes do the same but had never seen my mom do it—it must have been a family trait that had skipped a generation.

And now, looking at those photos, memories came unbidden from the depths of my mind but, thankfully, not the painful ones. When I was a kid, people—mostly grandma's female friends—would tell me how much I resembled her. The eyes, they'd say. I had no idea what they were talking about. To a kid, eyes are just eyes.

But now, looking at the photos of grandma and grandpa—yes, I had her eyes, definitely. The photo was black and white, so there was no way to tell nona's eyes had been blue, but I'd inherited them—and not just the color. Looking at the photo, my gaze focused on her eyes and there was something about their shape and the look in them...

I have my nona's eyes, and while we're at it, definitely grandpa's chin and jawline, even though my face is wider than his. I noticed now that mom had, funnily enough, inherited the opposite of me: she had grandpa's—well, her dad's—eyes, large and brown, and her mother's gently rounded chin.

I pulled myself back to the now and the graveyard. The headache had, once again, been gone for some minutes, and I enjoyed the reprieve because... well, I'd felt shitty enough already.

I raised my eyes from the headstone. Several rows forward, a small funeral was taking place. Just a dozen or so mourners, all in black, heads bowed. Young people, I realized, younger than me. A friend? And then I noticed the coffin. Small. The size a coffin should never need to be. A woman was at the front, sobbing, shaking, and as they began to lower the coffin, she let it all out. Her wail pierced my ears, and the headache stabbed me in the back of the head. I closed my eyes, willing it to go away, and the pain faded. The woman was still wailing but had obviously been sapped by the pain because it was so much quieter than just a moment before.

I noticed another person there, then, standing some meters away from the mourners. Something was wrong. It was a bearded man in a short, dark blue coat, with a cap on his head. Was it a man, though? The person was tall, slim, but something was off with the body, the face as well; even though they were too far away to make out the details my gut was telling me something was wrong, so wrong and—

The pain again, stabbing behind my eyes. I gritted my teeth, took a deep breath. When I looked again, there were just the mourners, the coffin now lowered into the ground. There was no tall man in a short coat there.

I hadn't slept properly in at least two days, what with travel arrangements and my insomnia making a comeback, and all my grief and guilt messing with my head. There had been no strange man—well no, there must have been someone visiting a grave there, but there was nothing strange about him. Just like there had been no dark, coiling shapes in the clouds we flew through yesterday; just like there had been no statues moving in the half-dark of the park outside my apartment building when I left it for the airport.

When I turned, Katrina was still there, a respectful couple of steps away, looking at the gravestone. I was either very subtle in my pain, or she thought it was just grief. She seemed sad—sadder than I'd expected her to be, I realized. She looked the way I felt and then some, actually.

"Paul, you okay?" she asked me, smiling softly through glistening eyes.

I nodded, finally realizing exactly how I felt, how I had been feeling ever since receiving the news of nona's death: sad but... at a remove.

"My mom kept up a correspondence," I said. "But, well, it's letters, it's not direct contact. You... drift apart. I know it sounds horrible, but it's just how it goes. We had plans to visit but long distance travel was expensive and there was always something more urgent to spend money on." I paused, shaking my head lightly. "The same way I wanted to keep in touch with you. And then you look at the calendar and it's been twenty years and more, and you have to travel to Croatia because there's a funeral and there's the will and your parents can't travel because of health reasons, so you have to do it all alone."

She put her hand on my shoulder. "Yeah, it sucks."

I chuckled. "Yep."

We left the graveyard in silence, the gravel crunching softly under our feet as we passed rows of weathered gravestones, cypresses and the occasional palm tree—which is something that always seemed so weird to me when I was a kid, visiting my great-grandparents' grave with grandma. And there were also the cats—quite a lot of them. They had no collars, so I guessed they were strays, but they all seemed well-fed and weren't mangy or one-eyed. Probably cared for by local grannies, I guessed, a time-honored Rijeka tradition.

The silence, not unpleasant, continued as we started downhill, back towards nona's apartment building, when a smell stopped me dead in my tracks. It was coming from a bakery we'd just passed and it was a siren call from the past. I turned to look at the shop, its open door inviting.

"A taste of home?" Katrina asked with a grin.

Inside, the smells swirled and melted into one another, a symphony of fresh pastry and powdered sugar and cinnamon and nuts and poppy and cheese. And there it was, in a round pan, on the other side of the glass: *burek*.

I ordered one, then turned around to ask Katrina if she'd join me, and she simply said, "I never say no to a free burek," and moments later we were outside again, and my burek, wrapped in butcher paper, was an intense but pleasant heat against my fingers.

It's a simple thing, really, stacked layers of thin pastry filled with cheese and stuck in the oven until they become this wedge of delight you need two hands to hold and eat with. There are many kinds, with meat and apple and, well, pretty much anything you care to fill it with (and depending on which part of the Balkans you're in, discussions on what is and isn't a proper burek can get quite heated), and when it's okay, it's okay but when it's great, it's divine. I unwrapped one end and started blowing on it, pure muscle memory from decades ago.

Before I took that first bite, the smell hijacked my brain again, barreling me straight back into the 90s. After a moment, I glanced at Katrina and saw her smiling.

"It smells as good as I remember," I said, as my salivary glands prepared to jump into overdrive. I finally bit into it and there was a brief pang of pain as the glands kicked in hard, and the tongue and the roof of my mouth complained about the hot cheese, and I chewed with my mouth open, huffing. It was divine. The crunch and the soft, melted cheese and, gods and saints, I could have spent a week eating nothing but this.

"You're okay staying here?" Katrina asked when we'd returned to the apartment.

"Yeah, sure," I said.

"A lot of people aren't okay sleeping in a place where someone died recently."

"Well, if her body were still there, yes, but I think I'm okay if the apartment is empty. She, uh, died in the bed, right? Not on the couch?"

She smiled. "Couch is safe to sleep on, yes."

"Good." I smiled back, but also felt incredibly tired all of a sudden. The headache was gone, but the lack of a full night's rest seemed ready to come down on me like a ton of bricks. "Look, I'd thought about asking you to accompany me to dinner or a drink later, but I think I'll fall asleep the moment I sit down. Jet lag is a bitch."

She nodded. "I understand perfectly. You go rest. Send me a message tomorrow if you like, I can take you to lunch somewhere."

"That sounds awesome," I said.

And with that she turned and went down the steps. I listened to her steady footsteps clack away against the stone as I unlocked the door and went inside.

So here's the thing. I was dead tired. But I couldn't fall asleep. After tossing and turning on the couch for a full hour, I finally gave up and started wandering around the apartment. It felt strange only for a few minutes, until the sensation that I was going through a stranger's things passed. Because I wasn't. This was grandma's apartment, grandma's things, and most of them were still where I remembered them.

Some things, though, were new and, well, unusual. The kitchen cupboards were full of food and spices and cooking ingredients, but there were also several ones full of bottles, with liquids of various colors. Each was labeled, but the handwriting was cursive and more scrawls than letters. Alcohol? I opened one of the bottles at the front, chosen at random, and my eyes immediately watered. An expression from my childhood came back to me, something grandpa used to say. *Prozoruša*. Homemade brandy that should really be used for window cleaning only.

Those bottles weren't the only unusual sight: there were also bits and lumps of stuff that smelled strange, roots and powders, as well as other colorful things that mostly resembled those large salt crystals I was used to seeing in hipster kitchens, but not so much in old ladies'. I'd seen, smelled and tasted my share of spices and herbs during the years when we never spent more than six months in the same country, but most of these were, at least at a glance, completely new to me.

Sort through it later, I told myself.

What for? I'll probably have to toss it all out.

Nona's unusual kitchen aside, there were other things around the apartment that would make me pause, but it was to stare at them with a lump in my throat. Clothes in the laundry basket, the smell just a little musty. A full washing machine, closed and set to wash but never turned on. A crossword magazine on the nightstand by the double bed, opened on a huge sudoku, half-finished.

For her it had been a day like any other.

The apartment was bigger than I remembered. I had, at first, thought it just seemed big because I'd been little back then. But after spending college years in small apartments in relatively new buildings, I had forgotten how big these old-timey apartments in Rijeka could be. The square footage of the living room/kitchen alone was bigger than some apartments I lived in while in college, *with roommates*.

I had no idea what to suggest to my parents that we do with the apartment, if grandma did, in the end, leave it to us. Do we sell it? Do we rent it out? I could maybe ask Katrina to be our intermediary, if we decided the latter. Short-term rentals were a huge thing right now and, this close to town center, it would probably get booked a lot, especially during summer...

But those were all things that would just complicate my life. You can't run a rental from another country. Okay, maybe you can, but I wasn't willing to put up with the hassle.

No, it would probably be sold. And all these things with it, or they'd just get thrown out.

On my way to the bathroom, I stopped in the long and narrow hallway with a high ceiling, my gut suddenly twisting in knots. Throwing everything in the trash, all the stuff grandma and grandpa had collected, which carried their invisible mark... god.

And then the tears finally came, in a slow, steady trickle. I pressed my head against the wall, closed my eyes and sobbed—at first softly, then out loud, once I'd told myself there was no one to disturb.

I cried, but not because grandma died. I cried because she'd lived for decades after we left, and in all that time I'd written her just a couple of letters, long ago, and talked to her over the phone a few times while in high school. I'd always planned on calling, writing... but tomorrow. Or next week. Soon.

It's always tomorrow until there's no tomorrow.

I wiped my eyes, took a deep breath. "I'm sorry," I said aloud. There was no one to hear.

I stood there, taking it all in. Were things still as I remembered them behind all the doors? The kitchen and the living room were pretty much the same, as well as the main bedroom they led into. The bathroom was the same, even though nona had at some point replaced the gas boiler that used to terrify me as a kid with an electric one. The toilet was the same as well, down to the hideous burgundy color of its walls and the ancient, wood-framed window looking out onto the inner courtyard.

There were two other doors I still hadn't opened since coming back. The one to my left as I looked down the corridor, was the door to what had long ago been my mom's room. It was also where I'd sleep and play while staying here on the weekends and during school breaks.

And the other, to my right, led into what had once, in my mother's youth, been a pantry, but had at some point been converted into a sort of general storage space. I opened the door, turned on the light—a bare bulb, hanging from a wire—and although the air was musty and the room cramped with brooms and cardboard boxes and stacks of bottles, I stepped in without thinking. I used to come in here when I was a kid, too. There were ladders here, leaning against the wall, and I would bring a book or comics and place them, open, on one of the ladder steps to read standing there, under the bare bulb.

Grandma would sometimes grumble about there not being enough air, but she never forbade it to me. Grandpa would ask what was wrong with reading in the living room, but it was nice here, quiet, and the small space felt kinda snug. The ceiling was as high as in the rest of the apartment, but the room was not very wide or long.

As I looked around, it felt more like a coffin stood up on its end than a room. What was I doing in there, with the door closed, the bulb shining its harsh yellow light over things that probably hadn't been moved in years, possibly decades? I should go back to the living room. Try to get some sleep and then, tomorrow, hopefully start sorting everything out so I can get on an airplane soon and leave.

And then I saw it: a book, stuck inside an empty, plastic beer crate. I leaned forward, pulled it out. It was a paperback, ancient; some science fiction novel from the sixties, yellow pages, brittle and coarse under my fingertips. The price tag from a second-hand bookshop slapped carelessly across the cover. I must have stuck it there for later the last time I was in here. It seemed like something I would do.

I felt it then, a slight breeze across my hand.

There was no way I could feel a draft in here.

And yet, there it was. And again.

I removed the crate, reached towards the wall behind it—yes, the draft was coming from that direction. From the bare surface of the wall.

What the... The crate had been resting on a small, wheeled cupboard, and now I rolled it out of the way. I stood in front of that bare section of the wall, another wall to my right, a tall stack of wooden boxes to my left. I felt the draft on my face, soft, cool.

I reached for the wall, just under half a meter away, feeling ridiculous, wondering if I were actually on the living room couch, and this was all just a very vivid dream. This was only a wall, for god's sake. I knew it was just a wall. There, at the height of a little over a meter were the lines I'd scribbled when I was five or six and was left to wander the apartment without supervision with a crayon in my hand.

The wall buckled under my touch. Only it wasn't a wall anymore, it was a curtain, the color of the wall, *patterned* like the wall and with the crayon marks still on it. The curtain was swaying from my touch ever so gently, covering a rectangular opening just about my width and a little over my height.

A hidden door.

I pulled the curtain to the side and a soft yellow light fell on me through the opening.

THE IMPOSSIBLE ROOM

It was a room with a table in the middle, covered in papers and books and notebooks. The leather swivel chair on the other side of the table had a knit sweater thrown over its back. Several large and in places dented metal cabinets with drawers lined the walls on both sides and there were cupboards and shelves as well. The floor was covered in a thick, dark red carpet that seemed ancient.

I realized that I'd entered the room only after the fact. A small glass chandelier hung from the ceiling, a perfect orb of milk-white glass.

But my attention was mostly on the table. The layer of dead tree matter on it was about half a meter tall, at least; like the contents of an entire used book store had been dumped there.

I approached it, slowly taking the room in. It was warm and pleasant and not at all stuffy, even though, by all rights, it should have been.

I felt a buzz in my fingertips, in my gut, in my neck and my temples, and the buzz was growing stronger the closer I got to the table.

In all that mess of pieces of paper and pages and notes, something drew my attention. It was either a book or a very large notebook, and it seemed handmade, its cover coarse leather and the pages inside neither of uniform size nor quality of paper, when I took it in my hands and leafed through it. It was also full of various other bits of paper stuck between the pages, some of them scraps of torn paper with notes, others cutouts from papers and maga-zines. I opened it at a random page and saw a detailed illustration of some kind of plant, hand drawn in ink, with something that looked like a bullet-point recipe in the lower left corner. Another random opening and there was a list of names with markings next to each. I turned the page and saw a map of Rijeka, but some old version of it, huge chunks of the town missing; there were thick lines of various colors drawn across the map, straight lines and swirls and irregular circles.

I closed the book—it was too big and thick for a notebook, I decided, so it was a book—and started browsing the rest of the huge pile. In fact, just next to the book was an open folder with several large sheets of paper covered in notes.

The notes were copious, to say the least. Scribbled in the mar-gins in neat handwriting, written on bits of paper attached with paperclips and sometimes jotted down over a sheet's content, such as a large photo captioned as a member of the town council, with a huge 'LAŽE K'O PAS' written in black marker across his fore-head. I smiled at the phrase, which was nona's favorite: literally 'lies like a dog', i.e. 'lying bastard.'

I took the sweater from the back of the chair. Soft, hand-knit-ted. Faint scent of lavender. Nona's perfume. I brought it to my face, breathed it in gently. Fought back a sob and tears and placed the sweater, gently, on the table.

This was all too much and my eyes suddenly hurt and some-thing keened in my ears. I sat in the chair, massaging my temples, eyes closed.

When I opened my eyes, the room was still there. I turned around slowly in the chair, taking it all in. It was like a madman's lair, wasn't it? I glanced at the table, noticing dozens of cutouts from newspapers and magazines.

The only thing missing is a cork board showing how it all con-nects into a conspiracy.

But it's not a madman's lair. It's nona's. And also, it shouldn't exist.

I returned my attention to the leather-bound book and saw something between the front cover and the first page. It was an envelope. Inside was a letter.

I knew the handwriting.

Moj najdraži unuče, it said. My dearest grandson. It had been our silly joke. I was her only grandson.

Ako ovo čitaš, nona je otišla Svetom Petru na račun. If you're reading this, then grandma is off to meet St. Peter.

Ne da vjerujem u njega, ali netko to od gore vidi sve, to oduvijek znam. Not that I believe in him, but I've always known there's someone up there, watching.

Sve ovo što si našao ovdje je istina. Nona ti je bila svašta, ali luda ne. All that you've found here is true. Your grandma was many things, but crazy was not one of them.

Sinko, imam ove moći od djetinjstva. Sonny, I've had these powers since childhood.

Sad su tvoje i žao mi je što ćeš toliko toga morati sam pohvatati, ali nažalost nisam bila u prilici pripremiti te. Ali ne sumnjam da ćeš se snaći. A imat ćeš i pomoć. Slušaj Katrinu, vjeruj joj. Ali vjeruj i u sebe. These powers are yours now, and I'm so sorry you'll have to figure out so much out on your own, but unfortunately I didn't have the chance to prepare you. But I have no doubt you'll figure it out. And you'll have help. Listen to Katrina, trust her. But trust yourself as well.

So nona was a—a what? What powers? The hell was going on? I looked back at the doorway, then around a room that... Well, that couldn't really exist, could it? The fact had been nagging at me, but the room itself and the table and the book had been a distraction.

On the other side of the wall, where the hidden doorway was, there should have been just the building's hallway. Where I was sitting now—I should have been on the steps. Floating above them, actually.

Bigger on the inside, I thought. *Not by much, but still...*

How the hell do you process something like that? The room, the letter, the implications.

Well, in my case you process it by staring dumbly at the letter and the book and then thinking *it's real but it can't be but it is.* Followed by cold fingers running up and down your spine and an internal Fuck.

I set the letter on the table, next to the book.

I took a deep breath, and then picked the book back up.

Grandma's handwriting stared back at me from the pages. My gut clenched a little and a tiny needle jabbed into my heart. I closed the book, held it firmly against my chest, eyes closed.

I felt so incredibly tired. I leaned forward, let my forehead press against the sweater. The gentle scent of lavender was a soothing touch on my very soul. I could almost imagine nona was here, next to me, about to say something, touch my shoulder.

And, against all good and common sense, I fell asleep.

I was running down the middle of a wide street. It was day and the sun was high in the sky and it was the bluest sky I'd ever seen. The road was in Rijeka, only not really, because it was next to the ocean and not the sea, and there was a school right to my left with a grassy hilltop instead of a gymnasium.

I stopped running. There was a door up ahead. In the middle of the road there was a door, large and red, and even though I was meters and meters away I could see the pattern on it. It wasn't wood, even though it felt like it should have been. It was deep red. It was carved, its surface all triangles and squares. The surface was, also, uneven, or maybe it was undulating like water.

I had to go through that door.

It was the last thing I wanted to do.

I turned and ran but it was always there, up ahead.

SEAFOOD WITH A SIDE OF MONSTER TALES

I woke up on the floor. At some point I'd obviously slid out of the chair and down onto the thick red carpet. Soft, soft carpet, I realized, impressed. I gently turned on my back, stretched lazily—and then finally remembered where I was.

I sat up fast, glanced around. The room was still around me, still impossible. The book was next to me. I gazed at it, took it into my hands to make sure it was real. Then I remembered why I was awake. I could hear a noise from my childhood: the apartment doorbell.

I looked at my watch, cursed softly, jumped to my feet and ran out of the room.

"Uh," I said as I opened the apartment door, "I'm sorry. I was asleep, didn't hear you ring the bell right away."

"No prob—" Katrina started saying as she stepped past me into the apartment, and then stopped short. She was staring at something. Was my fly undone?

I looked down and the book was still in my hand.

"Oh thank god, you found it," she said with a sigh of relief.

I blinked. "Uh, found—"

She nodded. "Yes, that."

"No, what—How did you—Wait. You know."

"Yes," she said.

I blinked again. "*How* did you know?"

"Lena helped me when I was a teenager." She paused. "This was a few years after you left. They wanted to send me off for treatments. Claimed I was batshit crazy. *Luda k'o kupus.* I had hallucinations; heard voices. Waking nightmares, almost. Saw dead people everywhere. Your grandma was the only one who didn't think I was insane." She looked at me firmly. "I wasn't. I *was* seeing dead people."

It took me a moment. "Ghosts? You were seeing ghosts?"

She took a breath. "She gave me something that temporarily blocked it, just long enough for me to calm down so they wouldn't send me to the nuthouse. Then she gave me a crash course during a single night. God, it was ridiculously hot, middle of July. She told me to sneak out of the apartment, meet her at the graveyard. By the time dawn came, I could deal with the voices and the sights. I could tell which people were real and which were, well, the ones only I could see and hear."

"Uh," I said then, "maybe we should sit down."

I took her into the kitchen and there was this brief silence as I made us some Cedevita, which had been another blast from the past, waiting for me in the cupboard. The powder was still as yellow as I remembered and the taste of the drink, after adding water, was still like fake lemon, only better. Some things hadn't changed. I was very grateful for that right now.

We sat and drank and just looked at each other. We had known each other long ago. Had been friends. But that was so long ago. And obviously, in all these years, she had changed even more than I could ever have guessed.

And yet: *trust her*, the letter had said.

The letter. The book. The *room*.

"So she was a witch." I finally said. "*Štriga.*"

Katrina very visibly tensed.

"What?" I asked.

"She—oh, she wouldn't like you saying that."

"No?"

"She wasn't that. A štriga does black magic, evil stuff. Your grandma bashed in the heads of a couple of them in her day, apparently."

"Literally or...?" I asked without thinking.

Katrina paused. "You know, I always thought she meant figuratively, but now that you mention it..."

"Well, she did box when she was in college." I chuckled, trying to distract myself. "So, just a witch, then?" As if *that* were a normal thing to be.

Katrina shook her head. "A krsnik," she said. "Well, *krsnica*, but they actually don't really care about the—oh, what's the word—masculine and feminine forms. In fact, she'd said that she preferred people thinking krsniks were just men. Said female krsniks had been using it to their advantage, flying under the radar."

Krsnik. I remembered that word, very dimly. Stories my grandma used to tell me: stories about them fighting *štriguns* and vampires and werewolves; stories about all kinds of supernatural creatures. Made up stories about made up things. About stuff that wasn't real.

This was a ridiculous conversation. Absolutely bonkers and—

"I know," she said and I stared at her for a moment.

Can—can you read minds? I thought, stunned.

"I'm not a mind reader," she said, shrugging, "but from the look on your face I guessed you were thinking this whole thing was nuts, right?"

"Uh, yeah." I glanced at the book on the table, next to my glass. "So... the letter said... am I a krsnik as well?"

"Yes," Katrina said. "Paul, she said you'd become one," she added quickly. "After she died."

"After she..."

"The way she explained it to me, it's—well, it's, er, *hereditary*. Like a title. A mantle, which is a *great* word in English. She told me that there are many ways a person can become a krsnik. Some are born that way, others inherit the powers. Your family is the kind that passes powers from one member to another upon death. She wasn't sure it'd be you, you know? She said the chances were great, but still..."

"Who would it have been then?" I asked, genuinely interested.

"Your mother. I had a letter I was supposed to put into the book if it was her. Or the mantle would wait for you to have kids."

"*Wait?*"

"Apparently," Katrina said, shrugging. "Look, I'm not an expert. It's probably in the book."

"But what—What am I supposed to—How do I—"

"I have no idea. I'm not a krsnik. She asked that I help you out and that you help me in return."

"Help you with what?"

"General supernatural affairs, I guess?"

We sat there, information stacking and stacking inside me without me really processing any of it.

"You see and hear dead people," I said because I had to say something.

"Often," she said.

I nodded, went to take a sip, stopped. "Wait. Do—do you see her? Can you hear her?"

She shook her head sadly. "No. Most people, they—they move on right after death. Just a few stay behind. Luckily for me, honestly."

"So she didn't stay."

"No."

"Unfinished business? But that room... You'd think she had unfinished business, all those maps and stuff..."

"I think... she knew her business wouldn't stay unfinished," Katrina said, looking at me.

I suddenly felt both hot and cold and I could swear there was a huge lizard running its slimy legs up and down my back.

"Would you like something stronger?" Katrina asked, getting up from the table.

"Um..." was all I said.

She opened a cupboard, took out two shot glasses, found a small plastic bottle in another cupboard. This I knew was alcohol just by looking at it: the bottle was orange, the cap was blue—and in the Balkans, an unmatched bottle and cap were always a sure sign the liquid inside was probably some kind of *rakija*, homemade brandy.

It tasted horrible, just as it smelled. I downed two shots. Then I looked at Katrina. "What am I supposed to do?"

She raised her hands. "Ask me something easier." She smiled. "But I think you should let me take you out to lunch."

So I did. But first I took a shower—a long, hot shower, hoping it would either clear my mind or that I would wake up again, this time for real. I'd been fully awake since Katrina rang the doorbell, but the shower did help a little with the clutter in my head, at least in the sense of allowing me to heap things into piles, giving me some maneuvering space.

Point: the room was real. It was still impossible, but it was real.

Point: if the room was real, then magic—well, *something* that might as well be called magic—was real.

Point: my grandma was magic. A krsnik. Who, I could dimly recall, was supposed to be something like monster slayer and magician all bundled into one, except not really—point was, grandma had been magic.

Aaaaand point... I was magic as well, or so she claimed in her letter. Otherwise I wouldn't have found the room.

Itemized like that, the list seemed manageable. I was certain anyone who'd ever been ever discovered with a wall full of cutouts linked by colored strings had also considered said wall—and the mental state it represented—manageable.

I changed into my only other set of clothes. I'd literally planned on coming here to visit the grave, attend the reading of the will and then travel back home. In and out, 72 hours max. I had barely crossed the 24-hour mark and my world was already turning upside down.

"Where to?" I asked, back in the living room. Katrina was sitting on the couch, leafing through grandma's book, smiling sadly. She looked up and her eyes were just a touch red at the edges.

"Well, what are you in the mood for?" she asked. "Apart from burek."

31

I smiled. "Um, honestly? Fish."

She cocked an eyebrow. "I know the perfect place."

As we descended the stairs to the ground floor, a young girl ran past us, legs pumping furiously as she rushed up. I stepped to the side so she didn't slam right into me and a bright red bow in her hair drew my attention for a moment. Hearing the loud babbling noises she was making to herself, I hoped she was just a very exuberant child and not, you know, possessed.

Katrina glanced after her, smiling and shaking her head as we continued our descent.

Outside, the weather was warm, the day bright, the sky clear. It was pleasant. It was normal. I held onto that as we walked down the street and rounded a corner.

I would have to continue the conversation, that was a given. But maybe, just for a moment, I could talk about something else? Something completely mundane? I glanced around, noticed that where a kiosk used to be when I was a kid, now there was just an empty space with several plastic dumpsters.

"So," I said, "your English is pretty great."

Katrina smiled. "Lena is to blame," she said.

"What do you mean?"

"I got a scholarship to go study in the UK when I was eighteen. Graphic design. She nagged me to apply. I did great on the application, but... I think she'd also pulled some strings to make sure I was one of the recipients."

I was nodding. Nona had been insistent I get good grades in school. She wouldn't ever force me to do my homework, but she did have this way of cajoling me into getting it done before playing or reading or watching TV.

"I never finished the degree, though," Katrina said.

I raised my eyebrow. "Changed your mind?"

"Not so much changed as realized my heart had never really been in it. I'd been pushed into it by my parents because I was kinda good at drawing in elementary and high school."

She was silent for a moment as we walked.

"Lena didn't judge me. She wasn't even angry. I was more concerned about her reaction than my parents', you know? But she helped me get a job in a grocery store and never once told me I'd wasted an opportunity."

"So, um, you still work there?"

She looked at me and laughed lightly. "Oh, no, no." She paused. "Right, I never told you what I do. I'm a legal translator, English to Croatian and back." She grinned. "Turned out those three years in the UK hadn't been a waste at all. My English got really good, especially written, but also, I'd met some people who later had to deal with Croatian bureaucracy and I translated a couple of things for them, and then I was asked by their Croatian lawyer if I could help him out some more and one thing led to another."

"You're freelance?"

"God bless the gig economy," she said, words dripping with irony.

I sniffed. "May it burn in hell?"

"Amen."

We both chuckled.

"I'm guessing you're freelance as well?" she asked.

I nodded. "Copywriting mostly, these days."

"So, let me ask you something: why does your Croatian suck?"

I chuckled again. "Well, my parents are to thank for that. You—wait, do you know why we moved?"

She pursed her lips. "Lena had told me bits and pieces over the years. Something about your dad working as an engineer?"

"Yes," I said. "Literally two days after the war ended he got an offer to go work for this huge international company. They were building bridges, hospitals, airports, housing complexes, dams—if it was concrete, they were building it. And dad was a really good engineer. He said yes, but it meant traveling all over the world.

33

Mom and I were supposed to stay in Croatia and he'd be coming back regularly, but then—well, they had a long talk and neither of them wanted to continue living here. So we all left."

Some crappy memories kept surfacing but I ignored them. Ignored the fights with my parents after they told me we were moving. Ignored me shouting at nona.

I looked around, taking a moment. The buildings were still the same as before I left Rijeka, but most shops I remembered had in the meantime been closed or turned into other shops.

"From 1995 to 2005 I'd seen more countries than most people do in their lifetime. I know what you're thinking, but when you're a kid, it's not cool, not really. Six months was the longest we'd ever spent in one place. Some places we'd come back to, but usually a year or two later. No way to make lasting friendships. Or, often, to even make short-term ones. You know who I hung out the most with? Other kids in my situation. The company had this program for families like ours, basically setting up makeshift private schools at their big, long-term construction sites."

"That sounds... sucky if you're a kid," she said. "The school was in English?"

I took a breath. "Yes. It was, for the most part, countries of the Commonwealth, so English was spoken everywhere we went. Now, Mom and Dad both knew English. Dad was self-taught; Mom had a degree in English Lit. So after about two years they decided not to confuse their poor kid's brain and so we started speaking exclusively English at home as well. When I started college I had some colleagues who were kids of Croatian expats and they got me into reading books and watching films in Croatian. That's why I can still read it at a certain level and understand most of it, but, well, you heard me yesterday."

Her eyes were a little wide as I finished the story. I'd skipped bits of it. Important ones, maybe. But not necessary for her to hear now. Or for me to dredge up.

"That... wow. I'm glad it didn't fuck you up, that kind of a childhood. Sounds rough on a kid."

Yeah, about that...

"I'm apparently fine, so it all worked out for the best, I guess," I said. "Well... I mean..." I glanced around, suddenly a little uncomfortable because I remembered why we were here and what the theme of the day was.

We walked on in silence. It wasn't exactly uncomfortable, but it definitely was a little weighed down.

I'm sure there are people from Rijeka who don't like seafood, just like there must be Neapolitans who don't like pizza, but I certainly never met one when I was a kid. Every single kid in my elementary school class would have choked on fried sardines if given the chance. My parents love seafood, my grandma and grandpa made sure I ate it every Sunday if I was staying with them for the weekend. And every time it would be fresh fish, which meant going to the fish market with grandpa just after breakfast.

The fish market was still alive and well: a building tall and wide, its windows and walls decorated in ways I never would have noticed as a kid if grandpa hadn't pointed them out to me. I smelled it before I saw it, just like all those times before. A square building that had once, long ago, stood directly on the edge of the shore (when it was still the shore, before they poured sand and rocks to push the sea back)—grandpa would often take me to the back entrance where, in the old days, fishermen would offload their catch directly from their trawlers.

As we passed by, I remembered the fountains inside and wondered if they were still there—and if people today noticed them at all. I certainly never would've had, if grandpa hadn't talked about them: four of them, one for each corner of the fish market, carved stone in the shape of the products being sold, providing water both for drinking and washing.

The walls and pillars were still decorated with reliefs of fish and squid and octopi, each creature on its own little shield, as if each were a coat of arms.

If it seemed to me, for a moment, that some of the animals up there moved just a bit, I ignored it. Just the sun playing tricks on me.

Years ago I'd seen Rijeka's fish market in a documentary by Michael Palin and it had brought nostalgic tears to my eyes. He'd called it 'a cathedral of fish' and I could understand why he'd say that: in my memories, the ceiling seemed sky high, and the stone tables and counters might have passed for altars. Considering that the seafood grandpa and I would bring back with us tasted divine once grandma had served it for lunch, Palin might have been on to something.

The smell in the restaurant Katrina led me into reminded me of those lunches. It was a tiny eatery in a side street directly next to the fish market, with just a couple of wooden tables outside and not that many more inside. Cozy, rustic, and I would have called it a tourist trap had the prices not actually seemed reasonable, the menu focused and the people inside ranged from business suits to, very clearly, people from the neighborhood out for a quick bite.

We sat down and for a moment there was an awkward silence. I was actively avoiding mentioning the... *thing* and Katrina was, gods bless her, playing along for now.

She was about to speak when the waitress suddenly appeared asking what we wanted to drink and showing us the menu; that is to say, a large metal platter filled with fresh fish the restaurant had in their daily offer. We placed our order—I hadn't eaten sea bream in a long time and it had been one of grandma's specialties—and a few moments later, when we were again alone, each of us had a glass of wine in hand and a knot in the gut.

"So it's real," I said finally because I had to start the conversation with something.

36

"Yep," Katrina replied. Then she frowned. "Wait, what part? A lot of folklore is based on real magic stuff, but there's also stuff that's misinterpreted and a *ton* that was straight up made up. At least that's what your grandma used to tell me."

She shook her head after a moment. "Lena," she said. "It's weird referring to her as your grandma."

I nodded. "We can call her Lena."

A pause as I glanced around, but the other patrons were deep in their own conversations and loud music played from the speakers. "So, aren't krsniks supposed to be shapeshifters? Turn into wolves?"

"Dogs," Katrina said. "They can also turn into dogs, not just wolves."

I stared. "Am I going to turn into a dog?"

"I have no idea," she said simply. "But I never saw Lena turn into any animal. I heard some people call her a bitch, though." She grinned.

I blinked.

"Bitch, dog..." she said.

"Oh," I said.

"Maybe you're not ready for jokes,"

"Sorry, my mind's all over the place," I said.

"That's why we're here," she said.

"I have no idea what to do," I admitted. "Am I—is anything expected from me? I mean, can I just leave and forget about all this?"

I could not decipher the look in her eyes. "You could," she said finally. There was a ton of subtext, just outside my reach.

"Okay, you're gonna have to tell me," I said, suddenly annoyed. "I didn't *ask* for this, alright? It's like finding out you've inherited a castle."

"It's not a bad comparison," Katrina said.

"It is if you live half a world away," I shot back.

"No, it's this: a castle comes with lands and, oh, what's the word, people living on the land, you have obligations to protect them—"

"Vassals. *Wait.* Grandma had—"

"No, no, not like that. But people did depend on her for help, sometimes protection. Okay, sorry, I've only now thought of the perfect comparison. Not a castle: a badge."

I blinked. "Like a sheriff's badge?"

"Yep," Katrina said. "Well, okay, there's no official organization behind the badge, so it's more like you've inherited a set of six-shooters from a wandering gunslinger with a heart of gold." She smirked awkwardly. "I discovered I like westerns in high school."

My head was buzzing, so I drank some wine. It was strong, yet pleasant, just what I needed to ground me a little. This was all so surreal—and yet, here we were. Last night had *definitely* been real. That room— although calling it a *room* definitely felt as if I were underselling it—was also definitely real, even though it shouldn't have been. And I was... yeah. What was I? I knew the word but that didn't help me much—didn't help me *at all*. I knew *who* I was, that was easy. I was Paul; once, long ago, called Pavle. I was from Rijeka. I was the son of an engineer and an English professor. I was a modestly successful freelance copywriter. I was single, I loved dogs and spicy food and hiking.

I wasn't... I wasn't a krsnik.

What was I supposed to do?

I asked Katrina that.

"Well, you can literally do anything you want, I guess," she said. "Within reason. I mean, you can't fly."

"That—that wasn't what I was—"

"I know," she said. She sighed lightly, obviously exasperated. "I don't know, Paul. Honestly. I want to help you because of Lena and because we were friends, but all the instructions Lena left me were, almost verbatim, '*Just look out for him and help him out*'. I guess you *could* leave and never come back."

"You just said I'd inherited—"

"Well, yes. But nowhere does it say you have to use the six-shooters here in Rijeka."

"Or at all," I said. "Can't I just hang them on a peg? Ignore them?"

She frowned and I felt a stab of momentary compulsion to apologize, to change tack. Then I realized it was *nonsense* and, now feeling more than a little cranky, I added, "I can, I know that. You don't have to tell me that. I'm human, I have rights, I have *the choice*. Free will and all that. So I could just get up and leave."

"So leave," she said curtly, staring me right in the eye.

A part of me—tiny but always impressively caustic—wanted to do just that. Ever since childhood I didn't like people springing important stuff on me out of nowhere and expecting me to react the way they wanted me to. And Katrina seemed full of just such expectations so she could go—

I was being an asshole. Luckily I was mostly being an asshole internally, but still...

I closed my eyes. "Ugh," I said.

"Ugh indeed," I heard Katrina say sympathetically.

The waitress brought our fish soup: the smell was pure heaven, and it was clear and full of pieces of fish and carrots and rice. I ate and for a blissful couple of minutes I completely forgot about grandma and the apartment and everything inside it.

But when I put the spoon down, it was all still there, patiently waiting.

"Tell me about her," I asked then, surprising myself.

Katrina's eyebrow twitched. "About Lena?"

"Yes," I said. "The Lena I never knew."

Katrina suddenly seemed so terribly sad. "No, Paul, you did. Your grandma was exactly the woman you remember, alright? Kind and loving, strict when it was needed, and helpful. None of that was an act."

And there was that pang of guilt again. She was right. Grandma had been a good woman. A kind woman. I could still remember my grandpa once telling me how happy he was to have found someone so good, full of love and able to always find a silver lining even in the worst moments. How she'd always lift him up, how she'd always look out for those in need.

And I'd left and hadn't called or written her a single letter in all those years. I had blamed her for leaving, even though it had been ridiculous even back then. And she—I was certain of this—had forgiven me for all that.

And that hurt so much more than knowing I'd ignored her.

"Paul?"

My eyes were full of tears. I wiped them, closed them for a moment.

"Alright," I said. "So tell me about Lena's secret life."

She smiled. "Now that I can tell you about." She looked around, leaned forward a little and started talking. "In fact, I can tell you something that might help you make up your mind."

Grandma had discovered our family's—I guess *legacy* is as good a word as any—when she was still just a girl. She'd had dreams, very vivid and very disturbing, for a full month prior to waking up one morning in the potato patch behind her parents' house, stark naked and with dirt under her fingernails, as if she'd been digging barehanded.

The dreams had been of someone stalking the people of her village, always behind a wall, under a window, peering through a crack in the door. And in the dreams she was the only one who could see that someone, although never in full: eyes in the darkness above the ceiling beams, watching a family at dinner; a hand resting on the window sill above the bed someone was sleeping in. A grin, sly and cruel, the teeth numerous and sharp.

Grandma had managed to get back into the house that morning without anyone noticing—through her bedroom window, the one her late mother had always made sure was closed before letting her daughter go to sleep. She'd washed as best she could, got dressed and prayed she'd find her nightgown before her stepmother discovered it was missing.

She did find it, later that day, in the woods not far from their farm. It wasn't torn and it wasn't very dirty but there was blood on it.

"Lena said, 'On the same night I became a krsnik and a woman.',' Katrina said. "*Sreća u nesreći*, to quote her," she added. *Fortune in misfortune*, my nona's favorite saying.

"Was it related?" I asked as Katrina was about to continue the story.

"Was what related?"

"Her getting her period for the first time and getting, er, getting her powers, I guess? Because in books magical powers are sometimes tied to the Moon and life blood and that stuff, so, er..."

Katrina smiled. "I don't think you understood what I meant," she said. "She was having periods already."

It took me a moment. "Oh," I said.

"Yes," Katrina said, smiling at my discomfort.

"Oh god," I said with a knot in my gut. "Was she—did some-one—"

"No, it wasn't rape," Katrina said, shaking her head. "She would remember what happened that night eventually, but it took some time. And if you let me finish the story..."

"Go on," I said. The main course had been served but we were barely eating, Katrina fully in storytelling mode and me engrossed by the tale, my nona losing her virginity notwithstanding.

Grandma had washed the nightgown the best she could, put it in the attic to dry and counted herself unbelievably lucky her stepmother didn't discover it.

As to how she'd found the nightgown in the first place: it had been her turn to take the cows out to pasture and she'd used the opportunity to clear her head, which was full of soft buzzing and vague feelings she couldn't grasp no matter how hard she tried.

The walk in the sun, under clear blue skies, in the middle of spring did her good, definitely. She'd felt reinvigorated walking barefoot in the grass.

And then, mid-step, she remembered running under the light of the full Moon, barefoot and still in her nightgown. In the memory, she wasn't being chased, she was running *towards* the woods under the craggy hill that dominated the view from her bedroom window. The woods she was now no more than a short walk away from.

Leaving the cows to their grazing, but still keeping an eye on them, grandma walked, slowly and full of apprehension. Then, at the very edge of the woods, she stopped and realized her apprehension had somehow turned into a strange excitement, as if she were coming back to a place where something amazing had happened.

And she remembered it: waking from a fever dream, sweaty and cold and hot and aching all over, as if her skin was too tight for her flesh and bones. Looking through the window slats, seeing the woods and the hill, pitch black and dark grey, bathed in blindingly white moonlight. And then realizing she could tell blades of grass apart under her window and make out individual leaves on the oak next to the water trough. She could hear her father and stepmother softly breathing in their sleep, and what was probably a mouse skittering across the attic floor. There'd been a soft whoosh and she saw something move in the oak's high branches: an owl had just landed there, its eyes enormous and deep as the bird looked straight at Lena.

None of that should have been possible for her to see, to hear, not even in full daylight. She must have still been asleep, dreaming. She fully expected to be, once again, transported into one of the houses in the village, to see him—something told her it was a *him*, not an *it*—observing people sleep or work, always near, menacing. Stalking. Preying.

The owl hooted. Lena flinched, felt pain in her fingertip from a splinter from the window.

She was *awake*.

And the owl was there, in the dark under the thick cover of leaves, yet she could see it clearly when she shouldn't have been able to.

Lena felt as if all the air in her bedroom had simply vanished. She opened the window, and then sat on the sill and jumped that meter or so down. The grass was soft and inviting under her bare feet.

The moonlight seemed to flow across her skin like oil on water. The owl hooted again, spread its wings and took silent flight. Lena ran after it. Towards the woods.

She'd realized it was ridiculous and dangerous only when she was already deep among the trees. The owl was gliding smoothly between the gangly trees before it suddenly perched on a tall tree's branch, high over a small campfire.

There was a man there, very surprised to see Lena. She remembered that clearly, the look of shock on his face as she stepped into the flickering light. He'd been sitting on a large stone, gazing deep into the fire.

He rose to his feet slowly, regally. He was tall and he was naked. "And apparently," Katrina added, "fine as fuck."

Which was to say slim but muscled; firelight danced over his pale skin, giving it a bronze sheen as he gently moved towards Lena, hands outstretched as if to say *"Don't be afraid."*

There were, Lena noticed then, horns on his head. No, *antlers*. Short and thin, encircling his head like a crown.

"But the rest of him was like any man," Katrina said. Then, with a wry grin, she added, "Well, to quote Lena fully: 'He was like any man, unfortunately very few men were like him.' If you know what she meant."

I think at that point Katrina was fully enjoying making me uncomfortable.

They spoke, even though Lena didn't know how, because she was certain he didn't know her language and she certainly couldn't speak any other. But talk they did. He'd asked who she was and what she was doing there. She just shot the questions back at him. He'd told her a girl had no business being in the woods at night, alone. She'd asked what business naked men with antlers had on her father's property.

And then the owl hooted and the naked man's eyes went wide. He asked her if she'd had bad dreams. Lena had said yes; she'd been having them for weeks now. He asked if, in those dreams, she ever saw the face of the man stalking the villagers. She'd said no; every time it seemed to her she finally would see it, she'd wake up, terror twisting her insides.

The antlered man asked her if she knew what she was.

To which my grandma, possibly for the first time in her life, had no smartass response.

Am I not... she started asking but he raised his hand gently.

I am not interested in what you are not, he'd said in a language Lena knew she couldn't speak even as she conversed with the man. *Tell me what you are.*

I... I feel something inside me, Lena said finally, after a long silence interrupted only by the crackling of fire and sparks flying through the night air. *I've felt it for some time. I cannot say what.*

The antlered man did not respond, but his eyes—dark, with flames reflecting amber in them—locked with hers.

I am Lena, grandma said finally. *Not a particularly obedient daughter to my father. A good friend to the few people I care about.* She took a deep breath, finally about to give, for the first time, voice to what she'd been keeping inside for more than a year at that point. *I am a girl who would be a terrible wife to the boy my father wishes me to marry. I am a girl who cares more for carving wood than milking the cows. I am a girl who would rather wear trousers and ride a horse than wear skirts and feed the chickens. I am a girl who loves to cook and eat but would do it for herself, not her husband. I am a girl who doesn't want a husband.*

A silence that seemed to last an eternity.

And I am a girl who has been having dreams of a man, a terrible man. A man moving in the shadows, just behind your back, always there, always watching, never seen. A man stalking the village—my village, my people. A man who is a threat, a monster, a demon.

I am a girl who would stop him.

These last words came as a shock to her but for only a heartbeat, after which they set like a stone slab and she knew they were true.

Then you feel it, the antlered man said. *The power that has become yours.*

What power?

The power gifted to your birth mother and her father and his father and his mother, a power bound to your blood for generations. You've finally come into it. The dreams are just a part of it.

He glanced around, spread his hands. *You feel all this. Your senses are sharp, almost painfully so. You see things you know you shouldn't. You hear what no ordinary man or woman ever could.*

What am I? Lena asked.

He frowned then. *'What' is for animals, creatures and things.*

Who am I, then? Lena asked, annoyed at this strange man in the woods.

A krsnik, he said simply. And she knew the word. The stories, the legends.

I can't—

He frowned.

Fine. You say I'm a krsnik. And my family are krsniks as well?

Some, yes. The power passed onto you when your mother left this world.

When Lena was six, her mother died, killed by a wolf. The beast had been sick, the hunter who killed it had said; it had attacked Lena's mother in a frenzy, tearing her apart. Father would not let Lena see the body, had made certain the casket they lowered into the earth had its lid nailed shut.

But that was long ago!

Those of your family come into their powers when their time comes, no sooner, no later.

That is it?

That is all I will say for now, girl. Apart from this: your powers will grow as you fully become a woman. You flowering was a step but there are some ways to go yet.

Who are you?

I am a shepherd of these woods. I've known your mother and her father. But that is all I will say for tonight.

The man. Can I stop him?

A krsnik can do many things.

Lena gritted her teeth. Can I stop him?

The antlered man nodded curtly. *Your family has been the end of creatures far worse than he. But he is still a formidable foe. Be careful, girl.*

The owl hooted again. The antlered man sighed.

I will help, but there are limits to what I can do and say. And I will not do it tonight. Come to me tomorrow, when the Moon is above the hill. I will help you, but I can only tell you what the path ahead of you holds, and even so I must remain vague. You will have to walk it alone, thorns and brambles and all.

Lena nodded.

She could feel it clearly now, the power inside her, like a hidden water well ready to burst. She could feel it thrum—*sing.*

The antlered man started to turn back to his fire when she stepped forward, closer to him.

What now?

She regarded his naked form, firelight dancing over it. She placed a hand on his skin, smooth as silk, hard as marble, pleasant to the touch. Inviting.

Girl…

You said my powers will grow as I move closer to fully being a woman, did you not?

Girl, I am not…

She smiled. *I am not interested in what you are not,* she said, mocking his stern tone. Her fingers traced the outline of his taut muscles.

He regarded her for a long moment, his eyes ablaze, reflecting the heat she felt inside —

"Okay, I get it, I get it," I burst out. "Get to the point, Katrina."

Katrina frowned, but smiled as well. "Sorry, I got carried away."

What grandma did that night didn't in fact speed up the process of her acquiring her full krsnik powers, Katrina pointed out, nor had grandma actually believed it would. In a daze, she returned home stark naked, completely forgetting her nightgown.

The next night she came to the woods again and the training, such as it was, began. The antlered man—he'd either refused to give his name or grandma never relayed it to Katrina—had done what he could to prepare her. Her senses were far sharper than any human's, that was apparent, so grandma was learning how to use them and how to adapt to them—at night with the antlered man's help, during the day on her own. She was also faster than ever before and stronger, with more stamina, but those were only the most basic, most noticeable aspects of her powers. And apparently the only ones her mentor was willing to help her with. He'd repeated that he was limited in what he could say to her and help her with, and was also adamant in not providing a reason why.

Lena could feel the power and potential in herself, the torrent about to break through the dam but she had no idea what the water would bring. Krsniks were supposed to be the enemy of witches and vampires and werewolves—but those were all just stories, surely?

No, not just stories, thought a young girl with preternaturally sharp senses, far faster and stronger than any other girl her age could ever be. A young girl being trained to fight by a man with antlers and an owl that seemed to be more a friend than a pet or familiar.

The dreams continued, as vivid and foreboding as before. In her dreams during that time she would call out to the villagers and, when they wouldn't respond, she would try to shake them, push them—but in vain. She could never get close to any one of them, no matter how much she walked or how hard she ran; they would always remain just outside her reach.

And that man in the dark would be there, always, watching. Only now Lena had the dreadful sensation he was *aware of her.*

The antlered man frustrated her the most, though, by refusing to talk about the threat the man posed, except in the most general, vaguest terms; repeating only that she had to be careful, watchful and not to underestimate him.

The man himself came for her on the seventh night after the night she ran into the woods. This time the threat in the dream seemed different; *imminent*. Foreboding was thick in the air, smothering, oppressive. In her dream, she was in a house in the village, watching a family at dinner, standing next to their fire-place. The fire crackled unnaturally loud, the family completely silent even though she could see their lips move as they talked to each other. She didn't hear him breathing but could sense his breath. He was in the rafters, watching the family.

And then he was watching her. For the first time ever in these dreams, she was completely and utterly aware of his gaze upon her. The fire fell silent. His breath caught.

Taking a step back, she reached behind herself, found a latch, pushed, and stepped into her own room through a closet door.

The room was hers, yes. She was standing at the foot of her bed. The only light came from a single candle next to the bed, one she'd forgotten to put out. The only sound was the distant cry of a fox she could hear through the window. The wide open window.

The man was crouching on the window sill, right above her pillow. Staring directly at her across the bed, he smiled. And leapt.

"And?" I asked, my entire skin turning into gooseflesh. Katrina shrugged. "Lena—she would never tell me that part of the story. The most I've ever gotten out of her were hints and tidbits, and even then she had to be drunk to let them slip."

"Nona, drunk?" I'd never seen her drink more than a little wine with water after a full lunch.

"Oh, Lena could *drink*," Katrina said, smiling wistfully. Then she shook her head. "But yes, the first time she told me that story was after about half a bottle of *šljiva*." Which was a *rakija* made from plums, a drink you didn't so much enjoy as suffer willingly.

"But when she got to the part about fighting the man, she fell silent and wouldn't speak to me for at least an hour."

"And you have no idea why?"

"No. Like I said, I can only give you the version I've pieced together over the years."

"Okay," I said.

"They fought, and it was hard and violent and vicious. I think it was possibly the first time Lena shifted into wolf form, and I think it happened when she was at death's door. The man wasn't human, that much is clear. He beat her within an inch of her life and she gave as good as she got, but even so... Well, I think he believed he'd won, so he stopped, took his time to gloat. It was enough to give her a moment to finally reach and break through whatever was blocking her from using her full powers. She killed him and, honestly, I hope his death was *nasty*. And that was it. She saved the village from the creature."

"What was it?" I asked.

"She didn't know back then, but over the years she came to believe it had been a *štrigun*."

And there it was—another thing that belonged in stories, but apparently wasn't just folklore.

"*Štrigun*," I said. "The eats kids, drinks blood, rises from the grave—that *štrigun*?"

"There's different kinds, Lena told me. She'd fought a few during her life and each was different from the others, but yes, that man had probably been a *štrigun*."

The fish was cold. We still ate it, in silence. Katrina's was a brooding silence, mine troubled.

When we finished, Katrina paid the check—she insisted—and as we walked away from the restaurant, the market already silent and empty, I broke the silence first.

"You loved her," I said.

She didn't break her stride. "Yes, I did," she said. "As much as you can love someone without being in love with them."

"I'm glad she had you," I said.

Now she stopped. "Paul..." she said.

"No, I—I've felt so guilty ever since I've heard of her death. It's only been worse since I came here, but I've been ignoring it. Fact of the matter is, I left and never called nor wrote, and now she's gone. I wasn't a part of her life, but I'm so, so glad you were." I paused. "And I wish—"

"No," she snapped then, staring daggers at me. "You don't get to say that. You don't get to think that."

It was as if she'd read my mind. "Katrina—"

"No, Paul," she said, her tone a dagger. "If you say you wish I were in your place because you think I would be better at it or some fucking bullshit like that, I'll fucking punch you. Understand?"

She was balling her fists. Probably completely unconsciously.

"I—"

"No. You've been trying *hard* to pity yourself, but you know what, Paul? Fuck. That. You were dealt these cards. I was dealt mine. Either play the game or fuck off from the field."

I glanced around. We'd stopped after crossing the street and were now just a dozen paces from the port. Several people had already done their damnedest to pretend they weren't paying attention to our argument as they passed us by.

"Paul, I'm sorry," she said.

"But you're right."

"Really, I have no right to—what?"

"I said you're right." And she was. "Look, I've... there's stuff I've very successfully not dealt with as a kid, and then I managed to completely bury deep inside as an adult. Only... now that stuff demands I deal with it. And combined with the last day or so... It's been a lot." I took a deep breath through my nose, the warm, salty scent of the sea in my nostrils. "We've both been under a lot of stress, I'd guess,"

I gestured, asking her to cross the road with me.

She nodded, sniffing, and in just a few seconds we were at the edge of the concrete berth. In front of us, the port of Rijeka spread out, the long shore to our distant right, the seawall to our left.

"This is new," I said, looking at the people walking along the seawall.

"Oh, yes, they turned it into a tourist attraction, in a way," Katrina said.

"The cranes are still there, but I'm guessing they're just for show?"

"Yep. The entire seawall is now a place to take a long walk," she said. "My dad used to take me here, you know? He worked as a customs inspector. I remember when ships would come to offload cargo here. The noise, the commotion. Kinda scary for a six year old, but also kinda exciting because I wasn't supposed to be there officially."

I looked to my left and the only ships I could see in the port were very fancy yachts. When we left Rijeka, there were still cargo ships here.

It was definitely much more quiet than I remembered.

"Not to mention I've been questioning everything I knew about Lena," I said, bringing us back to today's main topic of conversation. "And—"

"What?" Katrina asked.

"The story," I said, looking at her. "Lena's senses. I've been having these intermittent headaches the last few days, and my eyes get very sensitive. For a few moments, it can be like people are shouting, even though they're talking in a normal voice. Are my senses becoming sharper and I'm just handling it very badly?"

She nodded. "When I started seeing and hearing ghosts, it took me a while for their voices to stop feeling like they're screaming in my ear."

I fell silent then, thinking back to when these moments of sensory overload and their accompanying headaches started. I didn't have to think too much: the morning after nona died in her sleep I woke up feeling like the sun outside my apartment window was shoving hot knives into my eyes. It had passed after a few minutes but that had obviously been the beginning of... all this.

"It's been easier," I said, realizing now. "Today it's been much less painful than yesterday and the days before."

Katrina just nodded again.

"And... well, I've been seeing things these last few days." I smiled at her, uncomfortable.

Her eyebrows crept up a bit. "What kinds of things?"

"Shapes and shadows moving where there shouldn't be any. Stuff looking alive for a moment. Statues and such."

"It's going to get more pronounced," she said. "Well," she added, "depending how sharp your senses become."

"There was a man," I said then, remembering the graveyard. "Yesterday. That funeral?" I looked at her. She was staring at me intently. "I saw a man there. He looked strange to me. I can't explain how, but he just did, and then he was gone." Was I seeing ghosts as well?

"What kind of man? Paul, what did he look like?" There was incredulity in her voice but also a kind of alarm.

"Tall," I said. "In a coat, with a cap, and I think he had a gray beard. Dressed a bit like an old sea captain, now that I think of it."

Her eyes seemed ready to pop out of her head.

Then she smiled. Shook her head.

"Would you like to meet him?"

JUST A KIND
OLD MAN

Twenty minutes and a taxi ride later, we were, once again, in the graveyard. Katrina refused to tell me who the man was or why we were going to meet him, which was understandable because of the taxi driver. We spent the time chatting about the other kids from nona's building we used to play with long, long ago. Turned out Katrina was the only kid from that generation who stayed not just in Rijeka, but Croatia as well. All the others had moved at some point, either with their parents, or on their own.

We were walking between the graves, but not towards grandma and grandpa's plot. I was following Katrina, slowly winding between the graves. She seemed to be looking for something. I noticed only cats, and they were everywhere: lounging next to graves or at the foot of tall cypresses an the occasional palm tree. Not a single one of them moved, but *all* of them were watching us.

I stopped then, realizing where we were and dimly remembering the few times I'd been to this part of the graveyard with grandma. This was the old Jewish section of the graveyard. Grandma had once had a friend who had died and been buried here. We would sometimes come and grandma would stand in front of her friend's grave without a word, sometimes for minutes at a time. I would always wander off but I'd never disturb her. A few times I'd seen her bend down, take a pebble from the ground and place it on the gravestone just before leaving.

I looked at the graves now, trying to remember which one was her friend's, and also if they'd been like this back then: overgrown with lichen and moss. So few gravestones had any pebbles on them, and the few that had, had only one or two. I realized I couldn't remember which grave was my grandma's friend's anymore, couldn't recall the woman's name.

I looked up from the graves, saw Katrina standing nearby, waiting for me patiently. Then it hit me.

We were in a graveyard.

"Katrina," I said softly. "Are... are there any here?"

She looked at me. "Any what?"

"You know. Ghosts." I was glancing around as if I might see them skulking around, hiding behind gravestones and cypresses. There were no ghosts, but the sound of the wind in the treetops was definitely suddenly much, much louder. It grew in intensity even further, almost as if I were in a tunnel and then, just like that, it was back to being faint, barely noticeable.

"Oh," Katrina said. "Yes," she added offhandedly, glancing around. "Six or seven nearby." She pointed. "There's one sitting on that bench."

I looked and of course there was no one there.

"Are they—I mean, how does it work? You said not everyone stays."

"No, not everyone. Most of us leave into the light. But some stay." She thought for a moment. "It's hard to explain, there can be many different reasons someone stays. It depends on how you died, when you died, and yes, if you had any unfinished business, as cliché as it sounds. Trauma plays a huge part. Some ghosts are fully conscious and they're aware of what they are now. Some are fully conscious and refuse to believe they died. Some are, well, more like an afterimage, or an echo. Some look like they did in life; others are just a blur and a voice. I can tell you more later, but now I'd really like to find—"

"What is *that*?" I asked, pointing hard and not caring if I looked like a madman. It stood at the far end of the path, looking straight

54

at us. Several cats were there as well, pressing themselves lovingly against its legs for a few steps before leaving to wander among the graves.

The creature was tall, slim. It had the general shape of a human, two legs, two arms, hands, feet (bare), eyes, mouth, nose, hair, ears. A gray beard, full and thick. It wore dark pants and a dark pullover with an unbuttoned, short dark coat over it. There was a cap on its head. There was no way it was human. It simply radiated... non-humanness.

It moved towards us, casual, relaxed. I finally looked at Katrina, expecting her to seem as terrified as I was as it approached us, but Katrina was just nodding amiably.

"Katrina, *what is that?!*" I repeated. She stepped closer to me and gently lowered my hand down to my side. I had to fight the urge to run away and fight it *hard*. From meters away—like yesterday at the funeral—it could have passed for human in the same way a stunt double can pass for the actor. But it *wasn't* human.

Although, I realized as it came closer, it wasn't as terrifying as I'd felt. There was a symmetry to its features—*perfect* symmetry— and its movements were gentle, smooth, and its pants swished pleasantly as it walked—

No! I shouted at myself inside my head. This was something supernatural and I should be terrified and careful, not—

"*Bok, Barba,*" Katrina said to the creature.

"*Lijep dan za šetnju,*" the creature replied, nodding at her.

Hello? Nice day for a walk? They were exchanging pleasantries! In Croatian.

Katrina then nodded, indicating me with her head. "*Njen unuk,*" she said. Her grandson.

"*Oho,*" the creature said. Smiled broadly, as if happy to see me.

I felt the urge to take a step back but fought it because Katrina didn't seem alarmed and I grabbed onto that.

It offered me its hand.

I didn't want to touch it.

It looked like a man, really did, but it was absolutely not.

"Paul," Katrina hissed at me out of the corner of her lips.

The creature chuckled softly, waving any potential slight off. Then it looked at me and said, "You'd prefer English, yes?"

I nodded because it was a simple question with a simple answer.

"Then welcome to Rijeka, grandson of Lena," the creature said with a small bow of its capped head and a wry smile. "Your grandmother was a friend. May we both have the good fortune to become friends as well."

"You—you're not human," I said.

"Of course not," the creature said.

"You aren't speaking English," I said, stunned.

The creature's eyes—dark green—went a little wide, eyebrows twitching. "Why do you say that?"

"Your lips are moving but you're not talking in English," I said, although I was suddenly very uncertain of my own eyes.

It smiled. "My, my," it said. "You can see through glamour."

"Oh," I heard Katrina say softly, surprised.

"What are you?" I asked, immediately regretting it because who the hell would ever appreciate a question like that?

But it didn't seem to bother the—whatever it was. It smiled. "Everybody calls me Barba." It was a popular word up and down the Adriatic coast, used when you were addressing grown men older than you, whether total strangers or your family. When you were a kid, every older man who wasn't your dad or granddad was a barba. And also, I remembered, the word came from Italian for *beard* because, well, grown men wear beards.

Barba.

"I'm Paul," I said.

The creature smiled and then looked at me seriously. "You can see me, can't you? Not just my lips but my entire face is strange to you, isn't it?"

I nodded.

He returned the nod. Looked at Katrina. "What he sees is what you can see only when you use those glasses."

Katrina uttered another "Oh" and patted her handbag absently.

The creature smiled at me again. "Paul, I would like you to try something. It will make this conversation much more pleasant for the both of us. Try to focus on the way you see me. Take as much time as you need." His voice was a pleasant baritone, and there was this wonderful quality of a patient tutor to it that made me want to do whatever he said.

"So, as you focus on the way you see me, you might notice that my face seems to change."

And he was right. All this time it was as if I were watching two similar, but still distinct and different faces laid over one another in some kind of a visual effects cock-up.

"Now, your eyes and mind want to see what is real and are pushing the glamour aside. You can let it slide back over my face. Just relax, take your time."

The face on the surface was one of an old man, like you might see on any street in any town. Under that one was a face that was anything but: it was... well. It was as if someone had tried to make a human face but overdid it, made it too perfect, too smooth, too symmetrical. The longer I looked at that face, the more I was disturbed by it.

I focused, trying to make the top face the only one visible to me. It worked in the end, but only after I'd stopped trying to force it and let it—well, let the face flow towards where I gently tugged at it with my mind.

And just like that, there was a tall, friendly man in front of me, who looked like he fell out of the pages of some old book about a kind, old, retired sea captain, standing on the shore, looking at the ships sailing in the distance.

I tried pulling back the—the glamour, did he call it that?—and there it was again, the too-perfect, not human but trying to pass as one creature—and then I pulled the glamour back into place and it was just an old man... a barba.

"There," Barba said, smiling pleasantly. "Better?"

"Much," I said. "Oh god, sorry. I didn't mean it like that."

57

He chuckled. "It's all right." Again he offered me his hand. This time I took it. A firm handshake. Warm, callused fingers. Like any human's.

"I take it I shouldn't be able to see you at all," I said, glancing between him and Katrina. Seeing him as just an old man allowed me to focus back on other things and not solely on his wrongness. "The way you reacted before, when I told you I'd seen him yesterday."

She nodded.

I looked at Barba. "Are… are you dead? Are you a ghost? No, wait, she said there are ghosts around us. You're not a ghost, then. What are you? And why is it strange that I can see you?"

He smiled amiably. "I am not a ghost, no. What I am…" He paused. "I would rather not tell you. I am sorry, but I keep that to myself." He looked at Katrina. "I hope Katrina can speak to my reliability, even though you might find it suspicious I won't say what I am. I am not a threat to you, Paul."

Katrina shook her head when she saw doubt in my eyes. "Barba is the last person you should be afraid of," she said. "He's… well, he's like me, in a way."

The old man smiled. "She means I deal with the souls of the departed as well," he said.

"He helps dead kids," Katrina said.

I remembered the coffin. Too small a coffin.

"Help them?" I asked although I had my guesses already.

Barba's eyes filled with melancholy. "Death is almost always a shock, unless you have suffered long and embraced it when it came." He glanced at Katrina before returning his gaze to me. "Sometimes the souls—ghosts, as you prefer to call them—stay behind instead of going into the light. Some are unwilling to go, others are simply confused. She and I, we do our best to help them move on." He was silent for a moment, and then smiled sadly. "The little ones… it's hardest on them. They often stay behind, some because they don't want to leave their parents, brothers, sisters; others because they were broken in life and can't accept they deserve the peace and kindness on the other side of the light. There

58

are many reasons, really. What I do is help them. I look after them, take care of them until they are ready to leave."

I looked at Katrina. She was tearing up.

Barba smiled at her. "She thinks she could never do what I do," he said, sounding as if he doubted it very much.

"I never said I couldn't," Katrina replied. "I'm just grateful I don't have to." She looked at me. "Dealing with ghosts of grown ups is hard. Dead kids... are a special kind of heartbreak."

Barba smiled kindly at her. "Now, as to your question about seeing me, Paul. Your grandmother was never able to see me unaided."

I blinked.

"Katrina can see you, though, right?" I glanced at her. "And you mentioned some glasses? With them she can see the—the true you?"

Barba nodded. "As you delve deeper into this world, you'll find out that there are no simple, concrete rules to anything. Your grandmother was never able to see me like you do, but there will certainly be things that she was capable of that you will never be, at least not without some magical aid."

"So why can I see you and not ghosts, and Katrina can see both you and ghosts?" I asked.

Barba smiled like a teacher satisfied his student asked a very insightful question.

"She can see me because..." He paused, thinking and then nodded to himself and continued, "Because I have been part of the world of ghosts for so long it has rubbed off on me. But you... I believe you can see me because your eyes can see things that stand on both sides of the line between your mortal world and other ones." He raised a hand as if to give a caveat. "It does not mean you can see every such thing. As I've said; rules, if there are any, are mostly vague, at best. And your sight seems to be good enough to pierce my glamour. Don't take that lightly. But also, don't let it be known. It can be an advantage."

I nodded, wondering how many strange things I was about to see in the days to come and be the only one to see them.

"The way Lena explained to me," Katrina said, "magic isn't, uh... magic isn't maths, as much as a lot of it can be put into stuff resembling formulas and procedures."

"And even if a human is born with magic," Barba said, watching us both, "that magic can come in many different forms." He smiled wryly at Katrina, then looked at me as she rolled her eyes. "Your friend can see and hear the dead. She can also tell if there is bad food anywhere in her vicinity."

She sighed. "It's... not as cool as seeing ghosts."

Barba's attention focused on something behind me. I glanced over my shoulder but there was nothing there. *Nothing that I could see*, I corrected myself.

I saw Katrina looking the same way, her expression suddenly a little sad.

Barba looked at me, nodded. "I have to go, but I wish you luck, Paul, grandson of Lena." He clapped me on the shoulder. "We all have doubts," he said. "It is how we conquer them that matters in the end."

He walked off and I watched him go to the upper level of the graveyard and wave to someone before disappearing behind a wall. Only then did I notice that, at some point, dozens and dozens of cats had gathered around us in a wide, loose circle. Now they slowly turned and casually disappeared among the graves and the greenery.

"I'm guessing he saw some ghosts?" I asked Katrina.

She nodded. "Some stay in the graveyard."

"And others...? They wander around the town? Go back to their homes?"

"Both."

"So he's a... caretaker? Like a social worker, but for the dead?"

She looked at me. "As good an explanation as any. He's also protecting them."

"From what?" But again, I immediately had my guesses.

"Things that sometimes prey on ghosts," Katrina said.

"And humans?" I asked. "Black magic and that stuff?"

"Yes. Black witches and warlocks and... people like that." The derision in her voice could have cut stone.

I wondered. "When you say he protects them...?"

There was steel in her eyes for a moment. "Any black magic practitioners in this region know not to come for the dead kids of Rijeka. Most of them learned from others' examples."

"Because those that learned on their own hide..." I saw the answer in her eyes. "Don't have a hide left?"

"Their hide is the least of their problems," she said.

I decided to leave the natural follow-up to this for another day. "Can we leave now?" I asked her.

We walked out of the graveyard in silence. Katrina was obviously thinking about the dead kids, but my mind was a mess of all that was happening, all that seemed about to happen, and all that I wanted—and not wanted—to happen.

"Katrina," I said finally as we crossed the road and started slowly walking downhill.

"What if I choose not to use these... these powers?"

She didn't break her stride, but it was obvious it took a lot for her not to.

"Is there a way I could—I could transfer these powers to someone else? Or put them on hold for the next one in line?"

"The way Lena explained it to me, they will pass onto your kids. Or grandkids."

"Right, right. You said she wasn't sure if they would pass to me or my mom."

Kids. I'd always thought I would have kids one day. I still did, even though I wasn't even in a relationship.

And I would be saddling the kids with this.

She stopped suddenly, turned towards me. "*Transfer* them." There was an edge to her voice. "Paul, this is not a coat for you to take off and hand to someone else to go out into the cold while you warm your ass by the fire because you don't like winter."

It was an image that resonated with me.

"Paul, you're not normal. I'm not normal. You didn't want this. *I* didn't want this. *Lena* didn't want it either, back then. I doubt anyone in your entire bloodline wanted any of it at first."

She paused and then stared at me intently. "Paul, what are you afraid of?"

I didn't know where to begin. "Katrina," I said, "I'm just a guy, okay? Just an average guy, with an average job, and I can't be the protector of the innocent or the slayer of demons or whatever it is that krsniks are supposed to be."

A small part of me wondered if passers-by could hear us until it noticed the sidewalk was, fortunately, empty.

"Yes you can," Katrina said flatly. "Lena was just a girl from a farm. I was just a teenager with nothing on my mind apart from my next fix."

That took me aback, but before I could react, she plowed on; fire in her eyes and voice. "Yes, I was a junkie long ago. Paul... you've inherited Lena's powers. I've seen what she was able to do with them. I've heard stories from people she'd helped, she'd saved. I'm just asking you to try, Paul."

She took a step towards me, pleading with her eyes more than words. "Please, Paul, *just try*."

It was insane.

Then again, didn't I always fantasize about being a hero when I was a kid?

We all do. And then we grow up.

Only, people still do become heroes. Firemen, doctors and nurses, mountain rescuers, therapists, social workers, people who jump into a cold river to save a drowning man. Everyday, ordinary people who pull others out of fallen-down buildings and over-turned cars and burning houses... But I've never been one of them.

"Paul, in all your life, did you never help someone in need?" Katrina asked quietly. "At least once?"

I was about to say no but then a memory came storming back, unpleasant and raw.

"Elementary school," I said, looking at her. She shook her head in question. We hadn't gone to the same school, so of course she didn't know. Katrina's school was a few dozen meters from her apartment building, and mine had been on the other side of Rijeka.

"There was this kid. It was in the middle of the war. He was a refugee, scared shitless because he came from some tiny village, and Rijeka was bigger than he could imagine any place being. There was a school bully who loved fresh meat. He picked on the kid. We all did nothing because, you know, it was par for the course that kids get bullied. You just keep your head down, thankful it's not you.

"And then, one day, something snapped in me. I have no other explanation. The bully was pushing the kid around, kicking him, taunting him. And I was passing by, like a dozen times before, pretending I wasn't seeing it, like all the times before.

My gut was in knots now, squeezing and squeezing itself.

"Then I stopped, turned around. And I smashed my umbrella against the bully's side. And again. And again. The bullied kid was afraid. I was *beyond* afraid. But there was something in the bully's face that I'd never seen before. He was *terrified*."

I paused for a moment, remembering, so vividly, the silence that descended on the entire school hallway; the look on each and every child's face as they tried to comprehend what was happening.

"Of course, a moment later his fear turned into rage and he beat me up, mercilessly. The bullied kid escaped. Nobody intervened until a teacher came, just as the bully had started kicking me when I was down."

Katrina was watching me, and her shock was palpable.

"Those few weekends I didn't come to grandma's during that spring we were supposed to have a neighborhood dodgeball tournament?" I said. "I was at home, waiting for my bruises to heal. I didn't want to explain to you or the other kids what had happened."

I could now feel a slight tingling in my sides where, so long ago, a Doc Martens had almost cracked my ribs.

And then I remembered more.

"The bully got expelled," I said. "You see, that was the first time any teacher had seen him do something worse than just push someone around. He was reported for assault, the police talked to his parents; they claimed they'd had no idea he was a bully. A year later I'd found out that after the expulsion his mother had beat him so much she'd broken his arm and cracked his skull."

Katrina swallowed, visibly disturbed.

Then she nodded. "See, you were a hero."

I blinked. "You—you did hear the part about what his mother—"

"That," she said, compassionate but firm, "is a tragedy, and that mother was a monster. But if you've been blaming yourself for what happened to him, you're an—" She stopped herself. "Then you just want to see the worst in every good thing you do. And that is *a fucking dumb way to think.*

"You were a hero to that refugee kid," she said after a moment. "He ran away as the bully was beating you, and I'm sure he was deeply ashamed of it, but the point is that you *saved him.*"

"He didn't thank me," I said, half lost in memories I really didn't want to dwell on. "Nobody ever said a thing about all of that. Everyone just pretended nothing happened."

Katrina frowned. "Was everyone a little less stressed once the bully was expelled?"

She had a point I had to concede. "But he—"

"Yes," she said. "He probably suffered terrible abuse at home, which had made him into what he was in school. And yes, what his mother did, if what you heard was true, that's just monstrous. But you're not responsible for that. And yes, nobody acknowledging what you did is a shit thing as well." She paused, took a breath. "The dead people I help move on—their families have no idea I did something for their recently deceased dad, mom, son. I've helped so many, mostly on my own, a few times with Lena's help and, for the most part, my reward is silence. But it's a silence without whimpering or pleading for help or howling in phantom pain.

64

It's a good silence, Paul. I don't do my thing for the thanks. Lena didn't do her thing for the thanks. And you, when you helped that kid, when you swung that umbrella—and I love you for that, believe me, fucking love you for it and I wish you'd told me back then—did you do it so someone would praise you later?"

"No," I said.

"Why did you do it?"

She was looking straight at me, her eyes daring me to make the final step and admit it both aloud and to myself. "I just heard the kid cry out and I wanted it to stop and I wanted the fucking ass-hole to stop." Decades later, the rage was still in me. It was small and muted, but it was still there.

"And you stopped him," Katrina said. "Only this time," she continued after a beat, "you've got something far more potent, far more *badass* than an umbrella."

At some point she had reached out and was now holding my hands. Her dark brown eyes were making a fierce appeal. "Paul, I just want you to try. Not for Lena. I want you to try *for yourself.*"

I closed my eyes, feeling the warmth of her palms. I nodded. "Alright," I said, eyes open. "I'll try."

I gently pulled my hands from her grip. I raised a hand, making a point. "I'm willing to explore what this is. But I'm not committing to anything."

Explore, categorize, force it to make sense.

Katrina smiled in thanks.

I felt overwhelmed and I just wanted to be alone, in a quiet room.

"I'm going back to the apartment." After a moment I added, "I'll probably be reading that book nona left me."

She nodded, a hint of a smile tugging at the corners of her lips. We walked on in silence, since discontent was slowly brewing in my gut. I had no idea why, but I knew that, if I gave it a minute or two, it would become apparent.

In front of nona's building, Katrina broke the silence and said, "I'd like to take you out for pizza tonight, if you're up for it?"

I nodded. "Pizza sounds great," I said but somehow I felt... a little angry? At who, for god's sake? "But it's my treat this time."

Katrina was maybe two or three strides away when I called after her.

"Look, I... I appreciate what you were trying to do back there," I told her. I didn't really want to have this conversation, but the knot in my gut was making it clear it wasn't leaving unless I talked about it. The few minutes of walking in silence really did let me figure out what had been bothering me since we left the grave-yard. "But I... You jumped me."

She blinked.

"You cared for Lena. And what she did and what you two did together was important to you. But, Katrina, *I'm not Lena.*"

She was about to say something but I kept talking, "So here's what I'll do. I know what I said earlier, but I was thinking and—and this is what's going to happen." My voice was rougher than I wanted it to be but I couldn't help it. "I have to be honest, to you and to myself. When the meeting with the lawyer about the will is done, I'll most likely be leaving Rijeka. I promised I would think about it, and I will, but I don't really see myself doing any of this."

She held her head high but her eyes spoke volumes. She just nodded and turned and left.

SOME PREFER TO WORK UNSEEN

I stood in the apartment's living room, wondering what to do. I'd checked my email as I was climbing the stairs: there was a message from the lawyer's office, reminding me of the appointment tomorrow at two in the afternoon.

How to kill time until then? Answers presented themselves but I did my best to ignore them. The room. My grandma's book.

And there was that knot in my gut that made me act like an ass to Katrina moments ago; a knot that I had no desire to start untangling because I would have to face all kinds of things I'd made a lifelong habit of putting aside for tomorrow.

So I decided to do something to keep my mind off things, something that would busy my hands while pleasantly mind-numbing. I started taking stock. Every cupboard, closet, drawer—I opened it all, looked through it. I left the collection of bottles and herbs and spices for later.

Wait. Is it alcohol and herbs and spices or is it magical potions and spell ingredients?

I don't care.

So, wardrobes and chests, and in them clothes, old and only grandma's. She hadn't held onto grandpa's clothes after his death.

Taking stock took a while, and before I realized it, almost two hours had passed.

I had no idea what to do with her clothes. Give the lot to charity? Toss it into a dumpster? Leave it by the side of the dumpster, let the homeless pick and choose from the pile? I remembered people doing that when I was a kid, was that still a thing you could do?

I turned on the TV, found a music channel, left it on with music loud enough to be heard throughout the apartment but not so loud, I hoped, to disturb the neighbors. I went into the bathroom, saw the washing machine and thought I might as well wash my travel clothes so people next to me on the flight back don't think wrinkle their noses at me.

I got the clothes—but first I had to take nona's out of the drum.

I opened the door and crouched, looking at the jumble of sleeves and socks and dark fabrics, ignoring the mild smell of mildew.

And then I saw it.

Yesterday I would have said it was fatigue. Today, other things seemed like more probable explanations. Things no sane person should even consider probable.

I was certain I'd seen something move in there. I took out my phone, turned on the flashlight and pointed the beam inside.

"*Pizda ti materina!*" it cursed at me, shielding its eyes with one tiny hand. The voice threw me off, I have to admit, and I fell on my ass but still managed to keep the light and my eyes on the creature.

It was all tiny, to be fair, its back to the back of the steel drum, covered up to its waist with a sleeve of nona's shirt. It— well, it looked human in the same way Barba—with his glamour—looked human, while he obviously wasn't. It had a scruffy beard, its arms were gangly, fingers long and knobby. The front of its red tunic was straining over a pot belly and curls of greasy hair stuck out messily from under its short, red conical hat.

I lowered the beam so it wouldn't shine directly into the creature's eyes. It put its hand down. One of its eyes was brown while the other was green, but both stared right at me and blinked. Then it cleared its throat and straightened its back. "You're the grandson, then."

"And who are you?" I asked without thinking.

It climbed forward over the clothes and was now standing on the very edge of the washing machine opening. Its pant legs were of different lengths, its boots somehow both leathery and furry at the same time.

"I," the tiny creature said, puffing its chest, "am Lena's *domaći*."

"You're her what?" I asked, blinking.

The creature was scratching its head. "I... ugh, what is the word in English. *Jebemu, koja ono...* Ah. *Domovoi.*"

"That isn't an English word," I said.

It puffed. "Well, it's what they told me the English and the Americans use!"

But as it spoke, I remembered *domaći*. Another blast from the past, this time to my Croatian literature required reading list in elementary school and a collection of tales inspired by folklore. Domaći, the good spirits living in a house, helping out with cleaning and whatnot. I looked at the creature. *Of course,* I thought. *Of course.*

The domaći turned around and hopped onto the open washing machine door, and then leapt and somersaulted, landing on top of the machine. It looked at me, still on my ass on the cold bathroom floor. I put the phone down and, keeping my eyes on the tiny creature, managed to scramble up into a crouching position with at least some dignity.

"Do you, uh, have a name?" I asked.

The tiny creature nodded. "Lena gave me one. Bowie." Said with a proud grin.

I blinked. I once again noticed his eyes, one brown, one green. The teeth matched his namesake as well, in the early years of his career. I wondered if that was where the similarities ended.

"I'm Paul," I said. Then I asked, "Are... are you *my* domaći now?" *Do I have to take care of you? Pay you? Take you with me when I leave?*

Bowie seemed uncertain. "I've bound myself to Lena's hearth. Well, electric stove, but it's, *a u kurac*, ah, metaphorical. I serve her household. I'll serve yours." He looked at me for a moment. "I guess."

"Serve how?"

"Keep the house clean. Help you out with other domestic things."

"And you do that for free?"

"Well, you're expected to feed me, of course," he said.

I took a deep breath. "Look, I'm completely new to all of this. Last night I had no idea magic was real, and now my grandma was a krsnik and apparently I am one as well—"

He was nodding sympathetically. "Lena was worried the power might go to your mother instead but I see—"

"Yeah, honestly..." I stopped. What would Mom do with krsnik powers? She was coming up in years, led a peaceful life. True, she had a chronic illness but it wasn't life threatening and she could still move about, but... The hell would she do as a krsnik?

Heal herself? I made a mental note to check the book and ask Katrina if magical healing was possible. Then I thought of Dad and the kind of healing he needed. Could a krsnik do that as well? I had been trying to remember the stories from childhood, stories grandpa or nona would tell me during winter evenings—grandpa. Did he know what his wife really was, what she could do?

"How long were you Lena's domaći?"

Bowie, his legs dangling over the edge of the washing machine, said, "Five decades at least."

"Oh. That's long," I said. "Is it?" How long did domaći live?

"Domaći don't really feel time as you humans do."

"Fair enough," I said. "Did grandpa ever see you?"

"Ordinary humans see me only when I want them to," Bowie said.

"So he didn't?"

"Your grandfather never saw me."

"Did he know, about grandma being a krsnik?"

"No," Bowie said.

"How did she keep it so well hidden? I mean, that entire room, all that paper, the stuff she must have been doing over the years—decades—"

"Your grandmother was a very resourceful and cunning woman," Bowie said. I waited, but he didn't elaborate further.

I turned, saw the small wooden chair that had always been kept in the bathroom, pulled it close to the washing machine and sat down. "Okay, so now what?"

Bowie scratched his shaggy beard in confusion. "What do you mean?"

I sighed. "I don't know. I keep hoping I'll wake up, but no luck. Then I keep hoping someone will tell me what I need to do."

"You are a human and a krsnik," Bowie said. "You have not only free will, but also the means to enact it way beyond the powers of an ordinary man." He said it as if he had no idea what I was confused about.

"I don't want to be a krsnik," I said.

"Oh," Bowie said softly. His eyes regarded me warily. "Will you be leaving, then? Abandoning the hearth?" It sounded as if he was afraid for his job.

Or... existence? Fucking hell, was that it? ...God, I hope that's not it.

I looked at him for a long moment as other thoughts invaded my head once again. "I promised Katrina I'll try to... I honestly don't know what. She claims krsnik powers can help me do good, I guess? And that Lena's done good things—"

"Your grandmother had done much good, yes. Helped many, saved many."

"Yes, so I've been told. And now Katrina thinks I should be doing the same."

"I like that girl," Bowie said. "She always has candy in her pocket, leaves it for me. *Mmm, karamele.*" His eyes seemed to sparkle for a moment as he thought about caramels.

"Yes, well. I need to figure out what I want to do with this." I looked around. "All of this. The apartment, the sanctum—"

"The what?"

"The room that shouldn't exist, the one where Lena kept all—"

"Aaah, alright." He frowned. "She never called it that."

The word had only occurred to me but—well, that's what it would have been called in books I read as a kid, wouldn't it? The books in which I'd for a while found solace and escape, while my parents dragged me all over the world. The place where a mage would work. Nona wasn't a mage, but in my mind it was close enough. It needed a name and...

"What did she call it?" I asked.

"Her room," the domaći said flatly.

It was obvious Lena had a much more mundane view of all of this than I did. Then again, she'd had years and years to acquire such a view, hadn't she?

Bowie suddenly jumped to his feet and rubbed his hands. "Right, master, what shall we do? I've seen you walk the apartment, open closets and drawers. I can remove all of Lena's clothes, if you wish to make room for you own, and—"

"Wait," I said. "Just—wait. I can't stay here."

"We'll move?"

So he could travel with me?

"No, Bowie, in Rijeka. In Croatia."

"But you said you've told Katrina—"

I genuinely would have welcomed a headache because it would have paired nicely with my exasperation, but it stubbornly refused to return. "I know. But it's—god, it's ridiculous. I promised her something I know there's no way I can make good on. Yes, it's theoretically possible, but come on..."

I sighed, then groaned and got up.

Bowie was looking at me, seeming hopeful as much as full of apprehension.

"Can you remove her clothes from the washing machine? And then wash mine?" I asked, wanting to give him something to do because he seemed as lost as I felt. He nodded eagerly. But he kept standing there for a moment, and then he looked to the side, apparently uncomfortable. "If you could leave, please? I like to work unseen."

It sounded strange, but then again, what isn't these days?

"If you need me," he said as I was leaving the bathroom, "just call my name."

A DOJO ISN'T JUST FOR FACING OTHERS

Back in Lena's secret room, everything was still where it had been last night. Only, now it somehow felt as if all of it was waiting for me to take an action. *Expecting* me to take an action.

I looked at the table, the mess on it: pieces of paper, clippings, charts, maps, photos, printouts. And then I noticed it, in the far corner, atop a cabinet: a closed laptop. Its power cable actually snaked out of the room's door and into the storage space. I glanced out and saw it run along the bottom of the wall and out into the hallway and connect to a plug next to the fuse box. That cable had not been there yesterday.

No, I wasn't *able to see it* yesterday. That was it, wasn't it?

This was going to be my life now. Seeing things other people never could and never would.

I went back to the laptop. Another cable ran from it into one of the cabinet's drawers, connecting it to a small printer there.

I opened the laptop, switched it on. It asked for a password.

The user photo on the login screen was of my grandma holding a baby. Holding *me*. I was maybe a few months old, pink and grumpy-looking, but she had the biggest, happiest smile you've ever seen on a person. There was something in my eye as I clicked on the password field, wondering what to try. I doubted 'password' would work. Or '1234'. Grandma had been old, but something told me she'd also been a bit more tech savvy than that. After all, the apartment had Wi-Fi, and her TV had a USB port with

74

a thumb drive inserted—I'd noticed it while wandering around the apartment.

I was thinking hard, racking my brain for dates of birth and stuff like that until I realized I was, as usual, overthinking. The laptop was in a room I was pretty certain your average thief couldn't find nor enter. With all the stuff in the books and the notebooks and on the scraps of paper on the table behind me—well, I guessed grandma figured that her information was safe enough as it was.

I clicked login without entering a password.

And I was in.

The desktop background was a photo of my entire family. Mom, Dad, grandma, grandpa and me, sitting at a table. There was a lot of food, so it must have been some Christmas or Easter or someone's birthday. I looked to be about five or six years old.

The desktop itself was, well, a mirror image of the table behind my back, dozens of text files and folders with names ranging from 'Photos 2011' and 'Official documentation 2005', to 'Misc 1997 and 'asfwddee.'

Going through that would be like going through the stuff on the table.

So I clicked on the web browser instead, opening its browsing history.

Ten minutes later I had no idea what I was looking at, mostly because I didn't know what I was looking *for*. Most of the pages were in Croatian, some in English, but all of it didn't give me anything useful because grandma had been, in the week before her death, looking at everything from serious news sites to those claiming pyramids were portals to other dimensions. There were even a couple of Facebook pages in the history, near the very top of the page. Was nona on Facebook?

What *was* I looking for? I was going to leave—I'd said so to Katrina. After I told her I'd give all this a shot.

"*Krasni kurac i pizdu materinu, jebem li ti da ti jebem!*"

I had no idea where the curses had come from.

Well, that wasn't true. I knew where they'd come from: my frustration with everything. But they were in Croatian, and I hadn't cursed in Croatian, out loud... ever? I'd grown up hearing people curse but, as a kid, I'd always known it wouldn't be smart for me to curse because a slap would be incoming and fast.

It felt good, though. I felt just a tiny bit better.

Everybody wanted something—everyone was *expecting* something of me even though they wouldn't say it out loud. Katrina. Barba. Bowie. Nona.

Never mind if I had a life of my own I wanted to live.

It wouldn't be the first time, I thought bitterly, remembering the day I was told we were leaving Croatia.

I realized I was gritting my teeth. I forced my jaw to relax and turned my back to the laptop, taking in the room once again.

Yes, this—the room, being a krsnik, Bowie and Barba and seeing things—was all dumped on me without asking me if I wanted it.

Yes, leaving Croatia and the ten years of moving all over the world, that had been dumped on me as well.

No, it wasn't the same. As much as my instinct was to put an equal sign between those two things, it wasn't; I knew it and I had to admit it.

I was bitter, true. Bitter because I was being saddled with things I had no desire to have in my life. But also bitter because I felt it was happening to me again. And this time I wasn't a kid. I could choose for myself and nobody could force me to turn my life upside down and leave everything I knew and—

Oh, god.

The fuck am I doing?

I was breathing deep, my eyes closed. It wasn't helping.

I left the room. Standing in the hallway, trying to avoid thinking about things for a few moments more, I glanced to the right and saw the only door I still hadn't opened since coming back.

It was also the last door I should open if I wanted to avoid thinking about things.

Fuck it. I walked over and opened it.

76

The room had been my Mom's until she left for college and, subsequently, married my Dad. Then it became mine, when I started staying over on the weekends and during holidays. I'd inherited Mom's bed and furniture, her books and everything else, because, apparently, grandma and grandpa hadn't changed a thing in the room in the time between their daughter leaving and their grandson arriving.

I had wanted it to become my room, not for the weekends and holidays, but *for good*—I'd wanted to stay here, with nona; live with her instead of leaving Croatia with my parents. My parents wouldn't hear of it. And nona had said I had to go with them. Memories of that conversation, if you could call what I did a conversation, had been gnawing at the back of my mind ever since I stepped my foot into the apartment again.

But now they were, for the moment, dead silent. As were the rest of my churning thoughts.

The room was empty. There were the two windows and a lamp hanging from the high ceiling, and that was it. No furniture. Nothing but bare walls and floor, as far as I could see in the gloom because most of the window slats were closed, with only a few thin streams of daylight coming through.

I reached to the side instinctively, found the switch and flipped it.

The floor wasn't bare, and neither were the walls. The room was, in fact, covered in something thick and shiny: the entire floor and the walls, all the way up to the ceiling that was, I saw as I looked up, covered as well.

I took a tentative step over the threshold. As my foot sunk just a bit into the material, I realized what it was: mats. The entire room was covered in thick training mats.

I walked deeper into the room, towards the windows. The air was a little musty and quite warm. The windows weren't the ones I remembered from my childhood; those had been old and wooden, and these metal, double-paned, and I realized I couldn't hear a thing through them even as I stood right in front of them.

I turned and saw that I had been mistaken; there was some furniture in here. A single item of furniture, in fact: a large, rectangular wooden crate in the right-hand corner from the door.

The large iron lock on it was open so I lifted the lid, feeling a bit like opening a very large treasure chest.

There was no treasure inside. There were sticks, though, of various shapes and sizes. Bamboo, I realized when I took one in my hand.

"Oh," I said out loud. These were kendo sticks. This—this was nona's training room.

Only they weren't just kendo sticks, I saw as I returned the first one back into the crate. There were wooden replicas of other weapons in it as well. I took out what I guessed was a Roman legionnaire sword, uncovering what looked like a short spear under it.

In one of the treasure chest's corners was a metal box set on a wooden block. It was a cube of iron and it seemed very old, rusted in places, but the lid on the top slid to the side without a hitch. There was a stone inside, carved into some kind of geometric shape with lots of sides. It looked like it could fit into my palm.

It also... felt weird to look at. No, that wasn't it—it just felt weird in general. As if it was radiating something.

I looked around. The room wasn't locked. The crate wasn't locked. And the small box didn't seem to have a locking mechanism. Also, the crate was full of wooden replicas, not real weapons, and the room itself was, very obviously, a training room.

I reached, took the stone out.

Touching it felt weird, again, but not threatening. And then, as I held it between my fingers to have a better look, I felt the weirdness subside. I thought back to Barba and to seeing the stone reliefs on the fish market building move. It was the same impression. Something new and obviously magical and supernatural that—

—that my mind perceived as strange, and then accepted as part of the world.

I sighed inwardly.

The stone was about the size of a chicken egg, carved roughly into a—I counted—a twelve-sided shape. Each side had something engraved into its surface. At first I had no idea if these were symbols or letters from some alphabet I didn't know, but then I noticed one I was pretty certain was Chinese. Another that looked like a group of hieroglyphs, and another was in Latin script. *FLAVIUS AETIUS*, it said in very large letters, filling out the surface. The name meant nothing to me.

A side next to it had been inscribed with something in Arabic. As we traveled, my education was in English but since I had, after a while, accepted that this was my life for a while and staying inside Dad's company's compounds was getting very boring very fast. I'd started tentatively exploring the local cultures, which inevitably led to me picking up a smattering of various languages, mostly just for saying hello and buying food. My Arabic was very rusty, but it seemed to me that the small and elegant inscription was a name: *Qadira*.

Were all the inscriptions names? Whose names? And why were they inscribed on this piece of stone?

I put the stone back into the box. It didn't feel weird to me at all anymore.

I wanted to curse out loud again. The room, judging from the windows, was soundproof so I could curse up a storm, get really loud, *hysterical* even and—

—and what?

I plopped myself down on the floor, leaned my back against the crate. Knees drawn up, hands resting atop them, my chin on my hands, I let the thoughts back onstage.

This was supposed to be my room, in another life.

But it hadn't been.

My life had not been what I'd hoped for when I was a kid.

It wasn't moving in a direction I wanted it to even now.

But...

What was my life?

79

I had full control of it—well, I'd had full control of it until a few days ago. It was simple and I enjoyed it—well, I was content with it.

I wasn't bothered by it.

We used to live on the outskirts of Rijeka and I went to a local school there. But I never fit in there and I never really clicked with the kids in my neighborhood. I have no idea why.

I didn't really like the school either. Dad was often absent due to business trips and Mom worked from home, but was still very busy a lot of the time.

I wasn't a neglected kid, don't get the wrong impression. My parents loved me unconditionally and they showed it as much as they could.

But I was also a moody kid by nature—and kids are, in general, self-centered little asses and drama queens. Since grandma and grandpa always seemed to have time for me and the kids in their building—Katrina first—always seemed way more accepting of me than those on my own street, somewhere along the way I'd started feeling nona's building was my *home* and our own apartment was just this place where I lived during the week.

So naturally, when my parents decided to leave Croatia, I wanted to stay. I had it all planned out: move into nona's apartment, make this room mine and stay in Rijeka until I had to leave for college; maybe stay for college in Rijeka as well. I'd go visit Mom and Dad, of course—I wasn't a monster—but I didn't want to leave.

But I was told I was leaving. Mom and Dad were—I understood that when I grew up—aware how much I didn't want to leave, but they had the best of intentions.

Grandma must have had them as well, since she told me I can't stay, that I had to go.

I understood that now, as an adult. But back then, in '95? I screamed my head off at grandma. I felt betrayed. The stuff I told her, about how I hope I die or she die or we all die and how the building should just burn down and everything should just burn—

fuck me, I would have slapped myself if I could. But she didn't. She just took it calmly and then, when I was literally out of breath and had calmed down, she went to hug me.

And I didn't let her. I turned and left, walked out of the apartment and got onto the bus and went home. Two days later, we left Croatia. I heard grandma come to our apartment to say goodbye the day we left. I pretended I didn't hear Mom call for me. I heard nona tell her it's fine, to let me be.

I'd cooled off maybe a day after we left. I was so damn sorry and I wanted to tell nona that, but we were in transit and my parents were ridiculously busy and when Mom told me I should write nona a letter I didn't, because I wanted to *hear* her tell me she forgave me.

I finally did talk to her, but months later, and it was a very short conversation because international calls were ridiculously expensive. But she didn't let me apologize—three times I started, three times she gently brushed it aside, asking me how I was and how things were going and telling me I was just on a big adventure and to enjoy it.

Looking back, it was obvious she didn't want to relive that moment in the apartment, but that she'd also forgiven me for it.

It took me a long time to start enjoying that "big adventure", and it took me stopping resenting my parents and, well, the world.

Days turned to weeks, weeks somehow turned to months and years, and here I was, once again angry at nona and the world.

Somewhere in the middle of finally replaying those memories on the main stage of my brain, I started crying. I couldn't see the room around me. Everything was just a wet blur.

But with the tears came something else, something I didn't expect. There was no bitterness, no anxiety, no dark things coming from the depths of my mind to tear me apart because I've finally opened the door I kept all these memories behind.

Nona had forgiven me. I had forgiven her. I had forgiven my parents and they, I'm certain, had forgiven me for all I did as a moody kid and as an angry teenager.

I'd kept the thoughts back because I was terrified I would hate myself.

But... there was no hate. There wasn't even crippling regret, something I feared even more.

It was just life.

I wiped my eyes with my sleeves, took a deep breath with the back of my head against the crate.

"Alright, nona," I said, opening my eyes. "Alright." I stood up. I was still pretty certain I would be leaving and I wouldn't become a krsnik, but now I was willing to see what it was that she'd been doing in her secret life.

MEETING THE NEIGHBOURS

I sat in the chair next to the table covered in paper, rested the back of nona's book against the table's edge and started leafing through it. There didn't seem to be any rhyme or reason to it: what looked like recipes, instructions for carving metal and wood with strange symbols, drawings of what I guessed were plants and I hoped were not real creatures—all of it one after the other. There was no index, but there were dozens of places where she had left a note in the corner of one page referring to another page—not by number, of course, but by word or short description.

Nona's handwriting ran the gamut of almost calligraphic to what even a doctor would probably have a problem with. Her drawings were sometimes very detailed, almost like book cover illustrations, and other times no more than a rough sketch that seemed to be attempts at those pictures where you have to stare real hard until an image finally forms.

And then I turned a page and just sat there staring at it, dumbstruck.

It was a large drawing of a strange door. A strange red door, its surface carved into triangles and squares.

The door I had dreamed about—several times. I thought hard about it. When did it first appear in my dreams?

And I remembered then. I'd dreamed about it just before waking up on the day I got a call from Mom telling me grandma had died the night before.

I leaned forward, fully focusing on the drawing and the notes in Croatian surrounding it. I read and reread every line and every word, reaching several times for a translator app on my phone just to make sure I was interpreting the meaning correctly.

Nona had been dreaming about the same door. Although not just dreaming. My interpretation of the notes could have been way off, of course, but it seemed you could open the door and pass through them in your dream. There was no mention of what was on the other side, but there *was* mention that she'd been doing some kind of research: notes about talking to 'others' who 'also use dream doors', but that their doors don't look like hers.

Then there was another note saying that '*the door is the same for everyone in the family/blood line?*' followed by a '*YES*' in capitals.

I leaned back in the chair, the open book resting on my knees. Was this door something related to being a krsnik? Or was it something else, supernatural but not connected to my—my 'legacy'?

I skimmed the rest of the book, looking for any mention of doors in dreams or another drawing like that one, but didn't find any.

Well, next time I fall asleep, maybe I'll find out what's behind them. The thought wasn't exactly a pleasant one, but also—also, there was a small shiver of anticipation and excitement somewhere deep down.

I stood up, set the book down and looked at the table.

Was there actually some kind of a system here, and I just wasn't seeing it? Creative chaos and all that. Or was it just nona dumping stuff on the table and digging for it months later?

I started picking up pieces of paper and notes from the top. Just as with the book, I wasn't looking for anything specific, but hoping something would catch my eye and reveal more about what my krsnik grandma had actually been doing in her secret life.

It took some time, not just because the top layer alone was still dozens and dozens of notes, but also because my Croatian was rusty—although it would stop being so if I keep reading every damn thing I pick up from the pile.

There were articles cut out from newspapers, some with paragraphs underlined, some with photos circled, but nothing to reveal the meaning of the markings on the door.

There were copies of what looked like official documents, whose legalese was way above my current reading comprehension levels. Although, I could ask Katrina to take a look. Some of these legal documents also came with old aerial photos of plots and properties—survey maps, I realized, from some zoning department.

There were printouts and pages torn out from books and folded maps of Rijeka and other places I didn't recognize the names of; pages and pages of handwritten notes and drawings that seemed to belong in the book on the chair: plants and creatures and buildings and objects.

Some of these were old, which I could tell from dates (printed or handwritten on the backs, or in the corners) or from the paper being yellow and the images faint.

But some things were recent, stuff nona was obviously dealing with recently.

I found a three-page printout, the pages stapled together, each page with about a dozen names, each of them followed by a date and a place, and then a note in nona's handwriting. The oldest date was a little over a year and a half ago, the newest just four weeks ago. The places ranged all over Croatia, at least those that I recognized.

But the notes gave me chills: these were missing people, I realized after reading the first few entries. And nona was investigating them? Reading on, the thing became more confusing because some notes said a person had been reported missing, but for at least a third nona had written down something along the lines of people claiming they were just on holiday or business trips, or that they'd moved to another country.

I set the printout down. This was heavy stuff.

I glanced at the laptop and remembered the browser history. I walked over and clicked on those Facebook pages that were among the last things nona had opened in the browser. I didn't have a Facebook profile anymore, but I knew Mom did, and as the page was opening, for a moment I thought I might see Mom's face looking back at me from the profile photo—but it wasn't.

I had no idea who this woman was. *Snježana Remac*, according to her profile. And then I saw the note at the bottom of the screen and the first few posts on her wall. It was a memorialized account, the wall full of *'Rest in peace'* and *'There's another angel in heaven'* and *'Gone too soon but never forgotten'*. Judging from the dates of the posts, she had died recently. I looked at the photo again and felt a pang of sadness. This woman seemed to have been barely in her late forties. Far too soon to die. And she had this huge, bright smile and large, beaming eyes.

I looked at her personal information but all the fields were empty. I scrolled down but couldn't find any posts that were hers. It wasn't that odd, though; a lot of people on Facebook never post anything on their own wall.

Had she been a friend of nona's?

Or someone nona had helped?

Or *failed to help*?

The thought was fleeting, but it left a cold mark on my gut.

I opened the other Facebook pages in the browser history.

Two were broken links, but the third was another personal profile.

Snježana Remac had a husband. His name was Alen and, from the activity on his wall, he was still alive.

And she'd also had children: the first photo Facebook showed me was of Alen and Snježana with two young daughters, laughing as they sat on a seaside bench.

Who were these people and why had nona been interested in them?

I searched the browser history for *Remac* but the two Facebook profiles were all I got. Also—I checked, opening the Facebook login page—nona didn't have a Facebook profile, or at least hadn't saved the password.

I went through the photos on Alen Remac's profile and stopped mid-scroll. There she was. Nona. Sitting at what looked like a kitchen table with the two daughters, playing Ludo. I kept scrolling but there were no more photos of my grandma, but there was one that showed the two girls and a couple of other kids playing. The photo was taken from up high and the kids were looking up and waving at the camera—well, probably a mobile phone, not a real camera. And I knew where they were playing because, even after all these years, I still remembered the inner courtyard of nona's building, where I myself had played with Katrina and her friends so many times.

The photo had to have been taken from a window or a balcony. The Remac family lived in this building.

I turned back to the table. Where was it? Or maybe I was misremembering—no, there it was, a printout of a photo of the building, shot from inside the inner courtyard. A small balcony was circled, above what I recognized as nona's apartment's toilet window. Lines were drawn from the balcony, some down to the ground, others up towards the roof.

And there were a few handwritten notes.

'*Tavan ili podrum?*' Attic or basement?

'*Bosi otisci i zemlja u bebinoj sobi, ali ne po zidu.*' Barefoot footprints and earth in the baby's room, but not on the wall.

Footprints? Earth? What was going on?

Well, they were here, in this building, and nona had something to do with them and… and I could go talk to them?

And so I went back to the living room to get the apartment keys, after which I went upstairs to the Remac apartment.

I could hear faint music from behind the door, and voices that sounded like two girls and an older man.

I pressed the buzzer next to the little plastic tab saying *Remac*, thinking *What the hell am I doing?* The moment the door opened I realized I had no idea what *precisely* I wanted to do.

"*Da?*" a tall teenage girl with dark hair and a grim face asked, standing in the doorway.

"Hi," I said. "Sorry, do you speak English?"

"Yes. What d'ya want?" she asked, doing her best to sound like, I guess a New Yorker? But the accent was still very much Croatian.

"Hi, my name is Paul. I—"

"*Tko je?*" a voice came from behind the girl and Alan Remac appeared. He was at least fifteen years older than me. He seemed very tired and trying not to show it. The kitchen spatula in his hands added to an aroma of something sweet and savory which wafted off him. "*Vi ste?*"

"Hi, I'm Paul," I said.

"*Ne znam što hoće,*" his daughter said. Which was okay with me, because I, myself, didn't know what I wanted either.

"You need help?" the man asked.

"Well, kind of," I said, smiling awkwardly. "I came here yesterday. My grandmother lived here, two floors down. Lena."

The man's eyes went wide. The girl, up to that point the very image of a surly teenager, suddenly mellowed. But just a bit; she was, after all, still a teenagerl.

"Oh," she said. "I'm sorry."

"Oh," Alen Remac echoed and paused. "*A u klinac, kako se kaže moja sućut?*" he asked his daughter.

"He's sorry for your loss too," the daughter said, giving her dad the side eye.

"I was told you knew her," I said, putting on a hopeful smile. "Forgive me, I haven't lived in Croatia since the 1990s, my Croatian is very bad."

"No problem," Alen Remac said. "So is my English." He nodded then. "Lena was friends of my wife mother." He paused and a look of pain crossed his face. He glanced at his daughter then and pulled himself up, a smile back on his face.

"She was good woman," he said. "Helped us sometimes, when she and her sister was young," he said, nodding towards his daughter. "When we had no money for babysitter." Then he shook his head. "Sorry, you want come in? Making lunch for girls before school."

I smiled politely and entered, the teenage daughter not looking very pleased. In the kitchen, her sister, a few years younger, was holding a baby in her arms, cooing softly at it, poking its nose gently with her finger. A baby maybe a few months old.

Fucking hell.

She stopped playing with the baby when she saw me. And, for some reason, this young girl seemed familiar to me.

"Hi," I said, raising a hand.

"*Ovo ti je unuk od tete Lene,*" the father said, introducing me as Lena's grandson, and then he spit out a curse and ran to the stove, where fries were, guessing by the smell, burning in the pan.

The older daughter was looking at me, obviously not wanting me in the apartment, but also aware that she should be a good host, so she just said, "You want Cola?"

"Please, sit," the father said over his shoulders, dealing with the various pans and pots on the stove. "We have beer."

"No, Cola is fine, thank you," I said, taking a seat. The younger girl was still looking at me, as was now the baby in her arms. Huge blue eyes on both of them, I noticed. I glanced at the older daughter, blue-eyed as well; accentuated with dark makeup. Just like their mother.

"I'm Petra," the younger girl said. "And this is Ivo."

"Hi, I'm Paul," I said, feeling as if it was the only thing I've been saying the last few minutes.

The father was now next to me, showing me something. It was a large photo in an old plastic frame. "Here," he said, pointing. "This your grandmother." And so it was. There was nona, about a decade older than I remembered her, which put the photo in the early 2000s. The kind eyes were still there, even though there were many more lines on her face and her hair was fully grey. There were other people in the photo as well, all well dressed. And Alen Remac was there, too, in the middle of the shot, wearing a tuxedo.

It was a wedding photo. Snježana was next to him in a slim white dress and with a huge grin on her face; a tall woman, dark-haired and blue-eyed and very lovely. It was a smile, I guessed, this man had hoped to see every day for the rest of his life.

"She was at your wedding," I said, not knowing what to say.

"Yes," he said, smiling with sad eyes. He pointed out a woman next to Lena. "My wife mother."

"They were good friends?" I asked. Obviously, but I had to make conversation.

"Yes, yes," he said. "She die years ago," he added.

There was a long moment of silence and then the baby started making noises and Alen Remac turned, put the photo on a shelf next to the kitchen door and went back to the stove.

I realized that, at some point during my conversation with their father, the teenage daughter had taken over the baby holding duty, because the younger girl was nowhere to be seen.

Only she was, right next to me. I almost jumped from my chair.

And I recognized her then. She was the girl that dashed past me and Katrina yesterday, babbling merrily and loudly to herself. She was wearing the same red bow in her hair.

She was offering me something, hand awkwardly stretched out towards me, fist firmly holding something. She was smiling, but avoiding eye contact.

I smiled too, leaned forward a little and opened my hand.

She dropped it into my palm.

I hadn't seen one of those since childhood: a bracelet made of plastic strings woven together. Crudely made, but it's what gave it charm. Red and pink and yellow plastic threads crossing over each other, the weave mostly tight, but with the occasional gap.

"Thank—*hvala*," I said.

She looked at me, smiled brightly.

There were several of the bracelets on both her wrists. I noticed one around the dad's wrist as well as he cooked. I glanced at the teenage daughter and she saw me looking and pulled the edge of her sleeve down over the bracelet, no doubt annoyed at being caught actually caring about her stupid younger sister's gift.

I was holding the bracelet in my hand, feeling just a bit uncomfortable. I looked at the father but he was busy making a face at the baby. The younger daughter was looking at me very intensely, and so there was really just one thing I could do.

"*Pomogneš mi?*" I said, offering her my wrist. She nodded eagerly and proceeded to tie it around with expert movements. Obviously she'd had practice. Just a moment or two later I had a nice new bracelet.

I looked at the gift and then at the little girl. Her face was very solemn. She said something in Croatian, her voice soft but serious, her eyes locked onto mine. I couldn't make out what she'd said, though.

"She ask if you like it," her father explained, smiling.

I glanced at the bracelet; then put on a solemn expression to match the girl's. "Yes," I said. "*Da. Hvala,*" I told her.

She nodded, then her face broke into another smile and she ran back towards some of her toys nearby. Within a second I was forgotten.

At which point I reminded myself why I was here.

Well, why was I here exactly? Because Lena had circled their balcony door and written something about footprints and earth?

Maybe I should take a look at that room.

There was no way they'd give me a tour of the apartment, of course. But they were in the middle of lunch, so...

"Sorry," I said to the teenage girl as her father was busy with something in the fridge, "could I use your toilet?"

"No problem," Alen Remac said in her stead, glancing over his shoulder. "Go there," he pointed at a door that was slightly ajar. "Door on left."

"Thank you," I said, went through the door and closed it behind me. I was in a short hallway that seemed to run the length of the rest of the apartment. I took a few steps, saw various open and closed doorways. Unless my sense of direction was way off, the room with the balcony facing the inner courtyard had to be on my left.

And so it was: one of the open doors led into a small, but brightly colored room with a baby's cot in the middle and stacks of diapers in one corner. A mobile hung over the cot and some toys were scattered across the floor, probably left lying where the baby dropped or threw them.

There was a single, glass door in the outer wall, covered with blinds. A window next to it had its curtain open, giving me a view of the building's opposite wall with a row of windows, the same drab colour I remembered from childhood. I knew what else the window would give me a view of if I were standing closer: the inner courtyard formed by this row of buildings, making a sort of an elongated U-shape.

Glancing from the doorway, I couldn't see any earth or anything on the floor that wasn't old parquet or a relatively new, small rug in front of the crib.

"It's there," I heard behind my back. The teenage girl was standing in the now open kitchen doorway, frowning at me.

"Sorry," I said. I entered the toilet she'd pointed at, hoping I wasn't giving off a "creep" vibe.

I stayed in the toilet for about a minute, then flushed and washed my hands. The girl was back in the kitchen, grumpy at her father for filming her and her sister and the baby eating.

"*Ajde, smiješak za baku,*" Alen Remac said, obviously teasing them. Smile for grandma.

"*E, ajde nemoj opet stavit na Fejsbuk da svi vide da nas hraniš,*" the teenage daughter grumbled. Don't put it on Facebook just so people can see you're feeding us.

"Good?" her father asked me as he saw me come back into the kitchen.

"Yes," I said. Then I stood there for a moment, and finally forced a smile and said, "Thank you, and once again, I'm very sorry for your loss. I'm glad Lena was a good neighbour to you."

The teenage girl gave her dad the gist of it, and he smiled. He escorted me to the apartment door. We shook hands and he gave me a sympathetic clap on the shoulder and then I was alone on the stairs.

Back in nona's apartment, I went into the toilet. It was a small, square room with just the toilet itself and a large window you could look out of while doing your business if you wanted to.

The inner courtyard hadn't changed one bit in all these years. No, that wasn't true. There had been a section in one corner where the ground was not concrete, but soil covered in gravel, apparently intended to serve as kids' playground. When I was a kid, a tree had been growing there, but it was gone now, not even a stump left.

I leaned out the window, looking to the left and up. There was the tiny balcony of the baby's room—the only one on this side of the building. There were a couple places along the wall where balcony doors once stood, now just bricked-up outlines. Maybe half a meter to the left of the balcony the wall took a right-angle turn, stretching forward to where, some ten meters ahead, it would connect with the next building.

I looked down again—and I saw it. Tucked directly into the corner, still there after all these years: my grandpa's shed.

Luckily for me, nona kept all her keys on the same keychain, which hadn't changed its resting place for decades: a drawer in the cupboard right next to the kitchen door.

I had to try out several keys to open the metal door into the courtyard—the door was new; back when I was a kid it was just an ancient wooden one, its lock long gone. But the lock on the shed was literally the same one grandpa had put there decades ago, and there was no mistaking the key: it was an old-timey one, as if I were about to open a treasure chest or unlock a cell door in a castle's dungeon. It wasn't as big as those keys would be, of course, but the general shape of it was exactly the same.

I wondered how long ago the shed had been opened last. The door creaked gently as I stepped inside. The shed was long and narrow, jury-rigged from wooden and metal panels, using the side of the building as its back and right-hand wall. There was a short stack of chopped wood to the left, an old workbench to the right, and an equally old tool cabinet on the wall above it. Dust and dirt covered every surface. The chopped wood was old as well, and it was completely possible it had been there ever since grandpa died.

And there was a tarp on the floor at the very back of the shed. A hazy memory flickered in my mind, a reason I was told not to go to the back, not to stand there.

I made my way across the dust and dirt and saw that the tarp was actually bunched together and that there was something underneath it.

And there it was. The grille.

I remembered now: the grille over a square opening into the building's basement. A solid grille, set into concrete but—oh, right, it wasn't grandpa who'd been worried. It was nona, who was convinced it would give out just as I stood on it, so I was forbidden to go even near it. In fact, I remembered now, she'd nagged me about the grille so much I started avoiding other grilles like that. Back then, several streets in Rijeka we would often pass through had those grilles on the ground right next to the buildings. In fact, to this day I was uncomfortable walking over those things anywhere I saw them.

The tarp was obviously meant to cover it, but had, at one point been removed, pushed to uncover the grille.

I looked down the opening, but my light revealed only a concrete floor and even more dust and dirt.

It didn't feel pleasant. I was suddenly cold, and the air from down below was dusty and clammy. I stepped back, seized by a sudden feeling I might get vertigo.

I looked up and away from the thing and noticed that one of the irregular plastic panes that formed the makeshift roof of the shed wasn't aligned with the rest. There was an opening, at least the width of my fist. I could see the building wall through it, feel a hint of fresh air. Did someone use it to get inside the shed, and then didn't pull it back all the way? But there was nothing to steal in here.

Was there?

Or...

I looked down again.

I crouched.

The grille could be lifted. I saw hinges on the side of the grille closest to me as I remembered grandpa telling me that they used to store gold down there when Rijeka was a pirate's republic in the nineteenth century.

He liked to make things up to entertain me.

On the side opposite the hinges I could see where the padlock usually went, but there wasn't one there now. I couldn't remember if there'd been one there when I was a kid. Probably not. Luckily for me, I never noticed the hinges when I was a kid, or I would have—

Well, I would have done what I did now. I lifted the grille. The hinges squealed. I moved to the side to take another look into the building's basement, my view now unobstructed.

I took out my phone, turned on the flashlight. Just dark and dirt and the smell of mildew and old dust.

And then I heard a sound.

Mice? I thought.

Ugh, or rats?

And then a hand shot out from the darkness, grabbed me by the wrist and pulled hard.

I went headlong down into the dark.

IT'S WHAT WE DO FOR OTHERS, IN THE DARK...

I was on my back, breathing hard, looking at a square of light up above.

I fell in, didn't I? Just as nona said would happ—

I was pulled in.

I sat up, my heartbeat speeding up as I looked around, frantic, adrenaline making me want to jump up (I couldn't reach the opening!) or climb up the bare walls or—

I was alone, I realized as I looked around, sitting on the dirty concrete floor. There was no hand that had pulled me, no person the hand had been attached to, either. The basement seemed to be just a lot of concrete pillars and the occasional metal barrel or wooden crate. Lots and lots of dust and bits of decades' worth of detritus strewn across the floor, pieces of metal or wood or plastic or paper—

I was seeing all this as if under daylight that was dimmed, but still strong enough to let me see for meters and meters in every direction. The only source of light was the opening. It was impossible for me to see that well, and yet...

Was this a krsnik ability? Could I actually see in the dark? A car horn seemed to honk directly above me and for a moment I thought one had somehow crashed into the shed.

I heard more honking now, engines revving, drivers shouting, and it all seemed to be taking place directly above me, or next to me, only it couldn't be.

The nearest street was the one directly behind the building.

Something rumbled to the side of me and below me—a liquid sound—like water in pipes.

And there was also soft squeaking from somewhere in the distant parts of the basement. There *were* mice here, then.

The grit on the floor was like needles sticking into my palms as I pushed myself to my feet, doing my best to ignore all the sounds. *At least my head doesn't hurt*, I thought, thankful. I could feel the dust settling on my skin as I stood stock still.

My senses were stronger somehow.

And then they weren't. The sounds died out, apart from my own breathing. All I could see were the vague outlines of the closest pillars.

It was then I noticed I was in pain. My forearms were scraped in places, a little bloody. My forehead as well, which I found out when I touched it. The scrapes burned like any scrape would and there was so much filth here I couldn't not think about infections.

I looked up, thinking maybe, if I jumped up, maybe I could reach the opening—

I heard footsteps behind me, the crunching of dirt and grit.

I turned, ready for that same hand to grab for me again, to tear my face off—

There was someone there, maybe two meters away, peering at me from behind a concrete pillar. I couldn't make out anything apart from the general shape, and then my eyes adjusted a little to the dark and I saw a pair of eyes catching the light from the opening—

—and then I could see everything again and the woman was not just dirty, but caked in dirt, actual dirt, *soil*, and her dark hair was matted and the clothes on her were not what you'd expect from a homeless person. She was in pants and a blouse, crumpled and dirty but still fancy-looking under all that—

—and then she was nothing more than a dark shape again.

I was afraid, but also a little light-headed from my senses going into overdrive and then back to normal again, all within a second or two.

"Hello?" I called, straining to make out the person, watching intently for any sign they might rush me (maybe with a knife or a broken bottle).

The person—the woman, I reminded myself—moved from behind the pillar. She was shorter than I thought, a moment before.

She was shorter, but had appeared taller because she hadn't been standing behind the pillar. She had been holding *onto it*. She crawled across the side of the pillar, her palms and bare feet somehow finding purchase on the flat surface.

This is how she grabbed me, a tiny thought piped up. She was *on the ceiling*.

She stepped down onto the floor. Then she kept moving, creeping closer to me. The light was stronger where she stopped and I could see all I saw just a moment ago, only now I didn't need supercharged krsnik vision.

"I—I'm sorry if I scared you and you pulled me because you—" I stopped myself. One, I was babbling, and two, chances were great this woman couldn't speak English.

"*Oprostite*," I said. "*Nisam opasno.*" It seemed smart to let her know I'm no danger to her.

She took another step. I shrank back despite myself. She was fully in the light now. I could smell her, a strong whiff of—of freshly dug earth.

Her feet were bare.

And I could see her face very clearly now. Her blue eyes.

This was Snježana Remac. The *dead* wife and mother.

The face from the photos was there, the features present under the dirt. There was no smile or brightness in the eyes, though. The look in them was—not empty, *distant*. Not cold, *detached*.

I had no idea what to do. How was she alive? And why was she here?

I remembered nona's photo and the notes. Why was this woman climbing into her baby's room?

Never mind that, how was she here?!

Was she alive? Had she been buried alive—

But no, she was dead, I realized as I watched her, as she stood there, looking at me—or through me, it was hard to say. This was a corpse, and yet something was keeping her moving. And there was light inside those eyes, subdued but still there. There was, I guessed, a consciousness.

She took another step. I stepped back, this time intentionally and slowly, until I felt the basement wall against my back.

She reached for me and my hand shot up on its own, protecting my face. I felt her fingers touch my forearm, cold and bony.

She took hold of my forearm but she wasn't squeezing, wasn't crushing it or tearing the skin to get to the flesh and blood beneath.

She was holding it... gently. She was staring with an intensity I hadn't seen in her eyes so far.

Staring, I realized, at my wrist; at the twisted plastic string bracelet her daughter had given me.

I breathed out, slowly.

Her skin was cold and dry and coarse from dirt. *Earth.*

There was a glimmer in her eyes now. There was something new in there, something that softened her distant gaze just a fraction.

I could hear the water pipes rumbling again, and the wall was rough against my skin even through my shirt.

She wasn't breathing, I noticed as I focused. My once again superpowered eyes could make out each and every line of her face under the dirt—a face that had obviously been ravaged by some sickness prior to death. Death itself must have also taken its toll, but it was still Snježana Remac.

My senses went back to normal again, but this time it wasn't like a switch had been thrown. They faded fast, but this time I could feel them going away. I tried to reach out, pull them back, but they slipped from me.

Focus, for fuck's sake.

What... what was I supposed to do? She wasn't a threat to me, obviously. Was she a threat to her family?

Her finger played with the bracelet, pushing at the strings, pressing them gently.

No, if she was a threat, something would have happened already, surely.

Right?

Putting aside the fact she was obviously dead and yet moving about, there was absolutely nothing about her that seemed dangerous, threatening. Only... broken.

I looked into her eyes as she played with the bracelet. There was something there, definitely. A recognition, but only barely.

And then I had an idea.

I pulled out my phone with my free hand, slowly, because I was still afraid sudden movements might trigger an attack. She only seemed curious at the thing in my hand. No, *confused*. As if the phone now in my hand was familiar to her, but she couldn't place it. Just like the bracelet, it was another piece of a previous life.

Mercifully, the phone had bars—they were weak, but they were there. I turned on mobile data, waited what felt like an eternity for the Facebook app to load.

A white screen as the app searched and I thought the signal was too weak... but it wasn't. A list of accounts appeared. Third one from the top was him: smiling, hugging Snježana who'd been wearing comically large sunglasses.

His older daughter had grumbled at him for taking videos of them. As I tapped Photos, I held my breath.

There were photos. Dozens and dozens.

I tilted the screen to show it to her but still be able to see it myself.

"Look," I said. "This is your family. You know them, right?"

Will she understand it's a photo and not tiny people inside the object in my hand?

"Look," I repeated, putting the screen even closer to her face. Her gaze slowly changed, a transformation spreading from the pupils out, across her features. She let out a sigh—or was it, maybe, a word?

I swiped with my thumb again and again, slowly going through the photos. She was in some of them, with the kids and her husband. Some were selfies, others had obviously been taken by friends or passers-by during walks.

I got to the end of the album and hoped the next part would work. I had her in a kind of trance, and there was a flicker of hope that maybe, just maybe it might work.

God, I hoped it would work.

I opened the latest upload, the video I saw the making of, the video of the girls having lunch, the teenage daughter holding the baby in her lap, the baby doing its best to grab baked potatoes off her plate. The teenage daughter was annoyed but also doing her best not to chuckle as the younger girl intensely focused on her own plate, her eyes as wide as the potatoes themselves. I could hear the father laughing from behind the phone camera, saying something in Croatian I couldn't make out, and then the older daughter finally noticed him filming.

I looked at the dead Remac mother. Her eyes were rimmed with tears.

"They're okay. They'll be okay," I said. "Your baby will be okay."

I played the video again, increased the volume so she could hear the baby's cooing and giggling. It stuttered a few times because reception was getting shittier by the minute, but it played through the end without stopping.

"*Bit će dobro*," I said, hoping she could still understand Croatian. Hoping she could actually understand living people at all.

She was looking at me now. Her eyes went wide a little and my heart stopped and my gut clenched.

She gasped, so softly. No. *Whimpered.*

Her other hand reached up slowly until she was gently holding both my wrists. She gazed into my eyes. There was a vast space between us, a distance that wasn't physical and that I was only now fully aware of, a gulf between our two worlds. But there was something else there, too; I wasn't the same as her family, but I wasn't what she was either. I stood at that same edge, staring at her across the same expanse that separated her from her family's world but *I* was... a beacon?

It felt like that, somewhere deep down; that I was something that *could* reach her in a way her loved ones never could.

It seemed her eyes were really seeing me for the first time.

She said something, softly, her hands still holding mine, the tears flowing freely now. The blue of her eyes was suddenly alive with color and my breath caught when I saw it.

I removed my hands slowly from her grasp, undid the bracelet without fumbling with it for even a moment and then, not breathing, not thinking, just doing, I tied it around her right wrist.

I smiled, my vision blurry, her dirt-caked face returning the smile. She closed her eyes and a calmness seemed to wash over her. She looked as if an incredibly heavy burden had been lifted off her. And, I realized, it *had been*.

And then, before my very eyes, she fell apart, melted and disintegrated into dust and earth, and it was as if she had never been there at all.

I looked at the small mound at my feet, as if someone had shoveled a pile of fresh soil into the basement for some inexplicable reason.

I reached, digging gently through it with shaking fingers, but there was nothing in there, no scraps of clothes, no hair, nothing.

I wondered if a grave had its occupant back now. Did it work that way? *How did it work at all?!* And if the grave was full again, was there something in it that hadn't been there when they buried a dead mother and wife, strips of plastic thread intertwined, so simple and important?

I stood up, wiping my dirty hands on my trousers.

Then I looked around, wondering how the hell do I get out of the basement?

EVEN KRSNIKS DESERVE
A BREAK

Luckily for me, some of those old metal barrels in the basement helped me reach the opening and climb back out. After closing the grate and covering it once again with the tarp, I returned to the apartment and walked straight to the bathroom. The washing machine was still on. The domaći—Bowie—was sitting on the wooden chair, staring at the clothes tumbling inside the machine.

"It's amazing," he said without taking his eyes off the machine.

"I guess so," I said.

He glanced at me and then did a double take and stood up on the chair, confused. "What happened?"

I breathed out and shook my head, sat on the edge of the bathtub and told him what happened.

"You helped," Bowie said.

"I—I did, yes."

"You will stay?"

I didn't want to lie to him, but then again, I didn't know what to tell him because—well, I didn't know...

"I have a home and job to go back to," I said and it felt like I was doing it by rote.

The domaći frowned. "This was your home once. You lived here as much as you lived with your parents."

"You were here the whole time I was a kid, weren't you?"

"Yes. Before you were born, too. After you left as well." He sounded a bit judgmental.

"Now I have a new home."

"A home or just a house or apartment?"

"That—that's a home," I said.

"No. Home is more than a place where you live, where you sleep, where you keep your clothes and boots and pots and pans and books."

He looked straight up at me. "You know where home is in here," he said, hand pressed to his chest. "Your head *thinks* it knows, but your heart knows. Doesn't it?"

I was silent for a long time, those little eyes completely inscrutable.

"Will you come with me? You'd be more than welcome to."

"I'm a domaći. I'm bound to the hearth," Bowie said solemnly, regarding me without blinking.

"So you can't—or you won't?" I asked.

He hopped down from the chair. "I will answer you when you can answer me honestly." And then he was gone, vanished into thin air.

I sighed and proceeded to take my clothes off, looking forward to a long, hot shower and maybe shutting my brain off for a minute or two. I glanced at my forearms and stopped short. The scrapes were all scabbed over—and not only that, they seemed decidedly not fresh. In the bathroom mirror, the scrape on the forehead, as well, looked more like a week than an hour old.

But one thought wouldn't be ignored as the blessedly warm water flowed all over me: I had helped that woman. And it felt good.

Just as I took my pants to put them in the laundry hamper, my phone vibrated in the front pocket. It was Katrina.

"Hey," she said as I took the call and she sounded a little awkward. After all, she had no idea what mood she'd find me in. Then again, I had no idea what mood she was in.

"Hey," I replied.

"Everything okay?" she asked.

I blinked. Then I had to suppress a bitter laugh. "Er, yeah, everything's fine." I shook my head. I'd just told the entire story to Bowie and I just wanted to go and lie on the couch for a bit. I'd tell her later.

"Oh, good, I'm glad."

There was a pause, stretched out and a little tense on both ends. I sighed inwardly. I wasn't being fair to her. "Um, you calling just to check in on me or did something happen?" I asked to break the silence.

There was a smidge of gratitude in her voice as she said, "Yeah, I wanted to ask you if you'd like to join me for drinks tonight. I wanted to take you out to dinner but I can't make it. Anyways, I'm meeting up with a couple of friends and I thought you might like to meet them."

"Friends like Barba?" I asked, pretty certain I wasn't ready for more of that today.

She chuckled. "No, no, these are humans, I promise."

That piqued my interest. Hanging out with some normal people would be a great thing, I realized.

"Okay, sure," I said.

"Great," she replied and then gave me the time we'd meet in front of the bank on Korzo and then ended the call because she had a client calling.

I'll tell her what happened when I see her, I decided.

I looked at myself in the mirror. I looked tired, definitely. I felt tired, too, but more in my head than body. But what drew my attention was the lower part of my face, specifically the stubble that had, over the past few days, bloomed into something longer and messier. I was still very far from 'hobo' but was definitely inching towards my standard 'thinks he can pull a full beard off, but can't really' look. I was definitely my dad's son when it came to beards: anything under half a centimeter's length looked good on me, anything over a centimeter and people would assume I was wearing a bad fake beard.

I'd forgotten to bring my clippers, but luckily, nona had scissors that proved useful. I got to trimming, making myself at least a bit more presentable to Katrina's friends.

With just a towel tied around my hips and my phone in my hand I walked back to the kitchen/living room. I was hungry, but also sore all over from the fall into the basement. It was a miracle I hadn't broken anything or gotten a concussion—or maybe Mrs. Remac hadn't so much thrown me as laid me down very roughly. That bit of the entire encounter was still a blur to me.

I dug out an undershirt and a pair of boxer shorts from my backpack and sat on the couch. Then I lay on it and turned on the TV. The music channel was playing Croatian music and I had no idea who any of these musicians were. I had no idea if those I'd been listening to when I was a kid in the 90s were still active.

It was still hours before I had to start getting ready to meet Katrina. I'd just had a very eventful later morning and early afternoon, so I was due some peace and quiet and relaxation...

Somebody was knocking, someone very persistent. I was walking towards the apartment door but the hallway refused to stop, just kept stretching and stretching forward, the door out of reach no matter how hard I reached for them.

"I'm coming, for fuck's sake!" I shouted as the person on the other side started pounding on the door. Only I was outside now, on the docks where cargo ships used to moor, only there were cargo ships around me, and I knew they shouldn't be but there they were, to the side and stretching high into the sky, huge cranes lifting cargo, taking it from the ships and dropping it somewhere on the other side of the seawall.

I was standing there, watching the children playing in the sand, running on the grassy hilltop to my left.

And then I became aware. It was a dream and I knew it was a dream.

The space around me was still impossible, but the fact that I knew it was impossible didn't make it collapse into nothingness or make me wake up. The port was also the desert shore of a large lake and it was the rolling, grassy hills and there—there was a door.

A red door. *The* red door.

I closed my eyes. The door was still there when I opened them, bright red and standing there without a doorway or wall. Its surface was triangles and squares and it was *definitely* undulating gently; it wasn't a trick of the light.

I was still aware I was dreaming, which is something that's happened to me only twice or thrice in my entire life. I did the first thing I always did in those rare situations.

I looked down and smiled when I saw I was, indeed, floating, maybe half a meter above the sand. The sea was lapping the shore on my left; the grass was softly rustling in the breeze on my right. I flew then, slowly, staying upright as I circled the door. Its back was the same as its front. I floated up to it, touched it. The wood was warm, pleasant to the touch. Familiar. Inviting.

I reached for the doorknob, turned it—

I was looking at the ceiling and my phone was very loud in my ear. I must have been tossing in my sleep and, in doing so, I slid from half-sitting to a supine position, which placed the phone right next to my head.

"What, yes?" I answered and then realized it was the alarm. The alarm I'd set to start getting ready for drinks with Katrina.

"Oh," I said, turning the alarm off and sitting up.

"Oh," I said, louder and wide awake now. I'd fallen asleep. *I had a lucid dream.* And the red door was there again.

And if the alarm hadn't woken me up...

The light changed to green and I crossed the street, looking at the fountains that hadn't been there when I was a kid. There were two of them, large and square, and I immediately wondered if high school students used them as impromptu swimming pools on the last day of senior year. When I was a kid, there was only one fountain, at the other end of Korzo—the promenade through Rijeka's center—and *that* one would often be full of high schoolers on that particular day of the year, at least when I was in elementary school. There'd also be a lot of flour everywhere—for some reason people could never explain to me, high school seniors in Croatia loved throwing flour at each other and at younger students, especially, on that last day.

There were no high schoolers here, though, but there were a lot of other people, young and old, walking around. The few bars I could see with terraces or outside seating were all full. I looked at the old bank itself, a cube of metal, stone and glass. One of the walls was still covered in panels of polished glass, each effectively a mirror, and as I glanced at the slightly distorted reflection, I could almost imagine myself as a kid, stopping to look at the glass on my way to my grandparents. The bank's doors were now the sliding kind, but there was still a pile of big rocks in one corner of the patio-like entrance. I'd never found out what they were when I was a kid, and now I guessed they must have been the architect's idea of decoration. The rocks were smooth from generations of young people who'd congregate here during a night out—I'd sometimes see them when we'd be coming back from the cinema, which was, at least in my youth, just a street away from the bank. I was tempted to go sit on one of the rocks, a thing I'd wanted to do when I was a kid, but just as I was about to, I heard a voice from behind my back.

"Hey," Katrina said, smiling as I turned towards her.

"Hey," I said. Then I added, "Wow, you—you look great."

She grinned. "Thank you."

She was wearing jeans, but not black ones like earlier that day—these were dark blue, and went very well with the burgundy button-down she wore under a thin, black dress jacket.

"I feel underdressed," I said. I'd worn jeans as well, with a long-sleeved dark blue shirt, and while my clothes were nice, I still felt extremely not fancy compared to her.

"You look fine," she said. "So, my friends are going to be a bit late, so we can grab a drink on our own first."

"Lead the way," I said, glad I'd soon get the chance to tell her what my day had been like after we'd parted.

She led the way, first straight down Korzo, and then taking a left at a corner. Just as we were doing so, I said, "Oh, you have a McDonald's." It was my dear wish as a kid to try everything from the fabled McDonald's I'd only seen in movies and on TV. In college, my first apartment was just a short walk from three different fast food restaurants and let me tell you, the novelty wore off *fast*—which was for the best, because it probably spared me ballooning in size, something I'd struggled with during the ten years we'd spent traveling the world for my Dad's work.

Even though it was a work day, Korzo was busy in the evening. Bars and cafes were full and there were many people probably just taking a walk. We climbed up the stone steps next to a huge black-and-white building resembling a toy cube of some kind. "When did they do this?" I asked Katrina, looking at the hotel that I'd remembered from childhood, but that had, back then, looked much less fancy on the outside.

"Oh, a long time ago," she said. "Kinda sticks out now, doesn't it?"

And it did, since the surrounding buildings were, for the most part, from Austria-Hungary days. We climbed the steps, kept walking uphill but stopped after a few moments, when Katrina entered a doorway in the side of a building. A short corridor, another door, and then we were on the ground floor of a pub. It was all dark wood and robust furniture and tall ceiling, mostly cramped, but still likely able to fit more people than you'd ever guess.

We climbed another, narrow staircase to the upper floor. It was still early because there was only the bartender up there. She looked happy to see us, almost hopping over to us the moment we sat. I let Katrina order, saying I'd like to try whatever's popular. What came to the table a minute later was a tall glass of beer, pale and full of amazing flavor.

We were quiet as we drank those first few sips and I could feel both of us wanting to say something, but not knowing where to start.

And also, I noticed something in Katrina's demeanor. She was tense, avoiding eye contact for the most part.

I wanted to put her on ease, so I said the first thing that came to my mind, something that I'd remembered this morning but hadn't had a chance to mention back then at the restaurant.

"You know, when we were kids I remember people always thinking your name was Katarina, with two *As*."

"God, I hated my name when I was a kid," she said, scoffing, but with a smile. "You know how I got it?"

"I—you know, I just always guessed your parents wanted to make it special?"

She shook her head. "Nope. They were just huge fans of the song when they were picking out a name for me."

I was just about to ask when I figured it out. "Oh, Katrina and the Waves? Really?"

"Yep."

"And you hate *Walking on Sunshine*?"

She smiled. "It's... It's kinda neat, actually. Catchy. I wanted to hate it, trust me, but it's too damn *perky* to be disliked."

"Do you sing it at karaoke?" I asked, seeing the tension drain a bit from her and feeling the same was true for me.

"Not my song."

"Which one, then?"

"If I'm ever drunk enough to sing karaoke, you'll find out." She grinned.

"Fair enough." I took a sip of beer and glanced around. The music was a little louder now, a selection of 70s hits.

"Do you have anyone back home?" she asked then, a little suddenly. I noticed the word choice.

"Like a girlfriend?"

"Or boyfriend. Or both," she said, smiling still.

I shook my head. "No. It's…" I stopped, trying to phrase it. "It's been a bad couple of years, so to speak. I've kinda stopped dating about a year ago altogether."

"That bad?" she asked. Then she flinched, obviously feeling she was getting too familiar. "Oh, I'm so sorry, I shouldn't—"

"No, it's fine," I said. This wasn't what I had in mind as a topic of conversation before her friends arrived, but I found myself remembering the way we used to talk when we were kids.

Sometimes it'd been just the two of us playing in the inner courtyard and our conversations were always very open and relaxed. It didn't matter if we were talking about something serious like parents and school grades, or something absurd like would your spit freeze before hitting the ground if you spat from the building's roof in the middle of winter.

"Um, it was three crushes in a row that ended with the girl entering a relationship with someone else, and then two girls that… Well, one started flirting with me, I responded in kind, it seemed like things were going somewhere—and then she went back to the boyfriend she'd broken up with a month before. Yeah. I had no idea there'd been another guy in the picture. And then there was a girl a year ago who… I really liked her. *Really* liked her. We went on a couple of dates, everything seemed fine. Then one day she just stopped replying to my messages. We were literally on a date the day before. Dead silence."

"Ghosted you?" Katrina asked.

"Yeah."

She was nodding sympathetically. "I understand you taking a break," she said. "As long as you don't go all bitter asshole."

I smiled. "I'm way too scared of becoming that to ever become one. No, it's been fine. I think I was forcing myself to find someone simply because I felt I needed to, and it put me in this weird headspace. The day after I decided to take a break, my head cleared up. I haven't given up on romance and all that," I said, "but I'm very fine not actively pursuing anyone."

"Casual?" she asked.

"Cas—oh, you mean, er..."

"Sex, Paul, I mean sex."

"Yeah, no. Not doing any of that either."

"Men can do that?" she asked, laughing amiably.

I smiled, nodding. She definitely hadn't changed. Had it been anyone else that I hadn't seen in decades, I'd have told them to cool it with the personal questions. But Katrina had always been asking people stuff nobody shouldn't have, and there was—fortunately for her—something trustworthy in her manner, something that would make you aware she was genuinely interested in you as a person, even though she was several levels of intimacy away from those questions being appropriate.

"What about you?" I asked. "Any guys, gals, or non-binary pals?"

She blinked. "Any what?"

I chuckled. "I've heard that line somewhere and it stuck with me."

"Not at the moment, no," she said. "Well..." She was quiet for a second, with the barest of frowns on her face. "It's... complicated."

"Yeah," I said. "There's an expression that sums up our generation's take on romance."

"I'm the one complicating things, really. He's..." And she fell silent again.

I rushed to her aid because I felt she needed me to. "We don't have to talk about this," I said, smiling. "So, these friends of yours, who are they?"

She grinned, clearly relieved. "Two girls I think you'll like. I definitely think they'll like you."

"So, are they like... er, like us?"

"Well, they're not krsniks and they're not—" She paused suddenly, her brow creasing. "You know, I never thought about what I'd call myself. Psychic, I guess?"

"Ghost whisperer?" I asked, smirking.

"I don't whisper to them." She smirked back. "And I wish I had her figure. But yeah, psychic is fine, I guess."

"Ghost girl," I said.

She smiled, eyebrow cocked. "*Ghost girl*, I like that."

"And your other ability," I said. "You knowing that food's gone bad?"

She sniffed. "I have no idea why I have it. But it does come in handy. I've never had food poisoning or bought milk that was off ever since."

"So it works on any kind of food?"

"I think so. Food and drink—I think it works on anything edible and potable."

"Humans too?" I asked. It sounded way funnier in my head.

But she grinned. "I wondered that as well. I'm obviously not a cannibal because I get nothing off humans, living or dead. And I'd know, I spend a *lot* of time in graveyards."

We passed the next half hour pleasantly chatting about life in general, like two completely normal grown ups, and I'd decided to tell her about the Remac family and the red door later or tomorrow.

At one point I heard the pub's stairs creak through the music, and a moment later a woman appeared.

"This is Viktorija," Katrina said to me, smiling at the woman approaching us.

As she was taking a seat, the woman said, "Please, call me Viki."

She was also dressed for a night out, and not just a drink: her pants were a little baggy and peppered with sequins. Her checkered shirt was white and black, but also made of what seemed like very fine, silk fabric and, while loose, it was at the same time somehow cut to accentuate her figure. Herlong hair was dark and slightly curly, and there was a lot of it. Just as there was a lot of glitter around her eyes, which were lined with black eyeliner.

The conversation started with day jobs. Viki worked in graphic design and illustration, and there was a lot of talk about clients asking for hilariously dumb changes to logos and book cover artwork. It sounded familiar, definitely, reminding me of my own inbox full of 'could you write it like the previous version only completely differently' and 'our new project manager would like to offer some input.'

During those first few minutes I found out an important thing about Viki. She was the kind of person that didn't just love glitter. She was the kind of person that you could sit at the table with, with *no* physical contact, and somehow there'd be glitter *on you* almost immediately. Glitter seemed to surround her, invisible unless it touched your skin, a sentient cloud of stealthy sparkles that jumped on every person in her vicinity, spreading like a shiny plague. I knew this because *we didn't shake hands*, but when I looked at my phone, there was glitter on my fingertips and the screen. When I glanced at Katrina, who was sitting next to me, opposite from Viki, there was glitter on the tip of her nose, like a tiny drop of pixie dust.

"So, you're the krsnik," Viki said suddenly and casually.

"Er," I said, "yes, I am."

"I liked your grandma," she said. "I was sorry to hear she passed." She smiled and I could swear I detected a trace of discomfort hiding behind the sincerity and the casual smile. "Don't get me wrong, we clashed a few times, but that was a long time ago. We had a truce."

"And you're no longer in your wild phase," Katrina added, glancing at me before cocking an eyebrow at Viki.

Viki shrugged. "Well, that too." She nodded at me. "I should mention I'm a witch."

"A witch," I said. Gingerbread houses, warts and broomsticks flashed through my mind.

"I don't eat kids," Viki added. "They taste like shit."

There was a tense moment before I realized it was a joke.

Katrina laughed first, a little uncomfortably, to fill the silence. Then she glared at Viki.

I chuckled. "You got me there for a bit."

Viki frowned. "Nah, it's kinda shitty, isn't it? How could you know it's a joke?"

"This is all very new to me."

"He's picking it up fast," Katrina said.

"Tried out your powers yet?" Viki asked.

I glanced at Katrina as the encounter with the dead Remac mother came back to me for just a heartbeat. She must have read something in my expression because her eyes went a little wide.

"Well, I've tried out some," I said. I wasn't going to tell Viki anything specific—she was Katrina's friend, but not mine. And I was new to all this, and new guys have been an easy mark ever since there have been things to be new at.

"You should use them as much as possible," Viki said. "Powers, abilities, gifts—it's all just another kind of muscle. Take it for granted and you'll be shit at using it." She scowled for just a moment. "In fact, you can easily get the shit beaten out of you by someone who's technically weaker but more familiar with what they have."

I glanced at Katrina and saw she was looking at me with concern, obviously wondering what had happened to me after she'd left this morning. She was about to say something, but a sudden movement in the corner of my eye drew my attention.

I turned in time to see another woman sit down next to me. She was wearing a short-sleeved shirt with lace trimmings, her shoulders bare, and a necklace around her neck, with faux silver letters spelling out 'TIDEWAVE.' Her hair was dark red, with an undercut on her left and a flop of glossy mane on the right.

"Hi," she said to me, smiling pleasantly like we're old friends. "I'm Perdida."

I was certain it was either a nickname or a stage name. Surely no parent would put that on a birth certificate.

"Hi, I'm Paul."

"I like your shirt, Paul," Perdida said.

"Yes, well," I said, "If Katrina had told me we were dressing up..."

"No, it looks good," she said. "The color suits your eyes."

"Well," I said, not knowing what to say to that. "Either way, even if I dressed up, I couldn't compete with the three of you."

A chorus of *awwws* echoed around our table.

Perdida ordered a beer from the waitress and then turned to me. "Did you change yet?"

I blinked.

Katrina sighed. "Perdida—"

"What, I'm just asking," she said, smiling. "I wondered what kind of a dog you turn into."

"Um..."

"It doesn't *have* to be a dog," Viki said to Perdida, and it sounded as if it wasn't the first time she was explaining this to her. "It can be a wolf. Or an ox."

Perdida looked at Viki. "An ox."

"Yes, I knew a krsnik once who turned into an honest-to-gods ox."

Katrina sighed again, into her beer, apologizing to me with a glance.

"I haven't turned into anything yet," I told them.

"Well, it's still early days for you," Perdida said, making it sound as if I was still waiting for my growth spurt.

But shapeshifting had always been a huge part of krsnik stories I'd heard as a kid. Katrina did say she'd never seen my nona change shape, but it didn't have to mean she couldn't. Would I change shape? How? When?

"So, where are we going later?" Perdida asked, breaking my train of increasingly agitated thoughts.

Katrina downed the rest of her drink. "Not tonight, girls. I have a ton of work."

"What? We're not going out?" Perdida asked.

"You are two grown ass women, you can do whatever you want," Katrina said, smirking.

"But you're dressed so nice," Perdida said.

Katrina smiled. "Thank you. But I'm just here for a few beers and to get Paul out of the apartment for a bit."

"What about you?" Perdida asked me. "You want to go out with us, don't you, Paul?"

I had no idea what to say. I felt like in those stories, when a way-farer meets a fairy in disguise and learns a valuable lesson about answering deceptively simple questions. Or a witch, in this case, disguised as a girl ready to hit the dance clubs. Wait, was Perdida a witch as well? Or was she something else? And was it polite to ask?

"Girls, leave him alone," Katrina said. "He's tired and he's getting up early tomorrow." And she was right. The reading of the will.

"Oh," Perdida said, a little dejected. Then she looked at me and, in a very sincere voice, she said, "I am very sorry for your loss." She added, "Your grandma helped me out several times; I will always be grateful to her."

Viki was smirking at Perdida now, who glared at her and then rolled her eyes.

"What?" I asked, my curiosity moving my mouth faster than my brain could tell it to stay closed.

"Viki—" Katrina started but the witch grinned.

"Oh, Lena helped Perdida solve some problems with men."

I blinked. "What, with, like, a love spell or something?"

Both Perdida and Viki suddenly turned dead serious. I felt cold under their gaze.

"Love spells are bad stuff," Katrina said, fast, as if trying to de-fuse the situation.

"Love spells are fucking disgusting," Perdida agreed and the in-tensity in her voice and on her face was in complete contrast with her entire demeanor up to that point.

"I'm sorry, I didn't mean—" I stumbled.

Immediately, Perdida mellowed. Viki's gaze stopped being in-tense as well, but there was a slight tension in her now. No, I re-alized—there was more tension, just a little bit more, but on top of what had already been there before—what had been there from the start.

"It's alright," Perdida said. "It's just that, influencing people's minds and hearts—"

"That's been a fucking blight on the reputation of witches since the Dark Ages," Viki interjected. She smiled thinly. "So we get sensitive about it sometimes."

I made a mental note of that.

"But no," Perdida said, smiling herself, as if hoping to get the conversation on a more pleasant track. "No love spells or potions."

Viki chuckled. "You don't need spells, definitely." She looked at me. "She likes to be casual with men that inevitably get clingy and then she needs help getting rid of them."

Judging by her face, Perdida didn't find her friend amusing.

"So what you're saying is that my grandma was some kind of a relationship consultant as well?"

"You could say that," Perdida replied.

Katrina added, "Just to be clear, Paul, they're not talking about humans."

"She said men," I said.

"Men are the same, no matter the species or dimension they come from," Viki said. Then all three of the laughed and toasted to each other.

I was sipping my beer, wondering if they were just trying to get a rise out of me, a well not all men...

"But seriously, Lena was big on solving problems with her head," Katrina said to me.

Viki seemed to begrudgingly agree.

"Besides, we're still all people," Katrina said. "We can have problems that aren't just a matter of life and death or which need to be solved with violence or magic."

I found myself going back to the events of this afternoon as the conversation continued for some time—a very strange conversation, where they would be chatting about their day jobs and the weather and pop culture, and where I'd be asking questions about what had changed in the town since I left it, and then we'd veer into the magical and the supernatural. It was people getting to know each other, only the subject matter was a bit, well, not standard.

Perdida—who was a witch as well, I managed to piece together from the conversation—was a freelance architect, and had also been almost married, twice, to a Scandinavian werewolf. Viki loved pizza and gave me the names of six different restaurants to check out, and had also once had her soul stolen once. Katrina was baffled by the hate people had for the Star Wars prequels and had, two years ago, spent six months learning French from the ghost of a nineteenth-century scholar. And on and on it went: bad meals and terrible movies shoulder to shoulder with hexes and reflections in a mirror that move when you don't.

And all the while I felt as if I had almost nothing to offer, and was, at the same time, under the distinct impression the witches were not trying to pump me for information. They—well, they were just being friendly, hanging out.

Viki was definitely reserved, however, much more than Perdida. And as the evening went on, I decided it wasn't just because they had different personalities. There were moments where Viki would obviously forget herself and relax—her exuberance about the greatest pizza places in Rijeka was one such moment—and then she'd pull back, subtly, but still noticeable if you were paying attention, and I was. She was cautious, maybe a little suspicious of me. And that was fine, I realized. Nona had had clashes with her, unlike with Perdida—at least I gathered that much during the conversation—and maybe, just maybe, Viki was wondering how much like Lena I was or how I'd act when—

I caught myself then, realizing what I was thinking. But I wasn't staying here, was I? I thought as I sipped my fourth or fifth beer. So there was no need to be concerned whether a local witch was worried if I'll be the good cop nona was to her.

I turned to another, more pressing concern at the moment. Truth be told, I hadn't felt I had much to offer even when the conversation steered back to earthly matters. My life, ever since Dad had retired and we chose one country and stayed there for good so I could finally go to college—well, my life had been simple and devoid of spectacle, for the most part. I had a job I genuinely enjoyed even when clients tried to delay payments, I had my hobbies—reading as much as buying books, and hiking. No pets. No real drama in my life until, well, now.

And here were these three women who seemed like everyday women; smart, capable, resourceful; engaged in a conversation like good friends meeting for a drink after work—and also, all three of them had supernatural abilities and a metric ton of stories each that should belong in a paperback with a garish cover.

At one point I became aware that as much as I still found the supernatural aspect of it all unnerving, mostly because I wanted for it to not be there because that would mean I wouldn't have my own thing to deal with—I also enjoyed the rest of the evening immensely.

And then suddenly Katrina got up, smiling broadly, a little wobbly on her feet. "Girls, I'm afraid this is it for me."

"Nooo," Perdida said softly as Viki got up herself, to hug Katrina.

"I can't, hon," Katrina said. "I have to go home and drink a ton of coffee to sober up and finish my work before morning." She turned to me; put a hand on my shoulder. "Paul, if you stay with them, just remember we have the lawyer tomorrow." She grinned. "I'll be your wake up phone call if you don't text me you're awake."

I looked at Viki, who was finishing her beer, and Perdida, who was sitting back down. I still had half a beer left. "I'll just finish my drink and go home." Grandma's apartment, I had to remind myself. Home is far from here.

Katrina leaned down, hugged me, kissed me on the cheek and left.

I was alone now with the witches and suddenly Perdida was watching me as Viki fell silent and, for a moment, for some reason, I felt like a mouse in front of a cat.

But the moment passed and Perdida's face mellowed again and she took a sip and, smiling impishly over her glass said, "So, Paul, you're going out with us, right?"

It was obvious that the question mark was barely there.

"Uh, aren't we out already?" I asked, trying to wiggle out. I really wanted to just finish my beer and... Well, there was that red door. I was actually interested in what was behind it.

Viki shrugged. "Yeah, but we're going other places as well."

"Paul's coming with us, aren't you, Paul?" Perdida said, smiling still.

And I suddenly realized I hadn't been on a night out in what felt like an eternity. And I'd been enjoying both the company and the beer. Ah, what the hell. Besides, if they were Katrina's friends and she'd felt comfortable leaving me alone with them, I'd be fine.

I was certain I'd be fine.

The red door was there, right in front of me.

But I was sitting in a beanbag seat and someone was next to me in that same seat and she smelled so good. Her hands were around my waist and she was whispering, her face pressed against my shoulder. No matter how hard I tried, I couldn't make out anything except the soft, pleasant hum of her voice and the smell of her hair, long, so long, like silk across my chest, my face, me running my fingers through it...

The red door was there, but I was sitting and then I was on my back and she was still there, next to me, pressed against me, her body warm through the fabric of her dress, or maybe it was just a shirt...

A SHOWER CLEARS
YOUR HEAD

The music that woke me from a very pleasant dream was a woman singing in Croatian. She was belting out something about the morning bringing the end or something like that—I was dimly aware of the song through a haze inside my head. I opened my eyes and saw someone sitting close to my knees.

I was on the couch, still in yesterday's clothes.

"Good morning," Katrina said from the chair, sipping tea and looking at me.

"Hi," I mumbled, rubbing my temples and pulling myself up into a sitting position.

"Good night last night?" she said, teasingly.

"Ugh," I said. "We left that pub about an hour after you did." Memories of last night were slowly but steadily trickling back to me as I talked. Memories of drinking and partying and dancing, but also of something else.

My senses had been playing up again last night, but it hadn't been as bad as I'd feared when I felt the change coming on again.

We were on the dance floor—or what passed for one—in one of the bars Perdida and Viki had dragged me to when I suddenly noticed the dim ceiling lights becoming brighter. I reacted fast, looking at the floor until I felt my eyes adapted to my, once again supercharged, sight. Then I looked up and it was pretty freaky in a way, as much as it was amazing. It was like in the basement, seeing stuff nobody else around me could. This time, I was able to make out details that I normally couldn't even in full daylight. I could read the message on the phone screen of a man at least two meters away from me—although I was drunk enough to be unsure if the message in Croatian was a booty call or if somebody was cursing him out. I could make out the individual strands of Perdida's hair as she whipped her head back and forth in time to the beat; I could see specks of glitter float up from Viki's face and neck, and then vanish between the beams of colored light that had just started flashing all around the dance floor.

It finally felt comfortable, this new sight of mine. Then it faded away, even more slowly than in the basement, and this time I felt it halt, ever so briefly, when I tried to tug it back.

Another time during the night my hearing did amazing things too, as I could hear people talking from meters away when, moments before, I'd had trouble hearing what Perdida or Viki were shouting in my ear. The music was loud, of course, but I ignored the fact I was suddenly standing still on the dance floor. As I focused, and heartbeats passed, I was able to push the music back and draw other noises and sounds forward—not enough to pick just a specific one, but it felt possible, with practice.

When I opened my eyes at the dance floor, nobody seemed to have noticed or care, Perdida included—then again, she was so into the thumping music that she would have probably missed if I'd fallen unconscious.

"Viki left sometime during the night, but Perdida wouldn't give up," I said. "We went from place to place, closing time to closing time. And then she took me for a burek before it was finally over."

"Just a burek...?" Katrina asked. It took me a second to register the implication.

I shook my head, immediately regretting the movement because my gut complained. "No, nothing like that."

"I'm just asking. You're literally tall, dark and handsome; she's a sexy witch. People have been shipped for less," she said, grinning, so I just rolled my eyes at her and went to the kitchen to drink the biggest glass of water I could find.

"That woman can party," I said after I downed the water and felt significantly better.

"Viki didn't come back at some point?" Katrina asked.

"Nope."

"Did you hope she would?"

I looked at her, exasperated. "Why are you trying to play matchmaker?"

She tsked as she walked towards the kitchen. "No, I'm just teasing you. Trust me, if either of them were interested in you, you'd know."

I opened the fridge. I would need to go shopping soon—

"What's wrong?" Katrina asked, obviously noticing I was intently staring at the insides of the fridge.

"I just thought I would have to go shopping tomorrow or today because the food in the fridge won't last me through the weekend." I shook my head lightly. "My plan was to be home *before* the weekend."

Before she could say anything, it burst out of me, "I can't stay here, for fuck's sake; I have a job; my *entire life* is back there. How—I mean, even if I *wanted* to stay, how could I? I—I literally—This isn't my life—"

"Hey," Katrina said, stepping up to me, reaching up and grabbing my face between her palms, squeezing a little to ensure my full attention. "Relax. Paul, *relax*."

"Can't," I spoke through pursed lips. I focused on her face.

"Sure you can," she said with a no-nonsense frown. "It's literally a choice you can make in this situation, unless you have a diagnosis. You don't have one, do you, Paul?"

"No."

"Then you can choose to relax and *calm the fuck down*."

She let go of my face, but I could still feel the heat of her palms on my cheeks.

"It worked," I said, realizing I really did feel calmer. "How did you do that?"

124

"Stern words get through to people," she said. "Lena taught me that. You don't have to use magic if you learn how to use words."

I took a deep breath, and then a couple more.

"Better?" she asked.

"Yeah," I said.

"Okay, so, can you make us breakfast before we leave? We have some time."

Breakfast sounded great. Not only because I was hungry but also because it was a simple task I could lose myself in. Just a series of simple, familiar steps to go through.

I turned back to the still open fridge and started taking out eggs, bacon, cheese, milk.

And then I remembered.

"Katrina," I said, looking at her, eggs and bacon in my hand. "I need to tell you something."

She was leaning against the far end of the short kitchen counter, looking at me. "About yesterday?" she asked.

Right, there had been that look last night. She'd figured out something had happened.

I nodded.

"What happened?" she asked, sounding concerned.

"Well, I visited some neighbors and then went to the basement," I said.

Making breakfast, I went through the entire story of yesterday afternoon, starting with meeting Bowie ("Oh, good. I haven't seen him since Lena passed away, I was wondering if maybe he'd left. I'm glad he stayed," she said and then reached into her jeans pocket, took out a caramel, unwrapped it and left it behind the fruit bowl at the edge of the kitchen counter.) and ending with meeting her for drinks.

I skipped the dream doors, though, leaving that for later because the Remac family and their dead mother were the main point of the story.

By the time I was done with the telling, we were already eating bacon omelets I'd made. Katrina's face reactions had mostly been limited to the occasional eyebrow twitch.

When I finished, she regarded me with suddenly inscrutable eyes as I wondered if the Remac mother was really gone or if her family had found dirt on the baby's room carpet this morning as well.

"You did all that on your own?" she asked finally.

"By the time it turned out there was someone dead involved, it was too late to call you."

She stood up and went around the table. "Get up," she said.

I did, confused. She hugged me, hard, firm.

"Lena would be so proud," Katrina said, looking me in the eyes.

I smiled and did my best to suppress the tears that suddenly wanted to make an appearance. "I just did what I thought was best," I said. "Honestly, up until the very end I expected, well..."

"You'd fuck it up somehow?" she asked.

"She'd jump on me and eat my face because I'd misjudged her terribly."

"Yeah, that I can understand." She beamed proudly. "But you did it. Your first job as a krsnik. That's a cause for celebration."

"Ugh. I'll take a celebratory cup of coffee."

She grinned. "What, not even a shot of *rakija*?"

"Begone, devil," I said, more of last night coming back to me. "Your friends made me drink enough of it to last me a month. Swear to god, it's a wonder I'm up and walking. How the heck am I only this mildly hungover—" I stopped and looked at her, frowning.

"Did Perdida do something to me?" I asked then. "Made me more resilient so I could keep up with her or something? She insisted I match her drink for drink."

Katrina shook her head vehemently. "Perdida wouldn't do that without your permission." She then cocked her head lightly. "But you know, Lena was also pretty resilient to booze, now that I think about it. Way more resilient than an old lady should be. Drank me under the table a few times, as well as some, er, *people* who really should have lasted longer than her."

My eyes went wide. "You think it might be related to..."

She shrugged, smiled. "I'd say it is. I mean, Lena never got sick, never even had a cold or a runny nose in all the years I've known her."

I thought back to my childhood. Grandpa sick, yes, often, almost like clockwork every early autumn and early spring. But I couldn't remember a single time nona was anything but healthy and up and about.

"Damn," I said. "Must be some metabolism thing."

"Yeah," Katrina said. "Metabolism thing."

"But how—"

She shrugged again, this time frowning. "How the hell should I know? Not a doctor, Paul. *Metabolism thing* is pretty much what I was thinking even before you said it. Just enjoy the fact you can drink so much and get off lightly, you lucky bastard." She smiled and went to pour us both some coffee that she'd brewed while I'd been making the omelets.

I drank the coffee, wondering what other, well, *benefits* being a krsnik offered. Better sight and hearing, touch and smell, those I'd experienced already, if only in flashes so far. Probably taste as well, to round off the senses.

I wondered what else would change about me, physically..

Well, there's the whole thing about krsniks turning into animals...

"Paul?" Katrina said. "Penny for your thoughts?"

I shook my head. "I was just thinking..."

"About everything?" she asked.

"Yeah," I said. Then I looked at the clock on the kitchen wall. "I need to take a shower before we leave."

"Yes, you do," she said. "Can't take you to the lawyer looking like this. Well, smelling, to be precise."

I didn't need a supercharged nose to know what she meant.

"Thank you for coming with me," I said.

"Of course." She paused. "Oh, I didn't tell you, did I?" She smiled apologetically. "I'm not just going as your escort. I'm in the will as well. I have no idea what she left me." She grinned. "Hoping for a chest of gold or a ruby necklace."

"Is—uh, is that a real possibility?" I asked. "I know you're probably joking, but..."

Her grin turned into wondering. "Um, now that you mention it..."

It was my turn to grin as I walked to the bathroom.

The shower was long and glorious. It not only finished what the breakfast and the coffee had started, but also seemed to stretch time out. As almost-unbearably hot water sluiced all over me, I thought about the last few days—and how they seemed like a lifetime. I thought about the things I'd experienced and done, things I never thought I would do. But also things that I never thought I *could* do.

"Fuck me," I said, surrounded by steam. "I *could* actually do this."

I turned the water off. There was now just the slow drip-drip-drip from the showerhead and various parts of my body.

"Fuck."

"I could do this," I said as I entered the kitchen. Katrina was at the table, finishing off the omelet—*my* omelet.

"Sorry," she said with her mouth full. "I thought you were done."

"I was," I said.

"Could do what?" she asked.

"This krsnik thing."

Her mouth made a silent Oh.

"I can stay here for a bit," I said, raising my hand to curb her enthusiasm. "But only for a bit. My copywriting clients don't care which country I'm working from. So I'm willing to give this a try. If—if Lena was already helping someone out, or was just about to when she died, well... I can try and sort that out. And I'll gladly take any advice or training or whatever anyone who can be trusted can offer me." I paused. All of this—in my gut it felt right. "That's what I'm willing to do for now. It'll have to be enough for you."

Katrina smiled. "Paul, you're not doing this for me."

"I didn't mean it like that."

"I know you didn't," she said. "But I appreciate the sentiment. Of course I'd love for you to stay and take Lena's place, but..." She paused, shook her head lightly. "No, that's not fair. I'd love for you to do that, but it's selfish and stupid and I've been—well, I've been selfish and stupid. All that stuff I did yesterday really was to make you embrace your powers. You can do genuine good and the world desperately needs that, and there wasn't a shred of ill intent in me, but—it was horribly selfish."

She paused for a moment.

"I wanted Lena back and I wanted what she and I had back, and so, if I couldn't have *her* back, I was trying to make you—" She stopped. "Sorry, I'm incoherent."

"No, I understand," I said.

Bloody hell, I thought. *But at least she put it out in the open.*

"Lena was my mentor and she was my friend," Katrina said. "You can't replace her but, more importantly, you *shouldn't have to*. There are people who need help all over the world. Rijeka isn't all that special. I mean, it is to me, and there's stuff here that's rare and, okay, some of it is unique to Rijeka but... What I'm saying is, you being a krsnik, *that's* what's important. *Where* you'll be one is a distant second."

She sounded uncomfortable, awkward, and I understood her.

"That's—that's good to hear," I said finally. "I was thinking pretty much the same thing. But I'll be on my own when I get back—" *back home*, I reminded myself, because this wasn't my home, this was nona's apartment "—so, like I said, any tips or advice are appreciated." I thought about the hidden room. I'd have to organize the stuff there, see what I might use and take with me. I'd definitely need to upgrade my plane ticket, because I came to Rijeka with only carry-on luggage. Because I was supposed to stay just a few days.

"What is it?" Katrina asked, because I was smiling and shaking my head.

"Well, I was right when I looked in the fridge," I said. "I definitely need to go shopping. But now it's not just food, but also some extra clothes."

"I'll take you shopping after we're done with the lawyer," she said.

"You're taking me to lunch before shopping," I said. "You ate my breakfast."

WHERE THERE'S
A WILL...

It was my first reading of a will. Grandpa had left behind a will, but I was just a kid back then, so I was in school while my parents and Grandma went to some lawyer's office in the center of Rijeka—which was, Katrina told me as we walked down Korzo, apparently full of lawyer's offices.

We were the only ones in the small waiting room. It surprised me until I realized the surprise was solely me expecting something strange to happen because, well, of the past two days.

"Um, I should have mentioned this before," Katrina said quietly, probably so the lawyer's secretary couldn't hear us.

I leaned in, wondering *now what?*

"This would usually take much longer," she said. "The legal stuff, the bureaucracy in Croatia is—woof, give me a zombie invasion any day. Anyways, Lena made lots of friends over the years and some of them have been kind enough to, uh, speed up some processes." She looked around like she was expecting to see someone listening in from behind a potted plant or a corner. "I don't know those people personally, but Lena always told me that, once she's gone, there won't be any legal problems with the apartment or her will."

"Oh," I said.

"Friends in high places," she added.

I smiled. "When we were in Pakistan in the late 90s, I had a friend whose dad told me that a man needs to make sure to have at least four good friends in his life: a car mechanic, a doctor, a lawyer and a policeman."

"Sounds about right." Then she said, "Yesterday, in the pub. Why didn't you talk about traveling the world with your family?"

I shrugged and sighed. "I guess I didn't think anything that happened to me was a match for your stories."

She shook her head, frowning, but then the secretary told us we can go in.

Nothing strange happened when we sat down after shaking hands with the lawyer, a middle-aged woman with a pleasant smile. Well, at least in the sense that nobody suddenly broke into the office and the lawyer didn't reveal to us that my Grandma had another child apart from my mother with 'she's here now, come in meet your cousin.'

Apart from my mother, Katrina and I were the sole beneficiaries named in grandma's last will and testament. I'd asked the lawyer about the date of the last change to the will and she told me nona had updated the document less than two months ago. It was obvious that, just as with the message she'd left in the book, she had counted on me receiving the mantle instead of Mom.

I was also instructed to deliver something to my mother, nona's only child. Nona had left her a sealed envelope containing a letter that I was to personally deliver, as well as a small box with several pieces of jewelry. Not expensive ones, though, but pieces I did remember: most memorable of all, the golden necklace that grandpa had given grandma when they first met. The envelope was thick. I wondered what nona had written to Mom on the apparently substantial bundle of sheets of paper inside.

To Katrina, she'd left a sealed envelope as well, and had transferred to her the ownership of a bank account with—well, you know the thing about grannies keeping money under the mattress? Well, Lena had obviously trusted banks way more than your average granny because the sum in that account was—nice. It wasn't the kind of money Katrina could retire on, but definitely enough that she wouldn't have to worry about a roof over her head for a few years if her clients all abandoned her.

Katrina seemed uncomfortable. She avoided looking at me after the lawyer read out the sum. I was stunned, of course, but only objectively; only by the amount. There was no doubt in my mind that she deserved it.

"It's fine," I told her.

"Paul, I—"

"Katrina, stop being silly," I said, smiling. "You got your treasure chest."

She smiled back, relieved.

Bloody hell, I thought. *What did she leave me?*

Well, apart from the obvious...

I got the apartment and everything in it, which didn't surprise me. I got a bank account as well, which did. The sum was almost double of what Katrina had gotten. How much money had Lena earned when she was alive?

Does being a krsnik pay that well?

And I got something else.

"I'm sorry, what?" I asked, leaning forward.

The lawyer looked at me over her reading glasses. "All the papers are in order, I assure you," she said, her English only lightly accented. "The deeds to the house and the property are in your name. There are no outstanding taxes, no disputes with previous owners or their family, neighbors, the municipality or the Croatian government."

"But what house?" I asked. "Never in her life did she mentioned a house. My parents never mentioned a house."

The lawyer shrugged, very businesslike. "I just know what's written in the will, sir." She pushed a small envelope towards me across her desk. "Inside are the deeds, instructions on how to get there and a set of keys."

I took the envelope, confused as hell.

Once we left the lawyer's office, still on the stairs leading to the door that would take us out onto Korzo, I immediately opened the small envelope and read out the instructions. Katrina opened a GPS app on her phone, searching for the address I read out to her.

Rijeka is surrounded by several villages and smaller towns, and nona had apparently owned a house in one of those municipalities, a place called Čavle.

"What freaking house?" I asked. I looked at Katrina.

"Don't look at me, she never mentioned it."

"Did she ever go to Čavle?"

"Yeah, she worked all over Grobnik," Katrina said. Grobnik was the region making up a large part of Rijeka's hinterland: hills and forests and fields and dozens of settlements.

"Okay, I need to see this place," I said.

Katrina was already calling us a taxi.

Twenty minutes later, we were at the address.

Čavle was a municipality formed from several different villages that had, over the course of decades, melded into one big mess of houses covering a very hilly and wooded area. It was so close to Rijeka I wondered if, in a few decades, it might become its suburb.

The house I'd inherited was in one of those villages which were such only on paper and not in the least what most people still thought of when they hear the word village: there were no farms here, no fields being plowed, no huge stalls with cows or sheep, pig pens or chicken coops. There were houses though that most city apartment dwellers I know would kill to live in, and even the crappiest-looking house was surrounded by tons of greenery.

And in the middle of all that was the house I had the keys for.

It was a shithole.

It was stone and brick, with a roof that had several large holes in it; the windows were boarded up and, of its two doors, one led into the house proper, the other into what I guessed was some kind of basement. The house was built on an incline, so you actually had to walk up a few stone steps to get to what was technically the ground floor, while the basement door was at road level. Steep terrain surrounded the house on three sides—to the back, left and right when looking from the road—and the entire property was covered in tall grass, tangled brush and trees ranging from wild cherries to figs to walnuts.

Everything was overgrown and neglected and the house had, very obviously, been no one's home in a very, very long time. The property was surrounded by a low drywall on three sides, itself overgrown as well, while the road-facing side of it had a head-tall metal fence, rusted, with an equally rusted gate. The gate had at some point been forced open a bit, despite a chain and a pad-lock—the opening just wide enough for a small kid. God knows, as a kid, I'd have been among the first to sneak into an abandoned property. *Had done so, in fact*, I thought as I remembered Malta and South Africa.

Although, I wondered as I took in the property, *why did they bother with the gate since the drywall was low enough to climb over?*

Katrina and I stood there, looking at the house, baffled.

"Congrats, I guess?" she said finally.

"Yeah." I opened the envelope for what must have been the tenth time since receiving it, hoping that *now* a piece of paper might appear in it with an explanation. I took out the old-school metal keys. One was obviously for the padlock, but the rest were exactly the kinds of keys you'd expect to use on what looked to be at least a hundred year-old door, probably even more so.

"So she never—" I started, but Katrina shook her head vehe-mently. "As I've said, nope. Not even a hint."

"She never took you here?"

"We went to Čavle more than once," she said, "but I've only ever been to the center. Lena knew this woman there who used to sell her goat milk."

"Goat milk?" I frowned. "Nona never drank goat milk when I was a kid."

She shrugged. "People's tastes change. I can't stand the taste of the stuff but she claimed it's healthy."

Nona didn't like the taste, I remembered clearly.

But grandpa had loved it, I recalled then.

I held the padlock key, fingering it nervously.

"Alright," I said. "Alright."

I glanced around, noticed we were being observed. Nobody was looking directly at us, though; everyone seemed to be minding their own business, tending to their garden or walking their dogs or hanging laundry out to dry.

I unlocked the padlock. Katrina had to help me push the gate open and it squealed horribly as we tried to force it to wide enough for us to pass through.

The grass swished against my trouser legs as I walked towards the stone steps. I glanced at the basement door. Just from the look of it, the door was heavy wood, and it seemed very sturdy.

Closer to the house now, I looked at the roof as I climbed the steps to the house door—several birds flew out of various large holes, obviously disturbed by our presence.

The house door was hard, thick wood as well, dark and weathered. All the windows on that side of the house were firmly boarded up, and when I tried peeking through the small cracks between the boards of one, to the left of the door, all I could see, even using my phone's flashlight, was dust and bare walls. I tried summoning my super sight, but just thinking it, unfortunately, didn't actually activate it. I'd have to figure how to control it.

I heard someone say something in Croatian, and when I turned around I saw Katrina at the top of the steps, talking loudly to someone standing by the side of the road, looking through the half-open gate. It was a woman, old but spry, smiling widely. It took me a few moments to realize she was speaking in the local dialect, which was why I couldn't understand a word even though, at the same time, it seemed familiar. Even when I'd been a kid I'd a hard time understanding kids from Grobnik who went to my school when they'd be talking to each other.

Katrina obviously had no such problems, and at one point she pointed at me. The old woman waved at me, smiling.

"Say hi," Katrina told me. "She's a neighbor."

"*Bok*," I said in Croatian, smiling back.

The old woman repeated my word, smiling at Katrina, telling her something while nodding at me. I guessed it was something along the lines 'he hasn't forgotten everything, I see.'

Katrina and the neighbour conversed for a few moments more, and then the woman waved at us and was on her way. While they were talking, I looked at nearby houses. Some of the locals had stopped pretending and were now openly watching us through their windows or from their front yards. I could understand them completely; a quiet village will take any sort of entertainment it can get, and that's the truth in any part of the world.

"She was nice," Katrina said. "Talked a hundred miles an hour, though."

"I noticed," I said. "So, anything useful?"

Katrina shrugged. "Not much. Says people always say this is the oldest house in the village—at least the oldest still standing. There's nobody left alive who knew the old owners—says we're the first people to come in a very long time. Last time someone came was in the nineties, when workers put up the fence and changed the boards on the windows."

"So she's never seen Lena here?" I asked, looking back at the house door.

"Nope."

"Okay," I said. "I want to take a walk around the house before we go in."

We turned the corner to have a look at the side of the house and I saw the attic door in the middle of that wall. Due to the terrain—a little inclined and then a little flat until it inclined again—the entrance to the attic was just half a meter above the ground. I realized I must have seen the attic window while we were approaching the house. Built directly opposite the attic door, the entire length of the house between the two, it was a couple of meters above the road, at the very least. The attic door wasn't locked—it was boarded up as well, but one of the boards had been eaten partly by rot. When I peeked through, there was just dust and a couple of pieces of old furniture, nothing else.

We turned the corner again and faced the back of the house. Two windows only, both boarded up as well. The terrain surrounding the house was as sizeable, I noticed, as it had seemed in the deeds—the dense shrub and trees might fool you, but the property could have actually fit at least three more houses of similar size.

I wondered if there was an overgrown well somewhere. Then again, with how things had been going on recently, it would probably have a metal cover with a thick padlock at its top and a passage to Atlantis at its bottom.

"I don't know how it was before," Katrina said as we doubled back to the front door, "but this is *prime* real estate today." She looked at me and my skeptical eyebrow. "For the past ten years especially. I'm not joking. Everyone from Rijeka wants to move because people suddenly realized you can drive fifteen, twenty minutes to your workplace in Rijeka, and then drive back and be *away* from traffic and noise, in your own little garden. Relative peace and quiet, fresh air, all that. *Not* living in an apartment building."

"Hm," I said. "From what I remember from elementary school, all the kids from Grobnik wanted to move to Rijeka."

"Yeah, and those that did," Katrina said, "now most likely wish they hadn't."

"You think I should sell it?" I asked.

She looked at me, troubled. "Paul, if Lena left you this... I think we should first find out why she had it. And what's the deal with it."

We looked at each other in silence for a while, both aware that the last sentence could have a dozen weird answers.

It took me a few moments to identify which key was for the front door: there were five in the set, all on a metal hoop, almost identical to each other. Unless you were counting the teeth on each key, the only other way to differentiate between them was by a small, undecipherable marking each had just below the hole through which the key ring loop went.

A little fumbling and fiddling and then we were in.

The door creaked lightly and light fell into the short hallway in front of us, probably for the first time in decades. Dust swirled in shafts of light; the rest of it covered the wooden floor like a rug.

The hallway walls were bare, with no other doors I could see, only empty doorways: two to the left, two to the right, one straight ahead.

The floorboards creaked softly under us as we took our first steps inside, for some reason both breathing as softly as possible.

The doorways to the left led into rooms as bare as the hallway itself. The first one to the right revealed a room that seemed to be the mirror image of its counterpart on the left: long, rectangular, and with two boarded-up windows.

The next one was just a long, narrow corridor that seemed to stretch to the far end of the house. There were no doors there, no openings. Just bare walls.

The doorway straight ahead led into a large room with another boarded-up window and, finally, something more than just dust: a large dining room table, massive, seating at least ten people. There were no chairs, though.

"Probably couldn't be bothered to carry it out," I said.

Katrina let out a 'hmmm.'

"What?" I asked.

"How the hell did they get it inside in the first place?" she asked. "It's wider than the doorway."

"They assembled it here," I said.

"Hm," Katrina replied, shining her phone's flashlight at the wall closest to where we stood in the doorway: another open doorway, and a room behind it, with another boarded-up window.

Which left one final area, to the left of us as we stood: a small space with a very old bathtub and a toilet bowl. There had been a sink there as well, at some point, but the only evidence left was a short piece of pipe sticking out of the wall.

"All windows accounted for," I said, looking at the window above the bathtub. I hadn't realized I'd been counting them until now.

"Heh," Katrina said. "I was thinking the same thing."

There was a rustling sound from above, loud.

We both froze.

And suddenly I could see things as clearly as if I were standing outside on a bright, sunny day. *Better.* I could make out each and every individual speck of dust floating through our beams of light. Every shadow our phone lights threw had a sharp edge to it. And I saw light in the room overlooking the road: a thin sliver of it, on the floor, coming directly from above.

"Paul?" Katrina hissed as I walked into that room.

I saw it, then—the source of the rustling.

"What the..." Katrina said from behind me.

There was a hole in the ceiling, covered with a black plastic tarp. I had no idea what held the tarp in place in the attic, but one end was loose, gently flapping in the draft: the source of the rustling. It wasn't a wide opening, maybe a centimeter or two, but I could make out the blue sky outside, visible courtesy of a sizeable hole in the roof of the attic above me.

And suddenly the light was a sharp stab in my eyes, making me wince as I closed my eyes; it was still very bright, unpleasantly so—I felt Katrina's hand on my arm. "Just relax," she said.

Suddenly it was pitch black—she must have turned off her own phone's flashlight. I had mine in my hand, and I hadn't turned its light off, but Katrina's other hand was on it, blocking the light.

I took deep breaths and then cracked one eyelid open. Darkness, only the faintest outline of Katrina's head, illuminated by the bare trickle of light from the cracks between the boards covering the window.

"Thank you," I said in the dark.

"You're welcome." She sounded as if she was smiling.

"I thought I was done with the painful bit of having sharper senses," I said. "Obviously still growing pains."

We stood there, quiet, and it felt pleasant, having someone so close to me, especially in a dark, old, musty place that was completely unfamiliar to me.

She cleared her throat softly and I noticed my phone hand was free, its light illuminating my shoes. I raised it once again towards the ceiling. The edges of the tarp-covered hole were irregular.

"There," Katrina said, pointing with her own light. In a corner of the room we stood in there were some wooden boards on the floor, broken and splintered. I was certain they'd fit the hole in the ceiling like puzzle pieces.

"You think some kid fell through while snooping around?" I asked.

"Most likely," Katrina said. "Or, you know, kids needed some privacy, things got hot and heavy..." I could hear her grinning.

I chuckled. "Can you imagine falling through the floor mid—you know," I said.

"I'd probably die laughing," Katrina said. "Oh," she added then. "Look."

There were footprints in the dust. We hadn't really been paying attention before, but as I walked around and swept the floor with my light I saw footprints everywhere; this room, the dining room, the bathroom. They were covered in dust, but the layer didn't seem very thick, which meant someone had been here recently.

"Maybe it wasn't kids," I said, frowning. "Maybe somebody came looking for something."

"Why not break open a window or the front door?" Katrina said.

"Because they'd risk people noticing signs of a break-in from the road." I walked back into the room with the hole in the ceiling. I reached up, stretching as far as I could. I touched the center of the tarp with my fingertips, felt something hard on the other side "There's something up there," I said, moving left and right, feeling it around. "Boards or something else laid over most of the tarp. You can probably see into the attic through holes in the roof from the road out back. I'm guessing someone wanted to hide the hole from view as best as possible."

"Aren't you a proper Sherlock," Katrina said, teasing but impressed.

"Maybe we should end the tour," I said, wanting very much to be back outside, in the sun and fresh air, not surrounded by old walls, inside a house someone had broken into for—what the hell for? It must have been connected with Grandma.

Nona, what did you dump on me, huh?

"Maybe they thought there was something inside worth stealing," Katrina said.

"Yeah," I said. "Only, was it regular thieves or people like..."

"Like us?" she finished. I could hear her wry smile. She swept her light over the dining room table, then knelt and looked under it. I joined her, kneeling next to her, looking at—nothing; just the underside of a very old table. The table itself might have been antique and worth something, but it was still a completely normal table.

"Wait," I said as we started towards the open front door. I turned into the narrow corridor which apparently led nowhere, counting steps under my breath. At the far end, I swept the light over the walls and finally saw it. "There were doors here," I said, pointing to both my left and my right. "They were bricked up and painted over, but there's no plaster, so the doorways are still kinda visible."

One would have led into the room with the hole in the ceiling, the other into the large room on the left from the front door. Unless I'd miscounted my steps, but I was pretty certain I hadn't.

"Okay, so someone did some renovations at some point," Katrina said.

"Yeah," I said as I walked back to Katrina. "I'm glad."

She raised an eyebrow and nodded. "Because if it were just a long, narrow corridor that led nowhere, yeah, that would be freaky."

"Thank you," I said when we were outside. "For that thing back there."

Katrina smiled, under the clear blue sky. "Lena used to occasionally have problems with her senses in the past ten years."

I listened intently.

"She'd have these moments where light or sounds would be too much for her. Smell as well. She told me sometimes she'd feel it coming; other times it would jump her but, either way, she dealt with it the same manner. I don't think it was exactly you're experiencing, though. She said that, with her, it was her age. With you, it has to be your body adapting to your powers. Right?"

I shrugged.

"Well, my point is that Lena's technique is universal. And I quote: *smiri se, jebote.*" Stay the fuck calm.

I nodded, smiling. "I think it might've been because of the surroundings and the stress."

"It'll be like when I was learning to shut out the dead people's voices. You'll get the hang of it: you just need to remind yourself you're in control."

"So, um, did you see anyone or hear anything inside?" I asked.

She blinked at me. "I would have told you if I did, trust me," she said, smiling wryly.

"Would you sense if someone had died in there?" I finally asked. It had been on my mind for the past few minutes.

She shook her head. "Only if there's a ghost or an echo of one in there," she said. "There are people who can sense recent death but I'm just your straight up *sees, hears and talks to ghosts* girl."

"Ghost girl," I repeated.

She smiled. Then she glanced towards the bottom of the steps. "So, the basement?"

I nodded, as much as I wanted to leave it for another day.

When I was maybe two or three steps from the door, I felt it in my gut, suddenly and intensely: there was something on the other side. I had no idea what, but it was there.

It didn't feel like a threat, just a—a presence.

The basement door unlocked smoothly and opened without a creak. It was much heavier and bulkier than the front door of the house, and at least twice as thick if not more. Standing in the doorway, I swept my phone light over the interior, revealing a large open space. The doorway was set about half a meter below ground level, but the basement's floor was even lower than that. How much lower, I couldn't say, because of the something

143

I'd sensed moments before: the entire basement was flooded with dark water.

Katrina was looking over my shoulder, standing on the step behind me, her hands on the doorway.

"What the...?" she said as we took in that single open space that seemed to stretch the length and width of the house's foundation. Stone walls, rough, with rocks sticking out in some places, smooth and plastered over in others. No other doors, no windows, no openings of any kind; just a vast flooded space with only a few support pillars sticking out of the black, still surface.

The water was definitely what had sent my gut reacting moments before. It was reacting still; a tenseness, not like anxiety or fear, but something I couldn't put my finger on.

"Nope," I said. "Not today."

I felt Katrina move behind me. I glanced over my shoulder and saw her rummage through the brush next to the basement door. And I also noticed a pair of heads: two kids were peeking at us through the metal fence, trying to look inconspicuous. Glad to be distracted from the black water, I smiled and waved at them and they ran off.

"Here," Katrina said, offering me a stick.

"I'm sorry?"

"Check how deep the water is."

"Go right ahead."

"It's your house."

I sighed and took the stick. I was curious, despite my comfort zone screaming at me to leave. Nona hadn't left this house to me for nothing, and if she'd never ever mentioned it to Katrina in all those years... well then, there must have been a reason for that as well. It may have looked like just your average old, abandoned house, but I had been certain it was anything but. And now, this flooded basement seemed to be additional proof.

Standing at the very edge of the second step, the soles of my shoes just a centimeter or two above the surface, I crouched.

Katrina sat on the step behind me and I felt her hands on my shoulders. "In case something tries to pull you in," she said. It was supposed to be a joke, I was certain, but there wasn't much levity in those words.

I broke the surface gently, dipping the stick. Then I felt it encounter an obstacle. I dragged it to one side and then another, poked some more in different places.

My gut was reacting again, tensing, but there was something else now: something in the back of my mind *really* didn't want me to touch the water with my hand.

I listened to that voice.

"Okay, it's just about half a meter deep," I said, standing up as Katrina did the same. I glanced at the dark expanse of water. "At least here," I added.

"You'll need, oh, what's the word, those things you wear if you fish in the river, argh..."

"Waders," I said. "And no way am I going in there, waders or not."

I closed the door, locked it and climbed back to ground level. I couldn't get the image of that black water out of my mind, flat and smooth as glass. How long ago had the basement been flooded? And how did it get flooded?

Nona... what the hell?

"There's got to be something in her notes," I said. "In her book, or somewhere on that table, or on the laptop."

"I'm sure there is something, but she never told me. Then again, there's a lot of other stuff she didn't tell me as well." She didn't sound resentful. "There'll probably be a lot more stuff that's just for you," she said. "I mean, stuff I have no idea about."

"You mean I've inherited her problems as well as her powers," I said glumly.

"And real estate," Katrina added, tapping me on the shoulder playfully. She grew serious again. "But yes, you're right. The girls and I are here to help, if you need it."

"Thank you," I said, thinking back to last night. Perdida and Viki were friendly and they seemed to be good friends with Katrina, but once again I wondered how much I could trust anyone but Katrina.

We walked out of the front yard and I closed the gate behind us, relocking it. Curious eyes were still on us. I was pretty sure we'd be the talk of the village for at least a week.

We took a short walk downhill to the bus station maybe a hundred meters away from the house and waited there for the taxi. We sat on a low wall and chatted about how, when we were young, we used to think Grobnik was some godforsaken forest with the occasional wooden shack. Looking around, we could clearly see all the brick and mortar houses that had been here back then as well. The view from the bus station was also of hills both near and far—those near to us covered with a smattering of trees and various settlements that formed the Čavle municipality, the farther ones wooded and rocky. In the distance, the horizon was all low mountains under a clear blue sky.

"They call them the Grobnik Alps, you know," Katrina said. "Viki and Perdida once took me to the top of that one, there," she added, pointing.

"Hiking?" I asked.

"I thought it was just a nice walk. Turned out they wanted to show me where they'd fought a troll once, killed it and buried its body under a pile of rocks."

I frowned. "Is this the part where you tell me you ate it afterwards?"

She made a face. "What? No. Why the hell would you say that?!"

I smiled. "They do this thing in Iceland where they kill a puffin, stuff it under some rocks and then let it ferment for a few months before coming back to eat it. It tastes vile."

She laughed. "Oh, god, I'm glad I didn't know about that back then, I would have thought *exactly that*! No, there were just bones there, no flesh or skin. They said they use crushed troll bones for some powders, but that wasn't why they took me there. They gave me a piece of bone, in, like, a locket, as a gift."

"Like a friendship bracelet?"

"Pretty much."

"That's kind of sweet," I said.

She smiled. "They're good people," she said. "Don't get me wrong, you don't want to get on their bad side, but they never looked down on me, never made me feel like I was a kid even though—I mean, I kind of am, compared to them. They've always been there for me, including when Lena..."

I leaned in, hugged her. Her tears seemed to have surprised her as much as they surprised me. I heard her sob an apology but just told her to shush and let it out. And as she cried, my vision blurred as well.

When Katrina broke the embrace, gently, her eyes were puffy, but she was smiling. "Sorry, that wasn't supposed to happen."

"You don't have to be strong for me," I said, smiling.

"Har-har. No, I—I don't like crying in front of people in general."

"That I can understand," I said.

She took a handkerchief from her jacket pocket, wiped her eyes.

"Your eyes are red as well," she said then, eyebrow raised.

"It's the wind," I said.

"Mhm."

"Alright, your feminine sensitivity momentarily rubbed off on me," I sighed.

"Yes, you macho man, you, hopefully you don't get cooties."

A taxi pulled up, the driver asking us through an open window if we're the ones that called. We drove back to Rijeka in silence, but it was a pleasant one.

DECLUTTERING IS GOOD FOR YOU, THEY SAY...

We stood in front of the apartment building. "So, just so I know, are you planning on taking me out tonight as well? Because if your friends are coming, I'll need to get some sleep in the afternoon," I said jokingly.

"Busy afternoon and evening today," she said apologetically. "But tomorrow's Friday, and the girls and I usually go out, so you'll probably be invited as well."

"Yeah, that—I wouldn't mind that. It was fun. But I'd also like to talk to them about all this stuff. Maybe they know any other krsniks nearby?"

She nodded. "Lena never talked about any other krsniks specifically, but I think that was because she wanted to protect their privacy. I asked her a few times, but the only thing she'd say was that krsniks were rare. Well, rare in the context of our world."

My idea of finding a mentor suddenly felt very unlikely to happen. Then I remembered what I'd skipped when I told Katrina the story about the Remac family.

"So, one thing I haven't mentioned yet," I said. "I've been dreaming about this red door ever since Lena died. And I found a drawing of it in her book."

"Oh," she said.

"Now, I've been remembering bits and pieces of the stories about krsniks nona and grandpa used to tell me when I was a kid," I said. "And there's that story you told me about Lena becoming a krsnik, dreaming about that monster, finding it in a dream and fighting it in real life."

"Lena always said dreams are a really big thing with you guys," Katrina said. "Did you ever hear about the astral plane?"

"Of course," I said. "In books and movies."

"Yeah, it's real. People can enter it. Viki took me there a few times, it's trippy."

I blinked. *Of course the astral plane is,* I almost said.

Now is not the time to be snarky at people trying to help me.

"So if the astral plane is an actual place, this door, is it maybe— did Lena ever tell you about a red door in her dreams?"

She shook her head. "But I know that there are different ways to come and go from the astral plane. Maybe the red door is your way."

"From the notes in the book, it's our bloodline's way. Apparently."

Bloodline. I'm talking about bloodlines and inherited powers with a straight face.

"But she didn't leave me any instructions," I added. Which was, thinking back on the past few days, extremely on brand for nona.

"So what are you going to do?"

"Well, I had a lucid dream the other night and almost opened the door. I was woken up then, but I'm guessing if Lena and all our krsnik ancestors managed to open it, so will I. It's probably like my senses, just takes some time for it all to... manifest?" I shook my head, chuckling. "This is an insane conversation."

She grinned. "There'll be more. You're getting the hang of this, though."

"Har-har." I took a deep breath. "You know, Bowie might know something about the house."

"Possibly," she mused.

"I haven't seen him since yesterday afternoon, though," I said. "Honestly, I have no idea how to handle having him."

"Well—" she grinned "—he could be an Alfred to your Bruce Wayne."

I chuckled.

149

"I have to go," she said. "Call me if you need anything, otherwise I'll see you tomorrow night."

She hugged me and left. I stood in front of the building, searching my pocket for the keys, and then I glanced around and started walking towards one of the neighboring buildings.

I came into the apartment with both hands full of shopping bags, feeling like I'd bought half the grocery store. I set it all on the kitchen table and then froze. I wasn't short of breath, at all. Two days ago I would have been, but now I felt perfectly fine. My hands ached a little from the weight, but that was it, and the ache was already passing.

"Green peppers are better than red," the domaći said, peering critically into a shopping bag.

"Hey Bowie," I said. "I was wondering where you were."

"Busy. Cleaning. Maintenance." He looked at me.

"Tell me," I said, "why do you know English?"

He shrugged. "I learned it." He removed a curl of greasy hair from his eyes. "The first time I watched television, I realized how big the world is, how many different people there are. I couldn't travel, so I started reading. And Lena was always learning new things." He frowned. "I think it—how do they say it—it rubbed off on me? So I started learning languages. Lena bought me dictionaries and textbooks."

"How many do you speak?" I asked.

He puffed up his tiny chest. "English, Italian and German very well. French so-so."

I was impressed.

"Bowie, I was at the lawyer's office today, " I said then. "This apartment is now officially mine. And also a house."

His little eyebrows shot up. "House?"

"Yes. Lena had a house in Čavle. Do you know anything about it?"

"What house?" he asked. There was a gleam in his eyes, though. "Is it nice? A big hearth? An iron stove, maybe?"

"No. It's empty and full of dust and there's a basement flooded with black water."

His eyes were big as saucers.

"So you don't know anything about the house?"

He shook his head, now just confused. Good, so was I.

I sighed. "I keep thinking this would all be so much simpler if she'd left me more than just a note telling me to trust myself."

Bowie smiled sympathetically. "She was smart. You are her blood," he said. "You will figure things out."

"You think?" I asked, a hint of bitterness creeping into my voice.

He nodded firmly. "You will discover your powers on your own because not one of your ancestors, Lena included, could tell how their powers, or those of their heir, would manifest. It is up to you to hone your powers and abilities."

I sighed again. "And I don't suppose you can tell me how to open the red door in my dreams?"

He blinked. "The dream world is not for my kind," he said. "But I know this: a krsnik can be as powerful a force in dreams as in the waking world. That much Lena always said."

He then turned to the shopping bags, rubbed his hands all businesslike and started taking things out. He would stack items one atop the other, balancing them perfectly even though the stack was at least twice his height and width. Jumping from the table to the electric oven and then into the refrigerator, which was now somehow open, he began to distribute the items from his stack onto shelves.

I was tired, but I knew I wouldn't be able to fall asleep if I went for a nap, no matter how much I hoped to dream about the red door again, mostly to get it out of the way, whatever it was on the other side.

Well, there were still Lena's laptop and table.

And also, I should finally email my parents about what's been going on. I'd been postponing getting in touch, but it was time to tell them.

Well... tell them everything that shouldn't be kept a secret. Which meant... that the apartment was fine and that I've inherited a shit ton of money, so I wouldn't have to worry about the lean times as a freelancer for years to come. Everything else was out of the question. The house as well.

And there was the letter and the box nona had left for my mom; I'd have to get that to her at some point. '*Personally delivered*,' the will said. So I'd have to go back at some point in the near future, even for just a brief visit.

But first, I was hungry as hell.

Bowie was fast; he'd put away all the food in the amount of time it would have taken me to take everything out of a single bag. The refrigerator door closed by itself—I guessed Bowie was using some kind of domaći magic, which was a more pleasant thought than the fridge being alive. Then he turned, standing on the oven, nodded at me and was gone again, just like the day before.

I shook my head, opened the fridge and paused. I crouched and opened the freezer section. Frozen meat, small plastic tubs of frozen soup, and then I came across a large square plastic tub of ice cream. Only it wasn't ice cream inside. It was *sarma*. You take ground meet and rice, you roll it in cabbage leaves and you boil it in its own juices, water and some tomato puree. And then you eat until you burst.

I stood up, closed the freezer and went to find a pot. I filled it with just a bit of water, placed the frozen block of sarmas into it and set it to simmer. It didn't take long and soon I was at the table, my plate almost overflowing with the thick sauce, the pile of meat-stuffed cabbage rolls steaming pleasantly, smelling almost sinfully delicious.

"Thank you, nona," I said out loud and dug in. The taste was ridiculously amazing, once the equally amazing pain from putting a way too hot piece of sarma in my mouth finally passed.

Mid-meal, I remembered Katrina's caramels, as well as the stories nona would tell me when I was a kid. I had no idea what Bowie liked to eat, apart from caramels. Still, I took a saucer from the cupboard, put half a sarma on it and set it at the edge of the table.

I'd gone back to eating when a movement drew my attention. Bowie was there, peering at the offering. He looked at me, then smiled amiably and started eating with his hands. Messily, I might add; but somehow, despite all the grabbing fistfuls and the smacking and the slurping, not a bit of food went anywhere other than into his mouth. If I tried emulating him, I'd have half the dish down my shirt and the rest on the floor.

Bowie burped lightly, finished with his meal.

And so, with my belly full of food and my head full of thoughts, I went into the impossible room and got to work.

The first thing I did was see what else was in the cupboards and filing cabinets. There were papers and small notebooks and notepads aplenty, but there was one discovery that made me raise an eyebrow: a box made of dark wood—a box that I recognized. Not this particular box, though, but I knew the general type; it was a gramophone player. It was on a shelf, the rest of it filled with a row of records. I reached, pulled one out at random and chuckled to myself; a David Bowie album. I rifled through the records and realized nona had been a huge Bowie fan; also a fan of early Zappa and Blue Oyster Cult, among others.

I took out the gramophone player along with its tiny speakers and placed them all on the floor, next to the filing cabinet where the laptop was, and plugged them into the same extension cord that powered the computer. Then I took the Bowie album I had plucked out of the stack first and played the record. The gramophone's speakers crackled and hissed for a moment, just as I decided to leave the laptop's many folders for later and turned to the table. Then I stopped mid-stride as I recognized the song.

It was *Changes*.

Accepting it was as likely to be a coincidence as nona somehow trolling me from beyond the grave, I grabbed the first handful of papers from the table, sat in the chair and started skimming.

At one point I realized the room was silent, the gramophone having finished playing the record. I'd become completely oblivious to the music somewhere around the first chorus of *Changes*. Still, the silence was very noticeable now, so I chose a Blue Oyster Cult album and returned to Lena's notes.

So far I'd managed to make two distinct piles. One was made up of various newspaper clippings with notes; the other of different drawings of places, people and, erm, *creatures*, and notes in Lena's handwriting.

The piles were ridiculously tiny compared to the unsorted expanse of the table. *One paper at a time*, I thought to myself.

As time passed—me putting on albums one after the other and using that time to stretch my legs—I realized that the closer I got to the actual surface of the table, the older the dates on the newspaper clippings and in the corners of the handwritten pages were. I concentrated on one end and dug all the way down; 1965 was the oldest date I'd found. Decades upon decades of—what?

Finished jobs? Could it have been? Had there been that many?

I stood there, looking at the table. Daunted. And a little bit terrified.

I looked up to see Bowie sitting atop a cupboard next to the doorway, watching me. His eyes seemed to glow lightly.

"She would never let me clean it," he said. "I used to beg her. I hate to see such mess."

"Hey. How long have you been sitting there?" I asked.

"Since *Station to Station*," he said. "When she named me after him, I thought it was as a joke. But I grew to like his voice. It's impossible not to, I'd say."

"Yes," I said, "he was amazing."

"Was?" Bowie asked.

"Yes, uh, he died," I said.

He looked so sullen it broke my heart.

"Look, um, I could use some help," I said.

"Help cleaning the table?" Bowie asked, suddenly perking up.

"Yes. I've been putting these into stacks, but it's taking—"

He was just a blur for a moment and then he was on the table, looking intently at me. "Do you need to relieve yourself? Or perhaps eat something?"

I realized I was both hungry and in need of a piss. "Um, I do... You don't like people looking at you while you work?"

"I prefer to work unseen, yes."

"But in the kitchen—"

"That was just putting food away," Bowie said.

"And this is putting decades of paper into orderly piles," I retorted.

"It is not the same," Bowie said.

I sighed. "Alright, I'll leave you to it, then."

He smiled widely.

"Wait," I said. "How will you sort it?"

He blinked at me. "How do you want me to sort it?"

I thought for a moment. "Can you separate newspapers and magazines from handwritten notes?"

"I'll do my best," Bowie said.

"And if there's stuff that isn't newspapers or magazines or Lena's handwritten notes and drawings, put it in a separate pile?"

He nodded.

"Do you want me to do the cupboards and cabinets as well?" I heard him call after me as I passed through the curtain.

"Just the table for now," I said.

"As you wish," he said, sounding legitimately delighted.

When I came back, one trip to the bathroom and one sizable sandwich later, the table had four massive stacks of paper on it, one in each corner. The surface of the table was dark wood, painted with curves and loops in dark red and dark green, then lacquered.

155

"As you asked," Bowie said, standing in the centre of the table. "These—" he pointed to two stacks on his left "—are newspapers and magazines. These—" he pointed to one of the piles on the right "—are Lena's notes and sketches. And the fourth one is—"

"Miscellaneous," I said. "That... that's amazing. Thank you."

Bowie beamed.

"I left you something in the kitchen," I said. "You—you can go do your own thing now, if you want. Do—do you sleep?"

He didn't answer, just watched me. "You need sleep," he said.

I *did*. Eating the last few bites of the sandwich, I kept wondering if I should just call it a night, and I was pretty certain I would be doing just that very soon.

I found myself gazing at the fourth pile, the 'miscellaneous' one. It was the shortest of the four, with the documents I'd browsed earlier at the very top: the printouts and copies of old survey maps. Under those were some older ones, also printouts, this time of some legal documents from—I peered closer just to make sure I was reading it right—yes, it was a copy of some official missive from the Habsburg court.

The house, I thought. If it was nona's, then there must be something here. Maybe there was a buyer's contract somewhere in this pile.

I started digging, aware that Bowie was watching me from atop one of the other stacks. It took me some time, but eventually I found what I was looking for. It wasn't a buyer's contract, though.

It was a transfer of ownership.

"What the hell..." I said softly, reading it. I glanced up at Bowie. "The house was a gift to Lena," I said. I pointed at the bottom of the document, at nona's handwriting in black ink, as well as the signature of the person who gave her the house. "Do you know who Ilona Vranja is?" I asked Bowie.

He was deep in thought for a moment. "Oh," he said finally, looking terribly sad.

"What?" I asked.

"Lena helped her. This was long ago," he said.

I glanced at the document. "In 1984, according to this."

"There was a curse on a house and its family, I remember Lena telling me that," the domaći said. "She broke it."

I felt cold. "A curse. What kind of curse?" Was the water a part of it?

Bowie shrugged. "She never told me. I just know this: she had worked tirelessly on breaking it. There were six full moons between when she started working and when she was finally ready. Then she told your grandfather she was going for a weekend to the spa with some old friends. When she came back, she had nightmares for days before she was finally better."

Damn.

"Once the curse was broken, one day the woman—Ilona—came to Lena again, told her she could never repay her. She gave her something, a basket full of sweets." He seemed wistful until he frowned slightly. "And there were some pieces of paper as well, at the bottom, I remember now." He seemed a little uncomfortable as he said, "I was too occupied with the sweets to have a peek at them."

I wondered if the papers in question were the document I held in my hand, transferring the ownership of the Vranja house to my nona.

"Did the woman come back ever again?"

Bowie shook his head and sagged a little. "Some days later she took her own life."

That took me aback. "Why?"

"She was old and had been tortured by the curse all her life. When it was finally gone, she felt free. That is what Lena told me, that Ilona had finally felt free to leave this world."

I was silent for a long time.

Fuck me.

I shook my head, placing the document on the table. "Well, as Katrina said, Lena wouldn't have left the house to me if she hadn't considered it important." I rubbed my temples. "I just wish she'd left me a note explaining *why* it was important." I sighed. "We'll continue this tomorrow."

Bowie nodded and jumped onto the thick carpet.

"I've changed the sheets on the bed, if you'd like to sleep there," he said.

I wasn't comfortable with that thought, I realized.

"No, the couch is fine," I said.

He pointed at one of the tall cupboards in one of the corners. "There is a fold out bed in there. Lena would sometimes sleep in here."

Which made me pause and think about my recent dreams. Would sleeping here, in this impossible room, help me finally open that red door? I mean, the room was magical, and the door was something to do with being a krsnik—did it work that way? Or was I just trying to put an equal sign between things that had no connection whatsoever?

Well, I can try...

I went to the cupboard and was pleasantly surprised that the fold out bed wasn't something out of a hospital in a war movie, but sturdy and, when I sat on the mattress, incredibly, both firm and soft.

I turned to look for Bowie and noticed he wasn't in the room, but that there were now folded sheets and a pillow on one side of the bed. I smiled and started making the bed.

Then, before actually stripping down to my boxers, I remembered I have to charge my phone.

I'd seen earlier some USB cables in the drawer with the printer, so I connected my phone to the laptop. My eyes glazed over as I looked, once again, at the billion files and folders, but I also noticed something I'd missed the previous time: the email client was showing 20+ notifications. I clicked it open.

There was some spam, of course, and newsletters from various news outlets and assorted other web pages. But there was also one proper email, at the very bottom of the unread list. I checked the date and time. It had arrived less than twenty-four hours ago.

There was no subject, and that little bit of the message body that you could see without opening the email said something in Croatian about needing help.

I felt like I should open and read it. I didn't, because I also didn't feel capable of dealing with anything that wasn't lying down and closing my eyes.

As I did so, I found myself hoping the red door would skip this night.

'TESSERACT' IS NOT
A WEIRD WORD

"The word you're looking for is tesseract," Perdida said. "But it's fine, people don't really use it at all."

I looked down at the crossword puzzle, nodding. The sheet of paper the crossword was printed on was folded over, placed inside a large book as a bookmark. I tried reading the pages the book was open on, but couldn't make out a single word. The letters seemed to be crawling across the page, each line of each letter moving in its own direction.

"I don't like sitting," Viki was telling Katrina, standing on the coffee table in the corner, tapping one foot nervously.

"You should go for a walk, then," Katrina said, sitting on the floor next to me, her back against the couch.

I was on a stack of books and paper, and as much as they felt uncomfortable under my butt, they were also strangely smooth, like glass instead of paper, which made me think of church windows and the old orchard outside.

"Tesseract," Viki said, stepping down from the coffee table. "What will they think of next? Latin is a weird language, I tell you."

"It's not Latin," Katrina said. "And it works perfectly fine, doesn't it, Paul?"

I was trying to write the word down in the crossword. I knew where it was supposed to go, but there weren't enough little white squares to fit all the letters, so I decided to try and squeeze it in.

It wouldn't fit. I tried pushing the edges of the paper together. "If I make folds, it will look like there's less space than there actually is," I told Katrina.

A car honked outside the large window pane that made up the entirety of a wall of the room. It was the bedroom of my apartment from when I was in college, but it also held several rows of benches from a school in one of the company compounds we lived in long ago.

"Yes, it is," Perdida said. "It's Latin."

"It's just a box," Viki said.

"It's not," Katrina said, tapping me on the leg. "Paul, you're not trying, are you?"

I was doodling, trying to keep my mind off thinking about the crossword puzzle and the paper under my butt. I put the crossword on the coffee table and lay down on my side. The papers were flat and rustling even though my fingers slid across them like they were, indeed, glass.

I closed my eyes, thinking how to fit a word into a place that couldn't hold it. I wasn't happy Katrina kept insisting.

"I can't fit something just because you want me to," I told her, sitting up, frustrated.

"I'm not telling you to do it," Katrina said. "You took the crossword puzzle."

"It's still *tesseract*," Viki said.

"Weird word," Perdida said.

I was looking at the crossword, pen in my hand. Then I turned the folded paper over to the other side. It was blank. I started drawing.

"You can draw?" Katrina said.

"No," I said.

"There it is," I said, looking at the tesseract on the paper.

It wasn't a tesseract. It was a red door.

I looked up and saw that same door next to the couch. I was standing in front of it.

I was fully aware this was a dream.

161

The door felt more solid than anything else in the room. I turned and looked at the girls—it was weird to call them girls, they were grown women, but they called themselves that repeatedly, so I guessed it was okay—I stopped myself from babbling inside my own head.

They were all there, looking at me, smiling pleasantly. I knew they were just part of my dream.

"I have to go now," I said.

"Don't get lost," Perdida said as I opened the door and stepped through.

The air was cool and clear, and the darkness spread out evenly in front of me as I stood on the stone path. The stone under my feet was perfectly flat and uniformly dark grey. The door was behind me, closed. I peered into the darkness, turning this way and that, but it was everywhere and there was nothing in it.

No.

That wasn't it. It wasn't a black void. I knew it wasn't, something in my gut was telling me it wasn't... It felt as if I were in the wild on a moonless, starless night. There was stuff there, but I just couldn't see it at the moment; *that's* how it felt.

Then I noticed there was a piece of paper stuck to the door with a nail. In my grandma's handwriting, it simply said: '*Vjeruj u sebe. A sad idi gore.*' Trust yourself. Now get up there.

I looked up. There was nothing, just blackness.

The stone path led only forward; directly behind me was the door and behind it just empty space. Only it wasn't that, either; I reached and felt it. It was a wall, as smooth as the stone under my feet, maybe a hand's breadth behind the door. As I ran my palm across it, I could also see it, but it felt as if it were my mind forming an image of what my hand was touching, rather than my eyes actually seeing it.

I pulled my hand back and realized the wall was extending around me, that the path was a corridor—a corridor whose walls and ceiling I was aware of and that I could see but also not quite see.

It was frustrating until I realized it felt exactly like a dream: a thing you could see, but also didn't, was just like a kitchen that is also a classroom that is also a meadow. Or a bus driver who is also your father, even though he looks nothing like him, except he does. So I decided to ignore the fact it wasn't making sense.

Still, I *was* surrounded by walls and my only available directions were either down the corridor or—I looked and the door was now gone.

Of course.

I saw it then, there in the blackness where it hadn't been moments before: at least twenty meters above the path and about a hundred meters away stood the red door. Only now it was in the room—Lena's impossible room, which was also there, floating in the black. One wall of the room was either see-through or not there at all. The door was in the middle of the room, next to the table—which was back to its old state, covered in decades of paper.

Was this the astral plane Katrina had mentioned? Was that the astral version of the room? It was so far away, and yet I could make out details I knew I shouldn't have been able to. There was a desk lamp on the table, a lamp that wasn't there in the real world. Its light was so warm and clear.

It was calling to me.

I started walking down the corridor that was and wasn't there, down the gray stone path. Maybe a dozen steps later, I was suddenly at an intersection I couldn't see mere moments before. Left, right or straight ahead? All three directions seemed exactly the same.

I looked for the room. It was still there, to the right and ahead. So I took a right and started walking.

Then, at one point, I glanced up and the room wasn't there.

Panicking, I turned around wildly and saw it, very, very far away, just a small square of light floating in the dark.

I started running towards it and suddenly I was back at the intersection. The room vanished as I blinked, catching my breath. I turned and it was where it had been the first time I saw it.

Breathing hard, I closed my eyes and pushed the rising panic back. Panic is usually deadlier than the thing you're panicking about. One of my exes was a nature park ranger and she told me once that most people who fall through the ice into a frozen lake could easily make it out if they just stopped screaming and thrashing about. Now, of course, it's hard not to do that when you're suddenly in deathly cold water that's dragging you to the bottom, but once you know panic is what will kill you, that knowledge actually helps when you get yourself into a dangerous situation: being aware of the panic, you start looking past it.

At least that's what she'd claimed.

I couldn't say, never having been in a situation where panic almost killed me. I hoped tonight wouldn't mark the end of that streak.

I glanced around.

This has to be some kind of a test.

"Okay, nona," I said out loud. "You want me to prove myself worthy?"

I looked toward the room and its inviting light.

I was dreaming. It was a lucid dream, but still a place that obviously wasn't bound by earthly logic. Right?

I focused on myself, the stone under my feet, pushing myself up, trying to rise...

I looked down. I was floating maybe ten centimeters above the stone path. I willed myself just a little higher and I reached up and felt the ceiling of the corridor, there for my hands but not my eyes.

I descended, felt the stone under my feet again, firm.

I could brute-force it, I thought; take one corridor and then another and double back, rinse, repeat—but that would work with a puzzle book, or in a video game. Surely it wouldn't work here? First of all, there was no way for me to mark where I'd already

164

passed through. And I was *dead certain* nona wouldn't have made it that easy.

What did that leave? The path was still uniformly smooth and gray in all directions. No changes in color or texture that could serve as subtle pointers. The walls and the ceiling that were and weren't there also didn't provide me with any clues. I looked at the darkness, almost hoping for a faint point of light somewhere, something else to navigate by that wasn't the room. But there was nothing.

Trust yourself. A great sentiment, definitely, but some hint would have been—

Only it *was* a hint, wasn't it?

Relaxing, I closed my eyes and slowly reached inside myself with my mind, poking at my gut feeling. It had served me well ever since childhood, warning me of legitimate dangers and stopping me from making hasty decisions that would end badly. It had, of course, often been hard to distinguish it from that part of me that desperately wanted to stay in the comfort zone, urging me not to do a thing or say a thing, and I had to work hard on learning how to tell those two apart.

But here and now, it was the easiest thing of all: the comfort-zone-desiring part of me was at this moment basically catatonic. So I listened to the other voice.

And it said, *go left.*

I felt as if I'd been wandering around for hours, taking one wrong turn for every few right ones. Could your gut feeling get tired?

And then, at one intersection, I finally stopped.

It wasn't working. No way did nona intend for me to spend this much time wandering around just to teach me a lesson—that is, if there was a lesson here that I just hadn't figured it out. Wandering around and listening to my gut couldn't have been the point.

"What the hell *is* the point then?!" I shouted, startling myself. It had just burst out of me. I looked around. Nothing more than the stone path, the walls and the ceiling that were and weren't there.

I pressed my palm against the wall that was and wasn't. It hadn't changed. I pushed, gently. Nothing happened. I pushed harder, pressing both palms flat against the surface, giving it all I had.

I felt it buckle, just a little.

I pressed again, harder; then tried pushing with my shoulder, putting all my weight into it. The wall now felt not like stone but more as if it were some thick plastic sheet, taut, but with a little give.

It bent but wouldn't break.

Not if I kept pushing.

I stepped back. I threw a punch.

As I swung, I was certain this was the stupidest thing I'd ever done and I was about to find out if you could break your fist in the astral plane.

My fist connected. It hurt, but not nearly as much as I thought it would. *I'd accidentally tapped my hand against a door frame harder than thi*s, I thought.

There was a crack in the wall.

Why didn't it hurt more?

I pushed my fingers into the crack, tried to rip it open. The wall resisted, but I still managed to tear the crack wider. I strained and strained and finally it was wide enough—for what? I stuck my hand through the opening. It didn't feel any different on the other side.

Ah, fuck it.

Shaking my head at myself, I pushed through the crack in the wall.

It *was* different on the other side but almost unnoticeably. If I concentrated, I could feel the faintest sensation on my skin, as if from a breeze.

I headed for the room, slowly, because the last thing I wanted to do was splatter myself against an invisible wall.

And so there I was, flying slowly towards a room floating in the completely black sky. As I did, I started noticing movement in the far distance, as well as flickers of light, flashes of color. I wanted to take a closer look, but the room was my priority, I reminded myself.

Moments later, I was in front of that see-through wall of the room that turned out to be something like glass. The room was definitely not a direct copy of the real one: there was only the table, no cabinets or shelves or cupboards. And there was only the red door near the table—no doorway with the curtain leading back into the apartment. But, apart from it, there was one thing in there that wasn't present in the real world: a large corkboard on one wall, several pieces of paper pinned to it.

I touched the glass wall. I pushed hard, but it felt rock firm.

I tapped it with my fist but only felt a dull pain, as if I'd tapped—well, a rock. Something told me not to push my luck twice. It didn't feel like the same material the corridor walls were made of.

Although, that meant that, if there actually was a corridor leading into the room - even though the room was *up here* and the entire labyrinth was *down there* and the one didn't seem to connect to the other in any visible way whatsoever...

I spent some time flying slowly around the outside of the room, feeling with my outstretched hands for a corridor wall connecting to the room I was certain I looked like a total idiot, and if there was a way nona could see me from the afterlife, she must have been rolling her eyes and dying laughing at the same time.

But eventually I found it: on the ceiling of the room, in the middle of it, connecting *vertically*. I repeated the punching and tearing that I knew worked and dragged myself through the hole I'd made in the corridor wall, a few meters from the room's ceiling. I floated into the corridor and there was an opening at its end and through it I could see the table and the desk lamp on it, of course from above.

I floated through the opening and, for a moment, everything spun very unpleasantly, and then I was standing next to the table, staring at the lamp. I looked up, but there was nothing there except the flat surface of the ceiling.

I went to the red door, opened it. The room I'd been doing the crossword puzzle in was on the other side, but the girls weren't there, and neither was the large glass wall. The school benches were also missing, as were some other bits of that dream.

I closed the door, turned and walked up to the corkboard.

There was a large note pinned to its centre. Grandma's handwriting again: '*Bravo. Sve u ovoj sobi možeš mijenjati po želji. Naučit ćeš s vremenom, bez brige. Ploča te može povezati sa svakim koga smatraš svojim i sa svakim mjestom koje ti pripada i kojem pripadaš. Naučit ćeš putem kako to ostvariti. Pametan si ti momak, uvijek bio. Sretno, unuče moj najdraži. Nona te voli, jako.*'

'Well done. Everything in this room is yours to change as you wish. Don't worry, you'll get the hang of it with time. The board can connect you to everyone you consider yours and every place that belongs to you and where you belong. You'll learn how to do it on the go. You're a smart boy, you always have been. Good luck, my dearest grandson. Grandma loves you very much.'

There were dozens and dozens of other notes pinned to the corkboard, but the moment I finished reading nona's, they—well, they started melting away. They fell apart slowly, turning to ash, and then the ash faded away as it was floating down towards the floor.

The board was almost empty now, apart from two pieces of paper that looked like they'd been torn from a school kid's notebook. One was a drawing of the apartment, the other of—of the house I'd inherited.

I reached to take the drawing of the apartment off the board, see if there were any notes in the back. But the moment I touched, it my attention was drawn by a sudden change outside the room. The invisible wall no longer presented just a view of the blackness outside. There were now lights—real lights, and a lot of them. Some moved and zoomed about, others were stationary. It resembled a—well, a cityscape. And then I realized it was *exactly that*.

I approached the glass wall, taking it all in.

It was Rijeka, but a view of the city I could have never imagined seeing. The buildings were white and gray outlines, and the lights dotted all over the cityscape were of every color imaginable. I could make out nona's apartment building in the distance. The blackness was still there, but now it was just the dark sky and the horizon. A silvery haze seemed to permeate some parts of this version of Rijeka, flowing lazily between the buildings, down the roads. Where the Rječina river was in the real world, here bright purple flowed—and as I looked, it seemed to do so in both directions simultaneously. There was the sea, as well, a vast expanse of emerald, calm and glistening.

I looked back at the corkboard, a new source of light drawing my attention. The drawings of the apartment and the house glowed green, just like... I looked out the room, towards the part of Rijeka where nona's apartment building was—and yes, there it was; a green light glowing in the distance, identical in shade to the color now suffusing the paper.

I walked over and touched the other drawing. From this vantage point, I couldn't see the Rijeka hinterlands and the house there.

Wait. She said I can change anything in here...

I imagined another wall becoming transparent—and it did. And wouldn't you know it; in the distance there were lights and one of them was the same green as the drawing of the house.

Of course, I had no idea what it all meant nor how to go about finding it out.

I turned back to the table. Only the desk lamp remained there.

Was the room clearing itself of nona's stuff, getting ready for a new—occupant? User?

I thought about it, imagined it there—and it appeared: a large notebook and a fountain pen next to it. I smiled, impressed.

When I glanced up, there was a third piece of paper on the corkboard: a small, square note pinned to the drawing of the house. There was no writing on it, just a drawing of a symbol that held no meaning for me whatsoever.

I looked back at the town. And then I imagined an opening in the room wall. It appeared.

I stepped through and took to the air.

BRIGHT LIGHTS AND LONG COATS

As I looked down and around, I took in the immediate surroundings of the room. In the real world, it was in the apartment, but on the astral plane it apparently floated high over the Rječina canyon, directly above the point where the river flowed past the remains of Hartera, the defunct paper factory.

I flew down towards the Trsat fort, a small stone edifice overlooking the canyon and the town, built directly on the edge of a cliff. I'd never been there in my life while I lived in Rijeka. I personally hadn't been interested when I was a kid, even when they told us, in local history class, that there was a statue of a dragon there. My parents and grandparents also never took me there.

As I approached it, I started wondering if my eyes were tired. My vision seemed to blur. Then I realized I could still see the room in the distance, and I could see my hands perfectly fine. It was the town itself that was blurry. The outlines of the buildings were vague and the colored shapes fuzzy. Some of those shapes were places, maybe items, but many—so, so many—were people. People sleeping, I realized. I could just barely make out the head, the body, arms and legs of the first one I approached. I had no idea if it were a man or a woman. The only thing I was sure of was that their body was dark blue, and their head flashed in dark red and bright yellow.

There were tens of thousands of sleepers all over Rijeka.

I continued flying. And I flew fast. I might have even let out a gleeful "Weee!" as I sped up, feeling whatever passed for air here rushing around me. I was still breathing, but something was telling me that was just because my body thought I was supposed to be.

In just a few moments I was at nona's apartment building. There was the green light of the apartment, a glowing outline through the dark gray and white walls of the building. There were sleepers above and below it, and—no, not just sleepers.

It was the Remac family. I could see them through the walls, the same as all the others, everywhere around me. The large shape was the father. The tiny blob of light was the baby. And then there were the two daughters, each in her own room. But the younger one was not alone; there was a blood red shape scurrying around her restless form. It looked like it was slamming into her repeatedly—no, I realized then; it was *nipping* at her.

I flew closer, stopped at the building wall I could see through as if it were a dirty pane of glass. I pressed my fingertips against it and it was solid. I watched the scene and felt my guts squirm. The red thing I could see clearly, as detailed as my own body; it didn't look like anything I'd seen in real life. If a rat and a cockroach produced a kid, it would still win beauty pageants compared to this thing. It was the length and size of my forearm, with dozens of skittering, ratlike legs sticking out of a wriggly, hairy body. Its head was smooth, bare skin with faceted eyes, ending in a pointed snout with long, irregular teeth. It was absolutely disgusting to look at.

The girl was not sleeping peacefully; she was tossing and turning and her dark yellow body was shot through with emerald veins. And every time the creature nipped at her, I could see some of the emerald light flicker between its teeth.

Fuck. That.

I reached out on reflex and my hand went through the wall. I flew into the room. Tentatively, I touched the floor with my foot. It was solid. I focused and the tip of my shoe went through the floor.

Then I realized I was wasting time. "Get away from her!"

It stopped, turned, and its body flashed an even deeper red. It went straight for me. I kicked at it but it bit my leg, latched onto it.

And it *hurt*, a dozen needles stabbing. A moment later, it wasn't really as painful as it was deeply uncomfortable—which only meant I could focus. I grabbed the creature with both hands and immediately wanted to let go because it wriggled so repulsively in my grasp. But I gritted my teeth and pulled it off me. The sensation of stabbing stopped immediately—only to be replaced with a similar feeling in my left hand, as the creature dug its teeth into the flesh between my thumb and forefinger. I swear to god, I felt *the teeth wriggle.*

"Motherfucker!" I yelped and, still holding it in my right hand, I squeezed and twisted. The teeth let go and I launched the creature at the far wall of the room with all my might and anger. It slammed into it, fell to the floor. I leapt across the room and grabbed it just as it began flowing into the floor. Holding it by the neck, I slammed it again and again against the wall. When it went limp, I dropped it and squashed it under my foot.

I was breathing hard, angry and disgusted. Most of all, I was shocked at myself. I'd never felt as violent an urge as this one had been. I'd been in a couple of fights as a kid and later as a teenager—including the one with the bully—and I could remember being seethingly angry at assholes trying to push me around, but this... This was *bloodthirst.*

I wanted that thing dead.

I turned around, looked for the girl. Her shape was still yellow, but there were no longer emerald veins flashing inside. She'd turned on her side and wasn't restless any more. I'd done something good, apparently. It pulled me back from the rage that was bubbling inside me.

Which was good, because it meant that I was aware of my surroundings enough to notice something dark red coming my way. Several dark red things, actually; rushing through the air outside towards the room. The dead thing had obviously had siblings.

This isn't good. I glanced at my hand. The creature had bit me deep and hard, but the bite marks were barely there, already looking like faded felt tip pen marks.

"Oh," I said, a thin smile curving my lips.

I ran, ready to take them on—and I slammed into the room wall, fell squarely on my ass. I was about to scramble up to my feet when I remembered I could fly and imagined passing through the wall just in time to zip over the six or seven red rat-things that were about to enter the room.

They gave chase. And as they did, they chittered, making my skin crawl.

I flew in a straight line, and then took a hard right turn behind a building, where I stopped. I could hear them coming, so I readied myself and, just as they turned the corner, I flew straight at them as fast as I could, both fists swinging.

I'd misjudged. The maneuver sent me spinning and I didn't land a single punch, crashing instead into the pack. I scattered the rat-things, felt them bouncing off me. I managed to regain control of my trajectory a moment later, but they were already on me.

I was feeling them scratch and bite as I frantically grabbed at them, tearing them off me one by one and tossing them away. But for every one I threw off me, two more would dig its teeth into my flesh as the rest spun around me in a tight circle, keeping up with me even as I flew faster, trying to lose them.

"Get the fuck off me!" I screamed, now panicking, and grabbed one and held onto it instead of throwing it away. I squeezed and strained and finally tore it in half.

I'm going to die, I thought. *The fuck was I thinking?!*

Truth was, I hadn't been. I'd just expected I'd smash into them, scatter them like bowling pins with my punches and scare them off that way.

As I fought panic as much as I fought the creatures, another voice spoke up. It was the part of me that had stomped the first rat-thing into paste. *I'm not dying eaten by these things!*

I grabbed the one trying to chew through my thigh, tore it off, screamed from the pain and ripped the creature apart as I did so. I had to get away from them. I started picking up speed and, in just a few moments, managed to put some distance between me and most of the flying pack. There were only two still attached to me now, one clinging to my left ankle with its legs and another trying to bite through my shirt and get to my chest.

I grabbed the second one as I flew straight up to narrowly avoid slamming into the Korzo clock tower, missing the two-headed eagle at its top by maybe a hair's breadth, feeling the wings and the beaks almost graze my skin.

The fucker bit my forearm as I held it in my hand, extending its neck; I felt teeth piercing the fabric of my sleeve and stabbing into my skin.

I cursed, grabbed its head with my other hand and crushed it. Its limp body fell away as I kicked with my right foot at the remaining bastard still gnawing at my left shin. I missed. And then I missed again.

Then I realized it would be much easier if I stopped, so I did. I bent down and grabbed it with both hands. It bit and scratched and thrashed; I felt it ripping my palms into shreds with the tiny claws on its legs, but I didn't want to let go. I wanted to hurt it, *end* it. And I did, feeling its disgusting body crunch in my fists.

I turned around and saw that the rest of the pack was still pursuing me, was in fact just a few meters away. Then they turned and flew away, diving straight towards Korzo and disappearing among the buildings.

Floating and breathing hard, I looked at my palms, expecting something horrific. But while there were marks on them, they were just red welts, as if I'd been slapped by a ruler, not torn by sharp legs and crooked teeth.

It *hurt*, yes, but I could think through the pain instead of screaming in agony, which is what my mind was telling me I should have been doing—what I would have been doing if the attack had happened in the real world.

It must be some krsnik thing, I thought, trying to explain the healing taking place in front of my very eyes.

And the strength as well—I was *definitely* much stronger here.

I'm strong, I can fly and I heal from injuries.

Fuck me, I'm Superman.

I snorted at the thought, but also felt a mild rush of adrenaline. I mean, I *did* kick those things' asses. Yes, they gave almost as good as they got, but no real superhero ever got out of a fight without taking a few punches, right?

Was this also part of a krsnik's duty? Flying around the astral version of your town, punching monsters that attack people in their sleep?

I tried imagining nona doing just that, and while a part of me had a hard time with the mental image, it was the same part that had a hard time picturing Lena as anything but a caring grandmother who cooked her grandson's favorite dishes and read to him. But Lena had also, while still a girl, kicked the ass of a monster that preyed on her village. By all accounts, she'd kept kicking ass for decades, pretty much until the day she died in her sleep.

I floated there, high above the town, aching but strangely content. My head buzzed with thoughts of the fight in the girl's room and the one I'd ended by terrifying my enemies into fleeing. Maybe I should have gone after them? Those bastards would certainly go on to prey on someone else.

It was something to be kept in mind for later, I decided.

I started looking around for the room, but then I saw movement and a blood red light near one of the buildings below. I flew lower to get a better look. It still felt as if I were severely short-sighted, the buildings just outlines, the people I flew past only blurry humanoid shapes. The source of the movement and light wasn't blurry at all. Just as with the rat-things, I was able to make out its details perfectly.

It was floating next to an open window, seemingly completely focused on the person on the other side, sleeping in a bed maybe an

176

arm's reach the window. The person glowed light green and didn't toss and turn like the Remac girl had—no, they lay perfectly still.

And as I approached even closer, I noticed the dark red shape moving, ever so slightly. It was breathing, and with every deep and slow breath, a puff of emerald mist would rise from the sleeper and swirl towards the creature, disappearing under its hood.

At least I thought it was a hood, atop a long black robe, the body under it completely hidden.

I was now floating maybe two meters from it and I realized I was holding my breath. It wasn't a robe; it was wings, their feathers long and pitch black. And it wasn't a hood; that was its head, the feathers shorter and flat, peaked over the forehead. It had eyes, too—bulging eyes as big as footballs and blood crimson. It breathed in the emerald mist through a viciously curved beak, making a soft, wheezy sound as it did so. It sounded as if the act was... giving it pleasure.

"Hey!" I shouted suddenly. "Leave them alone!"

It didn't react to me at all. It breathed in again and its feathers ruffled ever so slightly this time as it took in more than it had with the previous breath.

"I said stop!" I bellowed, riled by it ignoring me.

It moved then, raising a long, armlike appendage and waving me off casually. Years ago, I'd spent a month working as a waiter at a five-star luxury sea resort. The richest assholes would often dismiss me with the same motion after I'd brought them their champagne and caviar and lobster. A week into the job, I'd had to teach myself fast not to grit my teeth for fear of spending all the money I earned on a good private dentist.

Fine, I thought. *Have it your way.*

I floated up to it, pushed it hard against the—well, what I guessed could be a shoulder.

It reacted. Oh boy, did it react. It turned fully towards me, its eyes growing bigger and glowing harder, two crimson discs that didn't have pupils but still seemed to bore into me. It spread its long, spindly arms even as it unfolded large wings. Talons gleamed at the end of each elongated finger—and toe, I saw as I looked down at its bare feet. It had a basic humanoid shape, but its limbs were longer and thinner, and every inch of its body was covered in those pitch black feathers.

It clacked its beak at me. Then it shrieked and I swear I heard it *inside* my head.

But while everything from the moment it turned towards me had made me stare in horror, the shriek snapped me out of it and allowed me to react.

I punched it squarely in the chest.

It flew backwards as I felt my entire arm hurt like that first time I'd been to a gym and punched a boxing bag without gloves.

The creature was now floating some distance away. Something in its demeanor that told me it was stunned by what had just happened. I was definitely shocked by it, but that shock was quickly disappearing. I was full of energy, ready to rumble.

Come on, run. You don't want to mess with me.

It slammed into me—although it would be more accurate to say it just appeared in front of me. I was thrown backwards and to the side by the impact, hitting the wall of the building, pain tearing through me. The creature was in front of me again, and it slashed at me with one of its arms. For a moment, I thought it had missed. Then my skin burned and I yelped, looking down to see a long gash across my chest—my shirt had been sliced, my skin and flesh as well, like with a fine razor.

And then the *real* pain came.

I screamed.

The creature shrieked again, whipped its other hand and stabbed my right shoulder with a long talon. I felt it pierce the muscle and I swear to god I felt the tip of the talon *push into the bone*, make a tiny crack in it.

This pain was unlike anything I'd ever felt before. Worse than a broken kneecap. Worse than a root canal. I screamed again. It shrieked in response.

Its right leg started coming up. It was about to eviscerate me with its talons, I was certain. Pushing through the pain, I reached with my left hand and managed to grab it by the ankle maybe a moment before the talons would have slashed through my belly.

It crooned now, its crimson eyes glowing darker. It clicked its beak softly. I was pretty certain it was mocking me.

Rage flared inside me and I latched onto it, let it power me. I grabbed the creature's wrist with my right hand, screaming as I tore the talon from my shoulder, as I felt it tear more flesh on its way out, and then, seeing red, I grabbed at the creature's ankle with both hands. With all my strength, I flipped the fucker.

It spun away from me, tumbling head over ass through the air. There was an invisible, white hot poker in my shoulder. I wanted it to stop burning. I wanted it to stop hurting.

The pain didn't stop. Luckily, I didn't have the time to think about the pain, because the creature was coming for me again, flying headfirst with its arms outstretched, talons gleaming, and eyes flashing with murderous hate as it let out an ear-piercing shriek that almost sent me running in blind panic.

I rose up, took a hard turn right and flew faster and faster and faster towards the Rječina. It followed, screaming for my blood, and no matter how fast I flew, it seemed to be gaining.

I dove hard as I passed over the river, until I was maybe two or three meters from the ground, following one of the downtown roads on the other side of the Rječina. Maybe I could lose it between the buildings?

I picked up even more speed as I followed the road uphill and then banked hard right over one of the long streets that, in the real world, would be the part of Rijeka called Krimeja. I swung left, then immediately took a right, then another left and a left again, weaving between the buildings. I stopped there for a moment, listening, doing my best to ignore all the pain and burning I felt. I heard the creature's shrieks now, approaching. I sped up downhill, hoping I'd lose it soon.

No luck. A moment later I heard it again—and it was close.

It flew out between two houses, slammed into me, and the impact launched me towards a building. I tried to avoid it, failed and slammed into a wall *again*.

I came to maybe a moment later. I was on the fuzzy white and gray ground. I was on my side, breathing hard, and now my entire body hurt, so the shoulder didn't bother me that much any more.

The creature was walking towards me, slowly, quite obviously relishing the moment. Its wings were draped around its long body, feathers once again giving the impression of a long coat. Its talons clicked on the asphalt as it came close. The entire scene made Katrina pop into my jumbled thoughts. She said she loved westerns. Well, here was a bad guy in a duster, coming for me. The creature bent down over me, crimson saucer-eyes now indigo, full of something I was pretty sure was cruel glee. Its feathers ruffled gently, as if it shivered in anticipation.

Some hero gunslinger I turned out to be.

It clicked its beak softly.

Can I die here? Will I wake up or will Bowie find me in the room dead?

Oh god. Did nona die like this?

I didn't want to die. I was terrified of dying. Had always been.

And I'd always wondered what I'd do if someone were about to knife me or shoot me. Well, here I was, staring down the proverbial gun barrel in the shape of a literal monstrous beak and the hideous eyes behind it.

Only...

In real life, I could only beg for my life. In real life I couldn't fly. Or hit things way, way harder than I could've ever imagined possible.

I was certain I couldn't fly away—it would stab me with its talons and... It was done. I was done.

Fuck that. If I'm dying, I'm leaving it something to remember me by forever.

The creature opened its beak, swung its head down towards me. My hands shot up, pushing the beak away. It clicked and crooned, almost as if annoyed. *It's pointless*, it seemed to say. But pushing the beak away wasn't the point. Getting a clear shot at its right eye *was*.

I pushed myself off the ground with my mind, flying up maybe just a few centimeters, but enough to make sure I'd hit my target. My fingers dug into the sides of that huge eye. It was moist and firm, like a huge, slimy grape. I squeezed and my fingers slipped as if I were trying to tear wet plastic.

The creature let out a shuddering sound. From the way its body lightly shook I was certain it was laughing.

It made my fear vanish, give place to blind fury. I pressed and squeezed and then felt the eye *give*. As it did, the crooning laughter cut off suddenly and the creature was stock-still for a moment. Its other eye went wide.

The one I was squeezing popped.

There was a scream and I was certain my head was about to burst; I closed my eyes, ready for the inevitable.

But it didn't come. I opened my eyes.

I was back on the ground, flat on my back. My hands were wet with clear fluid. The creature was nowhere to be seen.

Everything hurt.

But I was alive. That thought filled me with a pleasant buzz even as my shoulder threatened to fall off any moment now.

I pushed myself to my knees with my left hand, and then remembered I could fly.

Well, now it was more floating than flying; I didn't get more than half a meter above the ground before I felt like I might crash if I tried to go any higher. And so I slowly floated downhill. I just wanted to move away from where I'd fought the monster.

I'd fought a monster.

And I wo—

I survived. I forced the monster to run away. I hadn't won, even though a part of me very much wanted to claim it as victory.

I survived.

That was all that mattered to me in the haze threatening to wrap itself around me like a blanket, thick, comfortable, smothering.

And so I was sliding downhill, content to move and not pay much attention to the buildings and the lights and the shapes. I didn't know exactly where I was going, but downhill was good. My gut was telling me so.

At some point I realized I was on the bank of the purple Rječina in the centre of town, where, in real life, small boats would be moored. I was on my back, sliding slowly through the air above carved stone blocks that formed the bank. Why? I couldn't say, but it felt good, the downward motion, as I floated lower from the street, pushing myself backwards towards the river with my left arm, the right flat across my chest.

The purple stream glowed so pleasantly.

I pushed myself under a bridge, a tingling sensation spreading over me.

Was I in the river?

Why?

It felt good.

The blanket enveloped me, firmly and pleasantly.

I let it.

My gut told me to.

THEY CALL IT DUMB LUCK FOR A REASON

I felt hands on me, under my armpits. Someone was pulling me as a warmth slid off me. I forced my eyes to open, barely, and saw the purple-glowing Rječina and the white and gray outline of the bridge above me. I looked up, craning my neck.

"Oh, hi," I heard myself say. At least I thought I'd said it. I definitely thought it.

Viki was there, concern lining her face. Her eyes seemed angry, though. She was pulling me out of the river. Why?

"Good, you're still here," she said.

Why wouldn't I be?

Did I say that out loud?

I closed my eyes for just a moment.

I felt the rain on my face.

When I opened my eyes, it wasn't rain. It was water, pouring from a pitcher all over my head; a pitcher a dark shape was holding, standing over me. I made a sound, moved and flopped over the edge of the bed and onto the floor.

The rug was soft, which was good.

Katrina was standing over me, empty pitcher in her hand, a distressed look on her face.

"Hey," I said, laying on my back.

"Oh thank god," she said, setting the pitcher on the table and crouching next to me. "Are you alright? Here, let me help you up."

I wanted to say I was alright. But I wasn't. I reached with my hand, touched my right shoulder tentatively. It ached, like a days-old bruise. The rest of my body hurt as well, dully and not very much.

Why doesn't it hurt like hell?

I felt so incredibly tired. Just the thought of getting up was enough to make me want to curl up and fall asleep.

"Hey, you need to stay awake," Katrina snapped. "Come on."

She grabbed me under the armpits and helped me sit up, lean my back against the fold out bed.

"What happened?" I asked, trying to keep my eyes open.

"You're an idiot, that's what happened," Katrina said, angry.

I didn't fight her on that, memories of the fight—fights—coming back to me.

"Viki...?" I asked, looking around. "I saw her in the..."

"Yes, she found you, pulled you out of the river. Then she called me and said I needed to wake you up as fast as possible. I ran so fast people must have thought I was being chased by a killer."

I noticed movement behind her. Bowie stepped into my view. "Master," he said. "What did you do?"

I stared at them both. What didn't I do...

"Viki said I'm not to allow you to fall asleep." Katrina took a breath, now definitely more angry than concerned. "I sent her a message, she'll come over." She stopped then, frowned. "If—if you'll allow it."

I blinked. "Allow what?" Bowie suddenly seemed a little alarmed.

"Viki to come here. Into the apartment."

"Er, sure," I said. Sleep was pulling hard at me. "Uh, if you want me awake, I'll need—"

She was pulling me up to my feet. "Come on," she said when I was up, "Lena had a recipe; it must be in her book. It will help you."

I felt like I was moving through molasses. Like my *thoughts* were moving through molasses.

"It'll wake me up fully?"

"Oh, definitely."

Stumbling and leaning on Katrina, I made my way to the kitchen. Bowie was now on the kitchen table, Lena's book next to him.

"Katrina," I said, leaning with my hands against the back of a kitchen chair. "Thank you."

"Start brewing," she said.

It turned out that what I thought had been exotic spices and herbs in the kitchen cupboards were in fact Lena's ingredients for—well, potions. They were all neatly marked, and I only realized now that I could compare the writing and symbols on the labels with the honest-to-goodness recipes in the book. They were in the back, and I had to turn the book upside down—she'd obviously decided to use the back of the book for them.

It must've been the only part of the book that was in order.

Magic potions. Lena had been making them and now Katrina expected me to make one as well.

It was hard. It was worse than trying to type a message while half-asleep. But Katrina and Bowie stood there and looked very insistent.

The thing that Katrina had been talking about was called *Napitak za buđenje. Wake up potion.* I managed to find the ingredients and almost fell asleep only three times, twice with my head pressed against the cupboard, once while leaning against the kitchen table. Each time Katrina would shake me awake, force me to keep going.

I wanted to punch her only once.

There was no cauldron, only a simple kitchen pot that I stuffed with herbs and powders, added milk from a carton and waited for it all to boil.

Waiting for it to cool down enough for me to drink it seemed to take an eternity. I took a sip. It tasted of milk and earth and tree bark. Not in a bad way, though.

A moment later I felt my mind clearing. My body was still tired and every movement required focus—and I ached all over—but I was now wide awake.

"That... wow," I said.

"Yep," Katrina said. "Lena made it for me a few times."

"Is there anything in here for my body, though?" I asked, sitting down to leaf through the book.

The doorbell rang. I got up to answer it.

"Um, Katrina, could you?" I asked then, standing in the kitchen doorway. "I'll need a minute," I said. My legs were very close to giving up on me. Katrina hurried to open the apartment door.

"Hello," Viki said, from the outside of the doorway.

"Hi," I said.

Silence as Katrina and Viki looked at me.

"She cannot enter without an invitation," Bowie told me, somehow having climbed onto my left shoulder without me noticing. He weighed nothing.

"Invitation. Like when a vampire can't enter without being invited?"

"Some vampires," Katrina said.

"If she is coming as a guest," Bowie said softly, as if trying not to be heard by the two women, "she needs your permission to cross your home's threshold."

Viki seemed a bit uncomfortable as she waited. Katrina too.

"Master, you may extend an invitation to only specific parts of the apartment," Bowie whispered. "And she cannot enter Lena's— your room without another explicit permission from you."

"You need to know that I *could* enter without an invitation," Viki said then, looking at me. "But it would affect my powers. And also, because I'm sure Lena took precautions, there would be a big boom. I'd probably survive, but it wouldn't be good at all."

I cleared my throat. "Alright. Viktorija, I hereby invite you to enter my home," I said. "Specifically, you may pass through the apartment hallway and enter the kitchen and the living room." I paused and then said, "Also, you may enter the toilet if you need it."

Viki flashed a quick smile and stepped into the apartment. Then she paused. "I will not use my powers in any way, shape or form to cause harm to you or anyone else in your home, nor cause any damage to it, nor attempt to steal any item, nor leave anything here unless by your leave. This I swear by Hecate."

"Thank you?" I said.

"No, thank you for the toilet," Viki replied and rushed down the hallway. "Be right back," she called over her shoulder.

I turned and, with Katrina's help, went to the couch and sat down. She sat next to me. A few moments later, Viki came into the living room, looking around. "Haven't been here in a decade," she said. "Lena didn't paint the walls in the end, I see."

Katrina sniffed. "She wasn't willing to have workers in the apartment."

"Tea, coffee, waking up potion?" I asked Viki as she sat in one of the recliners opposite the couch.

"You made the potion?" she asked.

"Yes."

"Good," Viki said. "Your first magic potion and you didn't poison yourself. Well done."

I nodded. "Is there something for my body as well?"

She frowned. "There is, but it would be better if you'd let your body rest and heal naturally."

"Okay, *what happened*?" Katrina snapped.

"Well," I said.

I described entering the door—skipping the part where the three of them were in the dream—and wandering the maze. Viki was nodding as I described it.

I told them how I'd started listening to my gut feeling about where to go. Then I told them about giving up on that and breaking through the wall and flying to the room's astral version. Viki's eyebrows crept up.

"It worked," I said.

"It did," Viki said. "But it's obvious Lena had designed the maze believing you'd be more like her and..." She tsked. "You're not."

187

"What does that mean?" I asked, suddenly not appreciating her tone.

"Well, Lena was a good astral traveler," Viki said. "What I meant is—she never could have broken that wall on her own. I mean, not without spells or a boost from a magical item. You did it all by yourself?"

"It wasn't easy but, yeah, I did," I said. For a moment, I felt as if she might add an 'Are you sure?', but she didn't.

"Then what happened?" she just asked.

I told them about the room, the corkboard and the table, and only then did I think I'd maybe said too much.

But Viki seemed very businesslike, almost professorial. "The room reset itself for you, you're right. The corkboard is something Lena had created. She taught me how to make one." There was something warm in her voice now, and in her eyes as well.

"Never mind the board," Katrina said, visibly exasperated, "Paul, *what happened to you?*"

"Well, I decided to fly around Rijeka a bit..."

When I came to the part about everything looking blurry, Viki stopped me.

"Your body was the only thing you were able to see clearly?"

"Buildings and people—everything was as if I were severely shortsighted," I said.

"I see," Viki said. Then she shook her head. "Sorry. Yes, that makes sense."

"It does?" I asked.

"A person's astral form always has strengths and weaknesses," she said. "Your grandmother had exceptional senses and remarkable intuition. It's obvious that she believed the powers would manifest in you the same way. But your intuition, as the maze proved, will need a *lot* of work. Your astral senses, though, sight in particular—well, they're shit. And I'm sorry to say they'll probably remain so. Everything that's fully in the astral plane you'll see clearly, but reflections and projections will remain blurry." She regarded me for a long, silent moment. "But you're obviously way stronger than Lena ever was."

I continued my story. When I told them about the rat-thing in the Remac girl's room, they seemed surprised. Hearing about the pack of the creatures, Katrina seemed disturbed and Viki's eyebrows went all the way up, even though it was obvious she was trying not to react.

"Your wounds healed that fast?" Viki asked me. "You're certain?"

"Yes," I said. "Why?"

She shook her head lightly. "Strength, stamina, impressive regenerative powers." She leaned forward. "But it hurts where the wounds were, even though there's nothing there, right?"

"Not a mark on me," I said. "And the pain is more like old bruises."

"Your astral body heals by drawing the energy from your physical body," Viki said. "If Katrina did what you've done, she'd probably manifest the wounds in a much more serious way. But you're also a krsnik, which means your physical body regenerates on its own much better and much faster than any human's, including most humans with supernatural powers."

I stared at her. "It does?" I asked finally.

Then I remembered the scrapes and my eyes went to my forearm. Where the scabs had been last night, there was nothing, and I was just about to mention it when Viki rolled her eyes slightly, shaking her head again.

"Hey," I said sharply. "You might have noticed I'm kinda figuring things out as I go, here?"

Viki was silent for a moment. Then, as if she wanted to repair the mood, she said, "You'll be quite the fighter once you get some proper training."

"Erm," Katrina said, waving her hand at us. "If you two are done trying to pick a fight..."

"Look," I said to them both, "I'd love a manual, but I wasn't left one."

Katrina gave an exasperated sigh. "Yes. It's—that's so Lena. She said she'd prepare everything for you. She wrote that letter in the book for you three years ago. But she also... she liked leaving stuff for later—unless it was a job. And then she died. And now here we are, and apparently, you almost died as well."

Viki broke the silence that followed. "So, tell us what happened then," she said. But there was a look in her eyes that told me she knew already.

How did she find me? Why had she been there?

I told them about the black-feathered creature. Told them about getting cocky and almost dying.

Katrina gaped at me. Viki's face was stone.

"You fought a *mora*?" Katrina asked, stunned. "A fucking *mora*?"

"What, like a nightmare?" I asked. In Croatian, nightmare was 'noćna mora'.

"It's what nightmares are *named* after," Viki said, looking at me. "It feeds on people's astral energy, especially if they're having bad dreams or are in a bad mental state." She added, "It's also incredibly powerful and extremely dangerous."

She said it so matter-of-factly that it chilled me to the bone.

"*Jesus fucking Christ, Paul!*" Katrina yelled then, jumping to her feet. "What the—fuck the fucking fuck!" She very noticeably was doing her best not to grind her teeth in frustration. "You could have died."

Viki just nodded noncommittally.

I didn't argue.

And I wondered if nona really had died peacefully in her sleep, or had gone out fighting something nasty in the astral realm.

"If you're wondering how I found you," Viki said then, obviously reading in my eyes what the next question would be, "it's like this. I was in the astral realm myself, minding my own business at the edge of Rijeka when there was news of—a disturbance. A big, loud disturbance, moving through the center of town. Someone was fighting a mora, I was told, and the general impression was that the guy was insane. By the time I managed to get there, the

190

mora was gone and the man in question was under one of the bridges. And that's how I found you." She frowned then and, very somber, asked me, "Why did you submerge in the river?"

"Was that wrong?" I asked. "I honestly can't tell you why. It just felt right. But I was barely conscious from the fight."

"Well, it's not smart. If you'd fallen unconscious on the road, you'd have woken up in the real world. But because you were in the river, you..." She was searching for words. "Old rivers, old mountains, old forests; these things hold great power in the waking world, let alone in the astral plane. Our astral bodies will sometimes tap into that power on their own and then all kinds of stuff can happen, especially if it's an overwhelming amount of power."

"Like being submerged in a river," I said.

"Yes," she said. "The river kept you in the astral plane."

"Was," Katrina asked, "was he *stuck* there?"

"In a way, maybe," Viki said. "I've heard tales of people who got stuck between realms."

She straightened, looked at me squarely. "You're strong. Powerful. But what you did—the mora—that was incredibly fucking stupid. And you're incredibly fucking lucky."

My various aches agreed with her. "This was that thing where I pick a fight with the biggest bully on the block to show I'm not to be messed with, eh?" It didn't sound very funny in my head. It sounded even less so coming out of my mouth.

"No," Viki said curtly. "This was you walking into a forest and picking a fight with a grizzly bear."

"Super strength, zero fucking common sense," Katrina said. I'd never seen her so angry. I knew it was all from concern, but it was still weird seeing her almost ready to start slapping me.

Viki was frowning again, scrutinizing me. Then she finally spoke. "You need to—" She stopped herself, seemed to reconsider. "You should know that Lena was also a dreamwalker—she could see other people's dreams, even enter them. I'm mentioning this because you may or may not manifest that ability as well and, considering how you went about trying out your powers last night..."

191

She raised an eyebrow slightly. "You *should* be more careful, is what I'm trying to say."

I thought about last night. *Careful* was definitely not a word anyone would use when describing any part of what I've done.

Katrina tapped me on the thigh to get my attention. "Back when I started developing my abilities, Lena told me that people like me and you and Viki—" she glanced at her witch friend "—we all understand our powers at an instinctual level. If we have someone to teach us or guide us, it's faster and easier but, at the end of the day, we'd get there on our own."

"Unless we get ourselves killed," Viki interjected matter-of-factly.

I stared at her for a moment. Then I chuckled, and after a beat she returned the chuckle. We both laughed softly then, to Katrina's displeasure.

I leaned back on the couch. "Look," I said to them both. "It's obvious I need help." I glanced at Katrina. "Guidance, as you said." I pursed my lips for a moment. "I don't think I've ever been in a situation in my life where it's been more obvious that a little knowledge can do me more damage than not knowing anything."

They both gave me looks.

Viki said, "If you're asking for help figuring out your powers, I can do that. Perdida will probably be willing to pitch in as well." She glanced at Katrina, and then looked back at me, and if she had been hiding discomfort before, she wasn't doing so now. "But you're a krsnik and there—well, there is stuff that is just for you guys. Just as there is stuff that only we witches should know."

"Okay. Let's be specific, then. Can you give me some guidance with this astral stuff?"

She nodded. "As the kids used to say, I kick ass at astral magic."

"Great," I said. "Now, about my body regenerating. Is there something I can brew that will speed it up? Because I feel like shit."

"There is," Viki said. "But you shouldn't use it. It's like taking medicine. Sometimes it's best not to, even if you could. Let your body rest naturally any time you can."

I groaned, leaning forward.

"By tonight you should be fine," Viki added. "Just eat as much as you can."

I was hungry, I realized.

"You can find me tonight in the astral plane," Viki said, standing up. "Don't fight any dreambugs or another mora."

"Dreambugs?" I asked. "That's and almost a cute name for those things." I shivered remembering the hairy bodies squirming as I squeezed, and the teeth digging into my flesh.

"Once you leave the room, head for Pećine. Do you remember where to go?"

"Over the river, follow the road along the coast," I said, pulling stuff back from childhood.

"Good. When you see the shipyard, you've arrived. Just look around. You won't miss me, trust me."

"Thank you," I said. She nodded, gave Katrina a hug and left.

The moment the doors closed, Katrina rounded on me. "You are not leaving the apartment or doing anything except eating and resting until this evening. Understood?"

"Can't do much anyway," I said and I was completely honest.

"I'll be calling you regularly to check," she said. She turned to look at Bowie, still standing on the kitchen table. "He can only eat, drink, go to the toilet and lie here, watch TV or videos online or something. Understood?"

"I cannot force the master to—"

"Bowie."

"I appreciate your concern for him," Bowie said. "But I literally cannot command the master of the house."

She sighed. "But I can. Paul, swear to god, if you don't just stay here and rest, I'll have ghosts haunt you for a month."

I blinked. Could she do that?

193

I raised my hand to my heart. "I swear I won't do anything to make you sic a ghost on me."

"Good," she said and left.

Bowie inclined his head as I looked at him for a long moment.

"Bowie, could you not call me 'master'?" I was not comfortable at all with that.

He nodded slowly. "If you wish."

Then I asked, "Do you have to obey my commands?"

"No," Bowie said. "A domaći is a spirit of the hearth." He paused. "That is hearth with an 'h' at the end."

I nodded.

"We live alongside you, we help out if you treat us nice. If you're horrible enough, we can…"

"Go away?" I asked.

"Die," he said.

I swallowed. "You're serious?"

"It is what it is," he said. "Life and death do not hold the same meaning for a domaći as they do for a human."

"Still," I said, "you can't be thrilled about dying. Right?"

I couldn't decipher his look.

"You didn't seem comfortable having Viki here," I said, changing the topic. "Because she's a witch? Or was it her specifically?"

His eyes were still inscrutable. "Master Paul, you must be careful. A home is a terrible thing to lose. Mistresses Katrina and Viktorija are good women at their core, I am certain, but they are not of this hearth. You are. I cannot command you, but please don't hold it against me if I warn you to always be careful of who you let into your home." He paused for a moment. "And into your heart."

"Heart?" I asked, confused. I pressed a palm against my chest, just to make sure this time it was without an 'h' at the end.

"Lena cared deeply for Katrina," Bowie said. "But even from her, she kept many secrets. I do not believe she took any to her grave. Whatever they were, they will be in the room and in the book. Those secrets are now yours. You may choose who you will share them with but—"

194

The silence stretched.

"What is it?" I asked finally.

Bowie suddenly seemed—sad. "You must forgive me, master Paul," he said and I stopped myself from ruining the moment by reminding him not to call me 'master'. "But I'm old and I've seen people lose much because they were trusting and had their trust betrayed. Even your grandmother, and she was a woman—forgive me—much more wise and astute than you."

I chuckled.

Then I asked, "But I can trust you, can't I?"

He looked at me for a long moment, eyes glinting. "I am of your hearth, part of your home. Betraying you is something I am incapable of, as much as you are incapable of growing a horn in the middle of your head. Unaided, that is."

I wanted to take exception with the apartment being my home, but then he said, "You called it 'my home', master. When you allowed mistress Viktorija to enter."

I had, hadn't I?

It had just come out of me. I wanted to say it was just a thing I said but...

But.

It felt good, I had to admit. It felt good to my slightly buzzing mind and my aching and tired body, and there was a little prickle of energy deep inside my gut when I tried out the thought. *My home.*

Bowie was looking at me. The little bastard was smiling wryly, a gleam in his eye.

I was about to ask him once again not to call me 'master' when the doorbell rang.

I walked, feeling like I'd once again been convinced that running a marathon would be a good idea. When I opened the door I saw someone I really didn't expect.

It was the two Remac girls. The younger one was holding a plastic container, hugging it like she wanted to protect it. The older one seemed not thrilled to be here, at my door, but then again,

I remembered her demeanor the last time we met and it seemed to be her usual expression when dealing with people.

"Hello," I said, surprised.

The younger one mumbled something. The older one said, "We made too much cake. Dad told us to give you some. Unless you don't want it?"

"Uh, cake," I said. "Sure, I'd like some cake."

The older one nodded to her sister, who now offered the plastic container to me solemnly, like it contained royal jewels.

"Thank you," I said. This was very weird. It was also very sweet. Their mother came to the forefront of my mind then and I could recognize so much of her in their faces.

I noticed then that the younger daughter was looking at my wrist. At the lack of a bracelet there.

I looked at the older daughter. "Can you—er—can you tell her a friend of mine really liked the bracelet and I gave it to her as a gift?"

She crouched next to her sister and spoke softly to her. The younger daughter now looked me in the eyes and nodded, a very serious expression on her face. Then she removed a bracelet from her left wrist—there were at least four or five there, each in a different color combination of plastic strings—and offered it to me. I took it.

"*Hvala*," I told her. She smiled again and her eyes lit up and she ran off, babbling to herself all the way down the stairs.

Her older sister stood up. "Can you bring box back when you're done?" she asked.

"Of course. Tell your father I said thanks."

"Sure," she said. Then, just as she was about to turn and leave she paused. She looked at me, and dropped the grumpy teenager front for a moment. "I'm very sorry for your grandma. She was a good woman." Was that a hint of tears in the corner of her eyes? I wanted to spare her the embarrassment—I could still somewhat remember what it was like to be her age—so I thanked her and said, "Maybe you should catch your sister before she runs all the way to Korzo?"

196

She gave a sigh only a teen girl could give but there was a hint of a smile at the corner of her lips for just a moment before she turned and hurried down the stairs.

Back in the kitchen, I set the plastic container on the table and removed the lid.

"Chocolate and raspberries," Bowie said, nodding appreciatively, peering into the container from where he stood on an old apple in the fruit bowl on the table.

I broke off a piece of one slice with my fingers and placed it in front of the fruit bowl. His eyes seemed to glow.

I took out a fork from the utensils drawer and took the container with me to the couch.

There I sat, turned on the TV and tried not to think about anything in particular. It wasn't hard; a dozen thoughts roiled in my head, but they all blurred together, so nothing was standing out.

I took a bite of the cake. It was delicious as only a homemade cake can be.

THIS TIME WE'LL TAKE THINGS SLOWLY

By the time evening came, a strange reversal occurred: my body felt rested and the aches had gone away, but my mind was more tired than I'd ever thought it could get from just watching TV and videos. I ate a light dinner and then fell asleep on the couch, just as I was wondering if I'd have another bout of insomnia.

The red door was in the middle of a field of wheat, the stalks swaying in the breeze under a night sky with the sun burning brightly in the center of it. The moon slowly circled around it, a sea in the middle of the moon sparkling and dark blue.

I stepped through the door and was relieved to find myself in the room. The maze had obviously been a one time thing.

The corkboard was still empty, apart from the two drawings and that note pinned to the drawing of the house.

This time, as I looked over the drawings, I noticed a small symbol in the corner of the drawing of the Vranja house. The ink seemed still wet. I tentatively touched it with my thumb to check, and while the ink didn't smear, that same symbol was now on my fingertip. Then it moved. It slid gently over my thumb, up the back of my palm, over the wrist. Then it took a left turn and finally stopped in the middle of the inside of my forearm.

I didn't panic, because at this point I was guessing grandma wouldn't have left something for me in here that would cause me harm. Well, not direct harm, I guessed. I felt a slight irritation rise inside me. *Oh, I'm a smart kid, I'll figure things out. Yeah, about that. I almost died because she couldn't be bothered to leave a fucking—*

I stopped myself, taken aback by the aggression of these thoughts.

The symbol on my forearm already looked like an old tattoo.

It obviously had something to do with the Vranja house.

I glanced at the glass wall of the room, once again wondering what the house looked like in the astral plane—what was it Viki had said the buildings here were? Reflections, wasn't it?

Anyways, last time I got... distracted.

Sure, let's call it a distraction. Zooming around, tearing apart vermin and getting into fistfights with dream monsters—a distraction.

I passed through that opening in the glass wall I'd made last night, and as I floated in the air high above the canyon I once again took in the landscape before me. The white and gray buildings, the purple river flowing into an emerald sea, and all that under a black sky. The myriad lights and shapes, in motion and at rest.

I turned slowly and saw the green light of the Vranja house in the distance.

Okay. Let's see how fast I can move without someone chasing me.

Turned out I could move pretty fast. With the astral wind whipping around my ears, I was at the house in a matter of seconds. The village looked the same as it did in the waking world. The house, though...

It was glowing green, like the apartment, but the shade was different, a little darker, a little less friendly than the apartment's. I was close enough to make out the inside of the house through the hazy outline of its exterior walls.

Thing is, the inside of the house would... change as I blinked or shifted my position. It took me a few moments to figure out what I was probably seeing. Over the years the house had undergone renovations. Walls had been torn down, then built up again. Doors and windows put in, bricked up. Hallways expanding, shrinking; rooms combining and dividing. And it was all happening at once, simultaneously, in a loop. It was like watching an Escher painting, only... well, more like an Escher GIF, to be honest.

Except the basement. The basement wasn't changing at all; it was the same size and shape all through the loop. And it was full of water in the astral plane too, only here it was clear and full of tiny particles that floated around, reminding me of dust motes caught in a beam of sunlight.

And just like with the dark water in the real world, I had no desire to touch it.

Then I noticed it: a corkboard, floating in the air not that far from me. I flew up to it. It was tiny, maybe two palms wide, and it had a single piece of paper on it, with a symbol in the middle. I pressed it with a fingertip, wondering if this one would attach itself to me as well.

People appeared.

Figures were walking up to the house from the back. I flew closer and saw four of them—well, there was something strange about the way they moved, so I had trouble calling it 'walking'. It was more of a shamble or a stagger, as if they were drunk. There was also a van, parked right next to the property's drywall on the road leading uphill. Its side door was open and someone was leaning out of its back door. The van itself was glowing light indigo, as did the four figures shambling towards the house. The figure in the van pulsed with a sickly yellow gleam.

Of course it was all very blurry, so I had no chance of making out the model or the make of the van, let alone its license plate.

I turned towards the shambling figures, now climbing into the attic through the holes in the roof.

I flew closer. They were now kneeling around a spot on the attic floor. A moment later, they started pounding on it, prying open the boards. In just a few seconds, there was a hole in the attic floor—the hole, I realized.

Oh, I thought, my eyes going wide. The smaller corkboard, the symbol I'd touched that set this off—*it was some kind of security system*. And I was replaying the footage of a break-in.

That's fucking cool.

Immediately after which I thought, *If only I could make out the license plate, so I could find them and beat their faces in.*

But as the attic was being demolished, the figure in the van suddenly jumped out, vaulted over the drywall and ran towards the house, waving its hands.

What followed was... well, the sickly yellow figure seemed to be giving an earful to the shambling indigo assholes. After it was done, it forced them to go back to the van and get something—a rolled tarp, I guessed from the outline. While they were doing that, the yellow one climbed down into the bedroom and spent some time walking around the house. Even though I was looking at just a silhouette of a human being, I could still very clearly tell the person was frustrated.

Not finding what you're looking for, asshole?

I smiled, glad to see they were irritated, which was obvious from the way they moved, shook their head, waved their hand and the way their yellow churned and flashed. Then I flew through the wall and tried to touch the person. My fingers passed through it, of course, without even the slight resistance I'd feel while passing through walls.

They didn't go into the basement, though. Once the sickly yellow figure climbed out of the house the same way it had come in, the four indigo ones—with the yellow one waving its hands at them occasionally when they fumbled—covered the hole with the tarp and placed some old crates from the attic to keep it down. Afterwards, they all went back into the van and drove off. The van disappeared when it was some twenty meters from the house; that was obviously the range of this magical security system.

I saw the smaller corkboard where I'd left it. I willed it closer and it snapped into existence in front of me. I touched the symbol again. The 'footage' started playing once more. Then I willed it to stop. It did. I willed it to play. It did. Faster. Faster than that. Stop. Rewind. Faster. Play. Slower. Slower.

I shook my head, because I knew I was officially wasting time playing around. I had to go meet Viki. But this was a great thing, having a security system like this. I willed the piece of paper to go away and it did, dissolving into ash, the ash fading away into nothingness.

I turned and flew back towards Rijeka.

Pećine, the part of Rijeka Viki had told me to come to, was a place I'd only been to a handful of times as a kid. All I could really remember were these long stone steps that led from the road all the way down to a pebbled beach. As I flew and followed the shoreline, I was looking for that beach. The sea disturbed me, I won't lie; its shade of emerald was so vibrant and unlike anything I'd seen in real life, and the surface seemed to both shift gently and lie flat at the same time. It was ridiculously inviting as well, making me wonder what it would feel to dive in. *Later*, I told myself.

And then I saw the beach: it was still there, the long white and gray steps leading to a strip of what was probably still pebbles in the real world, but to my shitty astral sight just pale ground.

I landed there, feeling first with my bare feet—both times now I've appeared in the astral realm wearing the same clothes I'd worn that day, which meant I was dressed in sweatpants and a short sleeved shirt—and then my hands. It felt... undefined, but there was *something* under my fingertips. I grasped as if trying to pick something up. And I did. I had a large pebble in my palm, white and gray like everything else on the beach.

I hummed, turned and, without really thinking about it, threw it.

It hit the emerald surface and disappeared beneath it without a ripple.

Nothing happened. Nothing came out to attack me because I'd disturbed it. A part of me had been expecting that.

I soared back into the sky, continuing my search for Viki.

I saw her a moment later. Well, I saw what must have been her. It was a very bright multicolored light shining between buildings. I flew closer, until I reached a sphere of something iridescent and transparent floating in the air above a house. Viki was hovering in the dead centre of the sphere, surrounded by streams of multi-coloured—somethings. They resembled jellyfish.

I was now maybe a meter from the surface of what had—increasingly obvious to me—been designed to look like a gigantic soap bubble. Viki had her back to me at the moment, but she'd been slowly revolving in place all along, and now I could see her smiling as she waved her hands through the air. At first it looked as if she were dancing, but she was actually weaving something out of those streams of jellyfish.

I didn't want to interrupt her. It didn't seem polite. Also, her dance was not at all hard to look at; her hips swaying, her long dark hair glistening—

I managed to stop staring just a fraction of a second before she noticed me. She waved at me, still smiling widely as I wondered what the hell had I been thinking about just a moment ago.

"Hey," I said, smiling back.

Her face went cold serious in a flash. "Paul!" she shouted, pointing at something behind me. A liquid stream shot out of the bubble at the same moment, whooshing past me as I turned just in time to see it hit the mora in the chest.

Only it didn't, because the creature dipped just enough to avoid the attack but still keep flying straight at me.

"Fuck," I said, or maybe thought, as the monster slammed into me, bulging indigo eyes burning with hatred. Indigo eye.

Fuck.

Talons slashed, wings beat at me as I spun in the air, trying to block the attacks, separate myself from the mora and throw a punch, all at the same time. I achieved exactly none of those things. Panic was suddenly at my steering wheel and I couldn't help it, no matter how much my rage wanted to take over. That eye was the world now, with just the occasional flash of talon or beak and the terrible flutter of wings that seemed to press against me from all sides.

It shrieked, probably out loud and not just inside my head.

Its beak broke my skin, tore my flesh as the mora tried to take a chunk out of my collar bone.

"Paul!" I heard Viki call. She sounded so calm.

I just wanted to escape. A shriek tore my eardrums.

Run run run—

Dark.

... but no pain. Well, no new pain. My collar bone hurt, but the rest of my body was no longer under persistent assault. And it was so pleasantly quiet. Dead quiet, in fact. And I couldn't see a thing.

I was on my back.

Oh god, buried alive. I reached out, frantic, and the only thing that prevented a horrified scream was the fact that my hand hadn't been stopped by the wood of a coffin. I sat up, woozy, breathing hard.

Wait. Why was it dark? I was in the astral realm, everything was supposed to be white and gray.

Am I in the astral realm?

The floor under me felt like hardwood. I reached to the sides, felt something to the right. Something also made of wood. I followed its contours upward until I reached a wide, flat surface. A table?

I managed to get up, slowly and in stages, and I kept expecting to bump my head against something.

It wasn't really pitch black, though. I could make out shapes, but barely. There were glowing yellow lines, too, that I realized a moment later was light coming in through tiny cracks, some horizontal, others vertical.

Okay, so. I'm somewhere with walls and a hardwood floor. There's a table, and there must be some windows, but they're covered with something that has cracks—oh.

There was a smell, heavy and musty, filling my nostrils.

There were sounds, the hooting of an owl, very distant traffic.

I was in the Vranja house.

Not its astral version—reflection, whatever—the *real world* version.

I touched my collar bone. It throbbed, but it was whole, just like my shirt.

"What the hell?" I said out loud to no one in particular.

And then I could see. A moment ago I saw precisely shit. But now I could've read a book, easily. The white glow of streetlights lining the road by the house was seeping in through between the boards on the windows and it was suddenly enough for me to see *everything*. I could make out the details on the scratched and battered surface of the dining room table. I could hear people walking in silence down the road, two adults and one child. And a dog. I could smell not just the general mustiness of the house but also the slightly rotten wood of the boards and the ancient lacquer of the bedroom floor. I could even sense the tang of something rusty in my mouth when I breathed in.

And I could... *feel* something. It was a general sensation, something I seemed to detect with my whole body. Almost a thrumming, coursing through my body, as if I were standing close to a subwoofer on full blast. I closed my eyes, concentrating on the sensation. It *wasn't* coming from all directions at once, as I'd thought at first. It was stronger in my legs, and the more I focused, the more I felt it there. My legs—my feet—the floor—

Under the floor.

The thrumming was coming from the basement.

I pulled my senses back, instinctively, the image of that dark water so vivid in my mind.

It was then I noticed the hum of a car engine idling nearby. And then the soft rumble of doors sliding open. Footsteps, crunching on the asphalt. The sound of several someones climbing over a drywall, grass and brush rustling. They were full on running, and then there was the whoosh of bodies flying through the air.

The kitchen windows exploded, boards splintering and street-lights flaring as people dropped to the floor and then leapt and grabbed at me, silent and fast and strong.

I fought them.

Well, I tried to, but this was the real world, not the astral realm. They had me subdued in a matter of seconds. Cold hands, as hard as steel, pulled me out of the window, one firmly clamped over my mouth. They carried me to the van, threw me inside and the doors slammed closed as the vehicle was already speeding downhill.

The driver looked over his shoulder; the red light of the ceiling lamps in the back of the van making his eyes seem to gleam blackly as he grinned.

"*Zdravstvujte*," he said. "Thank you for coming here. I thought I wasted money." His accent was Slavic. "Don't fight my boys. They will break your bones like matchsticks."

I finally managed to have a proper look at my captors: four of them, all men, kneeling around me, holding my legs by the ankles and knees, and my arms by the wrists and elbows, pressed against my sides. Not one of them said a thing. In fact, not one of them had made a single sound this entire time. I could hear the engine drone, the tires on the asphalt. I could hear the driver breathe. But I couldn't hear them breathe. I concentrated, closing my eyes, glad my senses were still up to eleven. Their hearts didn't beat. I looked at them, under that red light. Their eyes looked through me, unblinking. Their hands weren't just as strong as steel; they were cold as stone.

I was pretty certain these four men were dead.

"These roads, much better than I was told," the driver called over his shoulder after maybe a minute. He turned the volume down on the music—some hysterical-sounding electronica—and looked over his shoulder. "They tell me this country proper

206

shithole, but fuck me, no holes in the road. New houses. Very pretty young girls. Beautiful weather."

I was listening to him praising Croatia while I was being held down by four undead men and wondered if I'd been abducted by a legitimate madman.

"And everybody speak English!" he exclaimed. "Great for me, I speak it good. I was afraid nobody understand me." He brayed laughing, making me twitch because I didn't expect such a sound to come from a human.

"Where are we going?" I asked.

"Ah, you're talking, good. Was afraid you died of fear!"

"No," I replied, the air in the back of the van becoming unpleasantly warm and stale by the minute.

"Well, we are going to a nice place. And then we have a pleasant chat."

I was certain I would not enjoy the talk at all.

"Look, that house, it's not mine. I was just—just looking around—"

He slammed a palm against the steering wheel, let out a string of what I guessed were curses. Was that Russian?

"Come on!" he shouted over his shoulder, angry. "Don't act like I'm idiot! I put a watchman on the house. The house is yours, don't talk shit, okay?"

"Look, man, I—"

"Yes?"

I didn't know what to say.

"Silent treatment now, eh?" He chuckled after a few moments. Then he said, "You'll talk. She's not here to talk, but you'll talk."

A PLEASANT CHAT

As the van drove along, I took stock of the situation. First: I was calm. Incredibly calm. My only possible explanation was that I was so terrified that some defense or survival mechanism triggered in my body and pushed me far away from panic.

Second: the driver was alive, but his—servants? They seemed to obey his commands, so servants for now. Or minions?—were definitely dead. And they felt dead in a... different way than Snježana Remac had. There had been something alive inside her still, a spark. These four were cold and empty.

Third: the driver had mentioned a 'her', and that was probably nona. I would be shocked if it turned out not to be nona.

Fourth: I was overpowered, outnumbered and with no way to call for help. Unless I fell asleep, when I could go looking for Viki, tell her what was happening. Only, there was no way to fall asleep in this situation.

I thought back to those last few moments before I'd inexplicably found myself in the house. The mora was about to shred me to ribbons and... something happened. What? How? Did Viki do something? I sure as hell didn't do anything, apart from wanting *hard* to get away from the monster, but that hadn't helped the first time either.

I listened—and heard only the engine. And the—were these guys actual zombies?—the dead men holding me down were just dark outlines under the, now much dimmer, red light. My senses had gone back to normal.

Great.

I thought of the dead Remac mother again. I'd gotten out of that situation by keeping cool and using my head. Sure, these guys didn't seem benevolent like she'd turned out to be, but if I paid attention and kept my shit together, I would maybe find a way out.

Besides, there was literally nothing else I could do.

The van drove on.

When the van finally stopped, it had been after what I guessed was the vehicle taking a turn from an asphalt road onto a dirt one. The transition was very noticeable, starting with a pretty strong bump and the driver cursing, continuing with the van shaking. But the dead men might've as well been steel shackles. Actually, as much as my senses had returned to normal, the four were still unnerving, and it wasn't just their dead—heh—stillness or the fact they made no sound. They gave off no smell, even though they looked like they *should*, under the dim red light in the back of the van. Their skin seemed to be rotting in places, and while there were no bones sticking out, nor raw flesh exposed, it looked like they weren't far from it. And yet, there was no stench of decay at all.

How the hell am I so calm? I asked myself again.

I was terrified, sure, but I was still keeping a tight lock on that fear. I found a strange satisfaction with myself in that, feeling almost smug I wasn't screaming and thrashing and calling for help—which is what I'd always been afraid I'd do if I was ever kidnapped.

Then again, I also wasn't the same person I'd been a few days ago. Or ever before.

The van crossed onto gravel and then stopped.

The driver got out and slid the side door open. The dead men carried me out.

"Oh come on," I said, looking up at the driver.

He grinned, nodded. "Boys, let him walk. Hold his arms. If he tries to run, tear them from shoulders."

They didn't make a sound as they lowered my feet to the ground and then stood me up. Two still held my arms, while the other two now stood behind me.

We were on a wide gravel path, under a starry sky and an almost full moon. Over my shoulder, I saw the van and the gravel giving way to a dirt road. Far behind, trees with lights between them: houses and street lights and distant, passing cars. In front of me, the gravel path ended at a house, low and wide, with a flat roof, generally giving off an unfinished vibe—no plaster on the walls and the windows covered in flat boards. The house was in the middle of a grassy field, with low hills and a thick forest a short walk from its back.

Middle of fucking nowhere.

If I ran, I'd have a long way to go until I reached the first house or a car I could stop for help. My gaze, as we walked towards the house, lingered on the dark outlines of those wooded hills.

What about running to the woods?

No way I'd make it.

And yet, something inside me seemed to think I'd have a shot between those trees, if I could just escape the viselike grip of the dead men.

We walked, gravel crunching under our feet. The driver—my height but more muscled, with an unkempt beard and giving off a faint smell of stale alcohol—kept next to me, grinning. He took in a lungful of air, savoring it.

"Fuck me, smells great here," he said. "I live mostly in big cities. I only go to country when I need fresh bodies." He looked around. "It's nice here. Quiet and dark. Maybe I could move here when I retire." He chuckled to himself and then he straightened up, pointed at the house ahead with his chin. "You know where we are?"

"No," I said.

"Hm," he replied. "Don't trust you."

We walked on. I didn't want to ask him anything. Let him talk. It was the smart thing, wasn't it? Trying to piece together what was going on?

Or did that work only in crime shows?

The driver opened the front door. The large space inside, bare walls and a concrete floor, was illuminated by a single light bulb, already turned on, hanging from a wire. There was a metal chair right under it and a coiled rope next to the chair.

Well. Fuck.

The dead men forced me into the chair, tied my hands behind the chair's back.

"So, you are not what she was?" my captor asked me, looking at me suspiciously."I mean, obvious you're not what the old hag was. If you were, you'd be a wolf by now or a dog or whatever else they turn into. So what are you?"

"What do you want from me?" I asked. I felt it was imperative he doesn't find out I actually was a krsnik, only, currently, without any useful powers. Turning into a wolf sounded great at the moment.

"I have to be honest, you are not who I came for. But the old hag is dead and there is no point I raise her." He smiled at me, pleasantly. "But, you are her apprentice, so you will help me."

I didn't say anything. Apprentice. How the hell had he found out I was Lena's heir?

He crouched in front of me. "No, but really, what are you? Witch?"

"What is it you think I know?" I asked.

He sniffed. "Don't like talking about yourself, huh?" He stood up. "Alright, I respect that. People like us, best we keep in-co-gni-to, eh?" He sighed. "Straight to business, then."

His face lost any trace of levity it had accumulated over the past few minutes. "You know I was at the house before," he burred, the Slavic tones dripping from each word.

My gut was telling me there was no point in trying to pretend I had nothing to do with the house. Besides, if I wanted to find out what was happening and also survive all this, then I'd have to participate in the conversation.

"I knew someone had broken in. Through the roof," I said finally.

He rolled his eyes, sighed exasperatedly. He pointed at the dead men nearby, standing around like sculptures. "No matter how fresh the body is, sometimes you just raise idiot." He cursed again in his language, which may have not exactly been Russian, but was definitely somewhere near it on the language tree. "I tell them, break boards and get inside. I obviously mean window boards. But board is fucking board to them. Window, floor, who gives fuck, eh?" He looked straight at me. "Where is it?"

"I don't know what you want," I said.

He frowned. "Don't fuck. You were her apprentice, you know what she did with it. It's not in the house. So where is it?"

"She didn't tell me everything," I said, and wasn't that the truth?

He sighed, cursed under his breath. "Look, I would rather not have my boys break your bones, but if you're going to be stubborn lying bastard—"

"I don't know what you're looking for," I repeated, and there was an irritated and aggressive edge to my voice that I immediately regretted. The dead men were still playing statues, but I remembered the intensity with which they'd broken into the house and caught me in their grip within heartbeats. If he let them loose on me, told them to hurt me because he didn't appreciate the tone of my voice...

But the fact he had, so far, taken great care not to hurt me made me think he could maybe be reasoned with.

Or distracted with talking long enough for me to figure something out.

I'd been testing the ropes at my wrists for the past minute or so. They weren't tight. The dead men had impressively fine motor skills for, well, dead men, but their master would've certainly made the bonds much tighter. I was working the ropes now, hoping to slip them over my wrists and—

And what? Make a run for the door? Yes, I was in better shape these last few days than in the many years prior, even with the strange, hangover-like feeling in my head, and the bone-deep tiredness the brief but brutal second fight with the mora had left me with. I had more stamina and more strength and I *probably could* make a run for it, but my gut was telling me there was no way I would outrun the dead men.

The man was nodding absently. "Alright, as you wish. I know what is like to lose your teacher. But if Vadim can give you piece of advice? Being noble, that's great. Being alive, much better. Trust me, dead men are something I know well. We," he said, pointing at himself and me, "are much better off." He tsked. "But alright. I'm going to make phone call. It will take some time, probably, so you have maybe half hour to change your mind. I leave the boys here, so don't try anything funny. Alright?"

He took a phone out of his jacket pocket and started typing as he exited the house, leaving me alone with the dead men.

I fiddled with the bonds but it was slow going, frustrating. So I closed my eyes and stopped doing everything except breathing. Slipping the ropes was my only way out. Sure, what I would do after was incredibly fuzzy, but I concentrated on the immediate check mark—getting my hands free. Eyes closed, I continued working the rope.

The door suddenly opened and my captor stormed in. "*Pizda*, this isn't me, alright? *Vadim*, they say, *you draw too much attention.* Be more subtle. *Po hui!* That is not me." He stopped in front of me, fuming. "So here's how it's going to be, *suka huilo*," he said, those last two words pronounced clearly enough that I could make out the sounds and dripping with so much derision I guessed they must be exceptionally juicy. "You talk or—" And then he stopped himself. He smiled, but it was a cold smile, only with his mouth.

He clicked his fingers impatiently and made another motion with his hand, and one of the dead men started moving and

213

walking up to me. Its master then barked something at it and the dead man knelt.

And bit me on the left forearm, the teeth pressing hard against my bare skin and then breaking through.

I screamed.

The teeth pulled out and the dead man stood up, its master waving it away with a curt motion.

The bite mark was big and round, blood welling in it. It was burning like hot needles. And there were black spots on the skin surrounding the bite now, visible through the blood that was already dripping on the floor and staining the fabric of my pants.

The leader grabbed my head with both hands, roughly turned me to face him.

"*Ne valyay duraka,*" he told me. "Stop fucking, okay? This was nothing. They will do horrible things if I tell them." His eyes were huge and completely insane. "I am not subtle man. I am blood and screaming and tearing limbs."

I punched him.

He staggered backwards and I slammed into his chest with my right shoulder. Pain was pulsating horribly through my left arm. The crazy lord of the undead landed flat on his ass as I stumbled past him, towards the door. His hands shot out, grabbed me by the leg and then I was down.

He was on top of me then, punching and screaming and cursing. Suddenly the light of that single bare light bulb was incredibly bright and his curses incredibly loud. The pain from his fists and in my left arm was incredible as well.

He must have punched me straight in the face, or slammed my head against the floor—either way, suddenly everything was very still and distant, except the pain.

The pain and something else.

There was a thrumming, reverberating oh, so gently through my entire body, flowing up my back from the concrete floor. *Not that different,* some distant part of me said, *from the one I'd felt in the*

Vranja house. It was much, much weaker, though. And this one—this one was calling to me.

I wanted to respond, pull it towards me, or maybe push myself towards it, I wasn't certain.

A sharp pain brought me back to the concrete floor. The man had slapped me again. He was screaming into my face now, holding my collar with both hands as he knelt next to me, shaking me and spitting at me—both curses and saliva. "That fucking bitch is dead but you will pay for what she did to my teacher! *You* will pay."

He went incoherent again after that, but his fists conveyed the message clearly, slamming into my chest and gut and sides. Through all that, I felt my left arm burning, but also going numb. I lashed out with my right, swinging blindly; one punch connected with the man's chin and he fell over on his back. The punch surprised him as much as me. Some part of me, somewhere deep inside, growled with satisfaction.

I staggered up to my feet. "Fuck. You," I said defiantly.

Still on his back, he kicked and his heel caught me straight in the solar plexus.

It felt like an eternity before I was able to breathe again. At some point during that eternity I'd ended up on my knees.

He was towering over me, shaking with barely controlled fury. "We are done," he said. He whistled, loud and piercing. The dead men changed in an instant. One moment they were eerie statues, the next growling monsters. Their eyes were no longer empty—now they were full of animal rage. Wild beasts, ready to pounce.

"This will hurt a lot, you cunt," the man said through bloodied teeth.

The door slammed open.

I felt a glimmer of hope as a figure stepped into the light.

"The fuck are you?" my captor growled.

"That's my friend Viki," I said, ridiculously happy to see her.

Viki stepped forward, smiling determinedly. The dead men hissed and slavered, rushing towards her. She planted her feet, raised a hand and extended the palm flat in front of her face, and blew very theatrically. Glitter flew through the air, forming tendrils that shot out towards the dead men, coiled around them. They stopped, stared in confusion, their heads twitching as they tried to follow the movements of the sparkles dancing and swirling about them.

Suddenly there was music. Pulsating beats, rich and manic as the tendrils of glitter wrapped themselves around the dead men. There was thrashing, there was shrieking, but the creatures could not break free. They flew into the air and ended up just beneath the ceiling.

For a moment, it was the weirdest tableau ever: the dead men up in the air, held in place by the shimmering coils; Viki standing there full of intent and with a wry grin on her face. The music squealed and scrambled, reaching a peak, sustaining—

"Aaand the beat *drops*," the glitter witch said and as the beat did, indeed, drop, so did the dead men, slammed into the floor with literal bone-breaking force. The glittering tentacles of some invisible force, still in tune with the music, slammed them into the walls and the floor, repeatedly, furiously. A second passed, two, three, and then the tune mellowed, just as the dead men stopped moving and making any noise whatsoever.

Viki stepped over the body directly in front of her, through a cloud of glitter that had just released from its grip what was probably the first doubly dead man I've ever seen in my life, smiling widely and *viciously* at the dead men's master.

Who promptly made a run for the door, reaching them in what seemed to be a heartbeat. A coil of glitter shot after him, struck him as he passed through the doorway, but there was a flicker of red light and the coil shrank back.

Viki sniffed, shook her head, then reached into her pocket and the music stopped.

"What did you think?" she asked me as she knelt next to me.

"That... was something," I said.

"Let me see." She reached for my left arm. There was so much blood. The wound was ragged, the skin surrounding blotched with black.

"*Kurac*," she growled. "You were bitten."

The pain wasn't burning anymore, just a dull throb that made it hard for me to focus on anything. A distant part of me noticed that the vibrations I'd felt from below the floor were gone now.

"The good thing is," she spoke as she pressed my flesh gently, examining the wound, "that you're a krsnik. If you were normal, your arm would already be gangrenous from fingertips to shoulder."

"Yay me," I spoke through my teeth, focusing hard on just talking to her, not anything else, say, the pain and the sudden numbness that was worrying me even more.

"Bites from the undead can't heal on their own even if you're a krsnik," she added. She looked me in the eyes. "Paul, I need to do something to your hand now. It's going to hurt. A lot."

"Will it be better after?" I asked, hoping I was smiling.

Viki nodded.

"Go for it."

And she did. She pulled something out of a pocket, sprinkled it over the wound. It was cold and prickly even through the dull throb. Then there was a flash of glitter over my arm.

And then—*pain* isn't even the word for it. It lasted just a heartbeat, but that heartbeat stretched into infinity and I swear I could hear colors and see sounds, and then I was leaning against her, my forehead on her shoulder.

"Take your time," Viki said. She was stiff, but she let me stay like that for a while, until I finally felt I could stand up without immediately keeling over.

The wound was now just a patch of skin the color of an uncooked hot dog sausage. It was very tender to the touch, but the dull throb was gone.

"It will change color several times during the next day or so. It may throb faintly occasionally. Also, tomorrow it will probably be very numb for a while. Don't slam it into things, okay?"

I nodded.

"You are incredibly lucky," she added a moment later.

"How—how did you find me?" My mouth was bone dry and I had trouble speaking because of it.

"Well," she said as she helped me walk out of the house, "once you teleported, I thought I'd have trouble finding you. Lucky for you, you're new to all this, so you don't know how to teleport without being followed. I tracked you to that house, saw it had been broken into. Lucky for you—*again*—the undead leave quite the necromantic trail during nighttime, so I didn't even need to wait for Perdida to give me a hand. I tracked you here."

Gravel crunched under our feet.

"So, who was that asshole?"

"I have no idea," I said. She was leading me towards a car. There was no van in sight. "He was here because of Lena. He thought I could give him something he wanted from her." I took a breath. "He didn't know who I was," I said. "I mean, he didn't know I was a krsnik; he thought I was her apprentice." I blinked. "Did he think I was *Katrina*?"

Viki raised an eyebrow. "She'd been helping Lena so much that people probably guessed she was being trained as a successor. By the time those rumors got to your friend, obviously, the part about the apprentice being female got left out." She waved her hand at me curtly. "Get in, will you?"

I sat down in the passenger seat of her car, feeling all the punches and kicks I'd received, as well as the pain in my left forearm.

"Oh, by the way," Viki said, putting on her seat belt, "what did you think about the music? It's my own track, I deejay on the side."

Because of course she did.

I looked at her. "I like the pounding beat."

Viki chuckled, then laughed. I joined her and, for a moment, all the pains and aches were gone.

"So, home or some other place?" she asked, starting the engine.

"Home," I said. I was incredibly tired and suddenly a little despondent. I turned to her as the car crunched its way over the path. "Thank you. If you hadn't come I... I have no idea what I would have done."

"You'll have to do something, and do it fast," she said. Her voice was hard and cold. "A krsnik could do all kinds of stuff to get out of what you got yourself into tonight. But a man with the occasional enhanced sense, which seems to be all you're exhibiting so far in the material world? Paul, you would've been dead within minutes if I hadn't come."

A knot was tightening in my gut. "I untied myself," I said. "I had this plan where I'd knock him down and make a run for the woods. But—maybe the powers don't really wor—"

"Oh fuck off," she interrupted. "I know what you were about to say because I've been you once, long ago. Your powers are not defective, they're not having second thoughts, you're not unworthy or any other nonsense you were ready to say." She glanced at me sharply before returning her attention to the road. "Paul. You need to get your shit together, *fast*. I don't mind helping you. I'm glad I was there in time to save you, but if word gets out that Rijeka's new krsnik can't handle a couple of revenants and their master on his own... it won't be good. You understand that, right?"

I felt a hot stab of resentment.

And yet it did make sense. If word got out that the new sheriff was a wimp, maybe all kinds of bandits and boogeymen might come breaking down doors.

Great, now I'm using Katrina's western analogy—again.

But still...

"One thing," I said, feeling the heat rising in me. "One thing goes right, then *bam!* Like that, another goes wrong!"

"I'm not the one you're angry with."

"I fucking know!" I shouted.

And with that I deflated.

"Look," I said. "I'm so—"

"It's okay, don't mention it," Viki cut me off. "You've been dropped into the deep end, I won't lie. Katrina had been hoping you'd prove to be a natural swimmer—hell, I think she still hopes that. But, right now, you're barely keeping your head above the water. And you're doing that with other people's help. And you're still holding firmly to the edge of the pool."

"I should just let go and drown?"

She didn't even glance at me as she simply said, "You should start swimming."

YOU CAN ONLY
PROCRASTINATE
SO MUCH

Back in the apartment, I drank water until I thought I might be sick and then went to the impossible room. I stopped short once inside, unsure of what exactly I wanted to do. I looked around, taking deep breaths to calm myself, suddenly aware of just how tense and pissed off I was. Almost as much as I was tired and as everything hurt. Again.

My left forearm was tender, unpleasantly so.

One breath and then another, deep, slow, closed eyes...

I stumbled and realized I had dozed off, on my feet. I put my general plan to start swimming on pause and more fell than laid down on the fold out bed.

"Viki told me about last night! How are you?!"

Phone nestled between my ear, a cup of coffee in my one good hand, I blinked the last bits of drowsiness away as I walked back into the impossible room from the kitchen.

"Good morning to you, too," I said. My body hurt, but again, not nearly as much as I felt it should have. Still, it didn't feel pleasant when I moved or breathed—he'd done a real number of my ribs, I only now realized. My forearm was a deep and very unpleasant shade of purple. It hung limply by my side, most of the sensation gone from my bicep down.

I had hit it against the doorway on accident when I walked into the kitchen and, for a moment, I was absolutely certain my skin had burst open and blood was gushing out, but it just pulsed with pain for a while. Finally the pain receded enough for me to make myself coffee with one hand.

Next time I see him...

"*Paul...*"

I took a deep breath as I sat back on the bed. "I'm... okay. I have no idea who that guy was, but he had a bone to pick with Lena. *Lena*, not me, Katrina."

The anger and bitterness in my voice were very clear.

"*Oh.*"

"He wanted something he expected to be at the house, but it wasn't." I remembered the psychotic eyes, so close to my face. "And—apparently Lena did something to his mother."

There was silence on the other end of the line.

"Katrina?"

"*I'm here. I just... don't know what to say.*"

I chuckled despite myself. "He wasn't from around here," I said. "Definitely Slavic, though. If I had to guess, I'd say maybe Russian or Ukrainian, something like that."

Silence again.

"Katrina?"

"*I'm thinking, but I don't remember Lena having... problems with anyone Russian or Ukrainian.*"

"Yeah, but you've said she didn't tell you everything she used to do."

Another silence, and then, "*Paul, why did you go to the house in the middle of the night?*" It was a perfectly reasonable question. And it also meant that Viki hadn't told her the whole story of her saving my ass last night.

"Well, you see..." I paused, collecting my thoughts as I drank a huge gulp of coffee. Then I rolled my aching shoulders and re-capped my night for her benefit.

"I... I didn't know you could do that," she said in the end. "*Lena never...*"

I swallowed another gulp—coffee never felt so good, swear.

There was a silence again, but different. "*You're angry,*" she said finally.

"No," I said, and it was true. "More bitter than angry."

As Katrina was quiet again for a long moment, I found myself glancing around the room. The table with its stacks; the shelves, the cabinets and the cupboards. My inheritance.

I breathed deep.

It was what it was, as Bowie had said, wasn't it? This was what I had to deal with.

My eyes fell on nona's laptop. I stood up, took the phone and switched the call to video.

Concern very visible on Katrina's face.

"Look," I said, shaking my head lightly as I walked towards the laptop.

Katrina was watching me, waiting.

"She knew this would come to pass some day, okay? She *must have known.* Maybe I would've had to deal with it, maybe my mom. Either way, grandma had done the bare minimum to make it easy for either of us... "It's like I've been stumbling through this—this fucking *obstacle course* for days now, only I can't see the obstacles until I slam face first into them."

Katrina was nodding lightly, the way you do so the other person knows you're listening.

"So yes, I'm bitter. I know she loved me and she believed in me, but goddammit, nona..."

"*She had a wall you couldn't get past,*" Katrina said suddenly. "*She kept things from people. From me, from other people she was close to in—in our world. When she was supposed to cooperate with someone, there'd always be problems, because she wouldn't share things in time or at all.*"

I was nodding now. Once again, it sounded very on brand for grandma.

"And now she's gone and... kurac i pizdu materinu."

I chuckled at her cursing and suddenly felt a little lighter. She was shaking her head.

"You don't know how many times I had to force Lena to tell me more about the things we were dealing with. It wasn't that she kept them from me on purpose, but... She was the worst combination, honestly. She was someone who just naturally does things on their own, which made her was shit at cooperating. She would also leave things for later—things she expected you to help her with, or needed you to help her with—but you wouldn't find that out until the very last minute, usually."

I chuckled again. "Honestly, I don't really remember her like that. But then again, I was a kid, so maybe I just didn't notice it." My thoughts went back to the message she'd left for me in the book. I said, "She probably was going to prepare the other stuff for me as well, not just leave me the occasional note and update her last will and testament. But, obviously, she never got around to it."

Katrina laughed then, and it was a short and honest laugh.

I shook my head, smiling now. "Fuck me," I said, rubbing my forehead. I placed my phone next to the laptop so I could still see Katrina and she me, as I clicked open the email client on that mess of a desktop screen.

"I'm glad you're alive," Katrina said then.

I snorted. My left arm throbbed faintly. "Not as much as I am."

"What are you doing?"

"There is an email on Lena's laptop. Somebody was asking her for help and I've been ignoring it, but I really shouldn't keep doing it."

There was a satisfied look on Katrina face when I glanced at the phone screen as the email loaded.

It was in Croatian, so it took me a few moments to read it. And then reread, to make sure it really said what I thought it did.

Fuck.

"Paul?" Katrina asked. She'd been patient as I read the email, but my face must have alarmed her.

"Katrina," I said, "what's a *vilenica*?"

224

REDIAL

I was resisting the thought that I might be too late as I redialed the number. It was the only contact we had for the woman who had asked for help—from a dead krsnik, but she couldn't have known that—apart from the email address itself. She hadn't responded to the *'I'm trying to reach you via mobile, but you're not responding. Please give me some other means of contacting you'* email Katrina had dictated to me in Croatian.

"Still nothing?" Katrina asked, sitting across from me at the kitchen table. She'd dropped her morning's work and come straight over the moment I told her what the email said.

"Nothing," I said, hoping to hear the sound of connection being made. But it was just ringing and ringing and ringing.

I wondered if there was a way to track the woman down. If she was being pursued, she'd probably do her best to hide, cover her tracks. Maybe there was something in nona's book that could help me.

There were also people I could ask, of course.

But...

"I know the girls wouldn't mind helping out," I said to Katrina, as much as myself. "But this woman asked Lena specifically. I don't know who is after her or why. I don't want to make things worse if..."

"If what?"

"I don't know," I said simply. "What if she's someone who Viki or Perdida are enemies with?"

She frowned. "Paul, what are you—" But I got her thinking, that was obvious. "Hum. I—okay, I wouldn't go that far, but relations in our world *can* be... complicated." She took a breath. "Viki and Perdida... okay, if you want, we can wait until we find out more."

"Lena said I can trust you," I said as I hit redial again. "She didn't say I shouldn't trust anyone else, but I don't want to make this into more of a problem than it currently is."

"Fair enough," Katrina said. Her phone rang, but she rejected the call after glancing at the screen. "What?" she asked me. I couldn't help either my smile or my eyebrow. She grunted. "Yes, it's what you think it is."

"*The Good, the Bad and the Ugly*, right?" I asked. Her phone had rung only for a second or two, but it was a very recognizable tune.

"Now, about what a vilenica is," she said. "I've never met one personally, but I know of them."

The phone in my hand still calling the number and getting no response, I listened to her intently.

"Well, they're healers. Like, they're both good at making working natural medicines and also have—legit *healing powers*. Literally healing by touch."

I blinked, my phone still trying to establish a connection. My forearm was now the color of aubergine where the wound had been. The tenderness had given place to very dull throbbing and a woman with healing powers sounded like a great person to meet.

"Bowie," I said. "Buddy, are you here?"

He dropped onto the kitchen table from atop the cupboard. "Hello," he said to Katrina.

"Hey." She smiled.

"A woman needs my help," I told him. He stared at me with a very serious look on his face. "Do you know anything about vilenicas?"

"I just know they heal by touch," Katrina offered, "and make superior medicine, so any additional info would be great. Oh,

226

wait" she added. "I think they're supposed to be daughters of a human mother and a fairy father."

Wait, do fairies *exist?*

Bowie seemed to shiver for the briefest moment. "No, no," he said, "a fairy and a human can't have offspring."

Oh. Fairies exist.

"They get their power from the fairies. Some as a gift, others because they, or their mother, ate or drank something made by a fairy."

I looked back at him after glancing at my phone. "That's it?"

"Unfortunately, that is all I know," Bowie said.

"Thank you," I told him. "So," I said as I hit redial, frustration mounting. "She's coming to Rijeka from Zagreb—she may already be here. Do you have any ideas how to find her if she's here?" I asked Katrina.

In the email she said someone was trying to force her into servitude, had been literally pursuing her. He had sent a dream monster to torture her until she gave in, and it was the monster she needed help with.

Help I was willing to try and give *if she picked up the damn phone.*

Katrina rose from the table. "I can ask around. I have contacts that most people don't."

My eyebrow crept up.

"Keep redialing," she said. "And come with me."

"Where are we going?" I asked as we exited the building. My arm had been feeling a little less numb the past few minutes, but it was still like a dead elephant's trunk hung from my shoulder. I just hoped people wouldn't notice.

The vilenica was still not answering. I was thinking of all the horrible things that might have happened to her—well, it was all very nebulous, because I had no idea who was chasing her, or what the dream monster was.

I just hoped it wasn't that mora again.

"The playground," she said, pointing as we rounded a corner. There was a school nearby, with a playground in front of it. There were kids there now, preschoolers mostly, accompanied by parents and grandparents. School was out this time of year in Croatia.

We walked into the playground and she pointed one of the benches in front of a low wall. The children were squealing and shouting, chasing each other and their balls and toys; the grown ups were chatting or just sitting, zoned out.

I could smell cigarettes, suddenly. A strong smell—well, stench, really—as if someone was shoving them up my nose. And the kids were *incredibly loud.*

"No, left," Katrina told me as I was sitting down. I had to focus on her voice and face to push back the almost overwhelming smells and sounds. I moved to the left, careful not to sit on a dried-out spot of pigeon shit. It stank as well, but much weaker than the cigarettes. Katrina sat on the bench next to mine, turned towards me.

I closed my eyes for a second, focusing on my senses. "Just a moment," I said.

"Oh," I heard her say. "Your senses flaring up again?"

"I'll be fine," I said as I felt the cigarette stench grow more powerful. Someone else had just lit one up. I knew because I also caught the smell of a kerosene lighter.

I let it all in. The cigarettes, the screaming kids, the dry pigeon shit, the cars passing by on the other side of the wall. Katrina's breathing. My own heartbeat. The muffled *beep-beep* of my phone calling the vilenica.

And now, it all felt less aggressive. It wasn't attacking me any more. It just... was. Gently, like putting on a pair of fine gloves, I pushed the senses back and they slid down to normal.

I opened my eyes. The only thing I could smell was the summer day.

"Okay," I said to Katrina. "I'm good now."

She smiled. She was still on the bench next to mine. I had no idea what she was doing. There was place enough for three people on my bench, at the very least.

I looked at my phone. Nothing.

"*Dobar dan*," a voice said next to us.

It was him.

"Hello," I said, surprised to see him.

Barba smiled kindly.

What was he doing here?

"Some of the little ones like to play here," he told me from where he was standing, next to Katrina. So I wouldn't look like I was staring at nothing and talking to air, I realized.

"I was hoping you'd be here," Katrina said, glancing sideways at him and smiling. "We need help."

"What can I do?" Barba asked.

Katrina turned towards me and said something in Croatian that I didn't catch, in a low voice and rather fast.

No, not to me. She was looking at someone next to me.

But there was no one there.

"I—I didn't catch that," I said.

"I'm not talking to you," she said. "Just keep looking at me."

I glanced at Barba, who smiled and looked at me expectantly.

Oh. Someone's next to me only they can see.

There's a ghost next to me.

She proceeded to talk for a minute or two and it was to both the person next to me—it seemed to be a woman—and Barba.

And while I didn't catch every word because she was talking fast, I definitely did get the gist of the conversation.

Finally Barba nodded at Katrina, then at me and walked away.

Katrina looked at me and said, "Okay, they'll help us find her."

"I was just sitting next to a ghost, wasn't I?"

"Yep."

I had, during the past minute or so, successfully suppressed the urge to reach out, try to feel the ghost, feel if there's any difference in the air.

229

"So," I said as I stood up. "If I understood that little conversation, you've just asked a ghost and Barba to help us find the vilenica?"

Katrina nodded as we walked back from the playground. "Over the years I've built a, uh, a network of ghosts who—who stayed instead of passing on. and who are, well, still *sane* enough. The woman who sat next to you is called Elizabeta. She'll ask other ghosts and they'll ask others in turn, and if anyone has heard anything that can help us, they'll let us know. Some will even actively search for her. Barba agreed to do the same—he'll ask the kid ghosts if they know anything, and to keep an eye open."

I smiled, impressed. "You have an informant network."

We had just closed the apartment building's front door behind us when Katrina's phone again whistled the Morricone theme, and this time she answered. After a very short conversation in Croatian, she looked at me, phone still against her ear. "Er, Perdida is at that house Viki saved you from yesterday. She wants to talk to you."

I stopped in the middle of the entry hall. "Me? Why?"

She shrugged and offered me the phone. "Hello?" I said and then it switched to a video call.

"*Hi, Paul.*" Perdida's voice and face were perky and bright. Just over her shoulder, I could see something that a moment later I realized was a corpse.

Perdida moved and now I saw the chair, still turned over, and the rope next to it—and all the other corpses, twisted and broken by Viki's magic.

Perdida positioned herself so I could see her and, behind her, all four corpses. It felt I was witnessing the weirdest selfie ever in the making.

"You, uh, you need something from me?" I asked.

She smiled briefly and nodded. "*I would like you to confirm that you are giving these corpses to me.*"

There was a sentence you don't hear every day. "They're not mine, you do know that?"

"*Viki defeated them, you were captured by them. She gave up her rights to them as spoils of battle. Now I need you to give up your rights to them as subjects of your revenge.*"

"I'm sorry, what?" I asked after a moment's silence.

Perdida smiled patiently. "*When someone raises something that once had a soul,*" she said, pointing with her free hand at the corpses behind her, "*it goes against the natural order of the universe.*" She stopped for a moment. "*Basically, when their master raised them from the grave, he' bound them to himself so he could control them. When he ran away from Viki, he cut that bond so that he couldn't be tracked. When Viki kicked their asses, the bond became available to her.*"

"...she could control them?"

"*She would have to do a ritual, but the point is that it would be much easier for her than for, say, Katrina.*"

I noticed Katrina straighten up next to me in a 'how did I become a part of this conversation' stance.

"Because Viki defeated them?"

I had just participated in a conversation with a ghost and a supernatural caretaker of dead children, and yet it obviously wasn't to be the weirdest conversation of the day.

"*Yes. But she gave up her claim on them.*"

"And I also have a claim?"

"*You are their latest victim, and as such, you could, too, take control over them more easily than Katrina.*" And again Katrina perked up, shaking her head in confusion. "*Revenge is a powerful metaphysical force,*" Perdida added.

Where Viki would probably be curt or give off the vibe she wasn't really in the mood to draw me a diagram, Perdida was very businesslike but also... affable.

For a moment, I imagined myself walking around with a retinue of zombie thugs. I shivered inside.

"*I'm asking you because it's polite,*" Perdida added.

"I understand that," I said. "So, what are you going to do with them?" I was curious and then some.

"*Take them apart,*" she answered immediately. "*Reuse some parts.*"

"Reuse."

"*Yes,*" she said, suddenly slightly embarrassed. "*I'm sorry, I should have mentioned what it is that I do.*"

"She crafts things from flesh and bone," Katrina said dramatically, but also with a smirk.

"*We call it biomancy. Sounds less scary than what she just said,*" Perdida shot back. But there was a smile on her lips.

"And that means you... can raise the dead?"

She made a disgusted sound and a face to match. "*I don't do necromancy,*" she said. "*I prefer living bodies, or creating new ones from base components.*"

There was a moment of silence.

"*So, can I have them?*" Perdida asked, pointing at the corpses again, then moving closer to give me a better look, which I could have done without. I realized I had no idea which one of them had bit me. My left arm throbbed a little at the memory of teeth tearing into my flesh.

"Didn't you just say you don't work with the dead?"

She shrugged. "*They've already been raised. I don't like things going to waste.*"

"But what will you do with them?" I repeated. I was glad nobody was around, that Katrina hadn't received the call while we were still in the playground.

"*Honestly? A few skin and body grafts are the biggest thing that might come out of them.*"

"...for whom?"

"*People from our world who have lost a part of their body or skin,*" she said, like it was very obvious.

"Oh. And... the rest?"

"*Well, I'll just decompose most of it with a decaying spell. Turn them into fertilizer. And what doesn't go into grafts will go into my other work.*"

"Other work."

"*I make creatures,*" Perdida said, nodding. "*Oh, would you like to see?*"

I wanted to say no, but it was too late. She turned the phone and switched to the back camera. A shape had been there all along, not that far from Perdida, just outside the frame. It was the size of a bullmastiff. It was swollen with muscles like one as well. But it wasn't a dog, the same way a sabertooth tiger isn't a house cat. It started moving towards Perdida.

"What the fuck is that?!" I breathed.

"*Don't worry, he won't hurt you,*" Perdida's voice said as the creature sat on its haunches next to her. The creature's muzzle pressed against Perdida's shins for a moment, and she cooed something to it in Croatian that I couldn't make out. "*Before you ask,*" she continued, "*he's all living flesh and bone, one hundred percent. But there's other creatures that I'm working on which I can use bits of their bone and sinew for. Not flesh itself. I don't like working with dead flesh unless I have to.*"

I was quiet for a long moment.

I glanced at Katrina. She gave me a look that said, 'his is strange to you, but not to me.'

"Do you need me to say specific words?" I asked. "If not, I give up any claim whatsoever to these four corpses."

"*Yep, it worked,*" Perdida said, camera again pointed at the corpses. "*I can see they're free of any claims.*"

The corpses still looked the same, twisted and broken and doubly dead.

"Well," I said. "We should probably leave you to your work."

She smiled and there was a glint in her eye.

"See you later, Didi," Katrina said, taking back her phone.

I looked at my phone. The vilenica hadn't called back while we were talking to Perdida.

WORKING WITH YOUR HANDS CAN BE REWARDING

Back in the apartment, I stood in the hallway for a moment, thinking. Katrina had left because she had business meetings to attend in the afternoon, ones she'd preferred no to postpone, but would also drop immediately if her ghost network brought her news, or if I managed to get hold of the vilenica.

For my part, I wanted to be prepared, and that, I decided, meant providing protection in the real world as well. The way things had been going, I had a feeling I might find the vilenica under siege by an army of real world creepy things, not just tortured by a dream monster.

I went into the impossible room and picked up the book, my left hand feeling good enough for me to actually be able to hold things in it now. I started looking for something I vaguely remembered from my first time leafing through it.

I found something interesting after a few moments: several pages labeled with 'ZAŠTITA' at the top. Protection. Spells that seemed to provide anything from skin becoming temporarily impervious fire and heat, to... was I reading it right? I used the translator app to check and yes, there was a spell that could *turn skin into iron.*

But I soon realized there was no way I could perform any of these spells. Each involved a very detailed ritual that required items and ingredients. I not only had no idea where to find them, but also *what they were.* The last thing anyone needed was for me to botch something so horribly I turn someone into iron. Not just skin but *the whole body.*

But then, reading on, flipping pages in search of something I actually can do, I discovered a section about protective charms and they seemed... well, much simpler than the ritual spells. 'Protects the wearer from physical harm,' Lena's notes said about one of them. '*Temporarily.*' Of course. '*Cuts and stabs and attacks with clubs—works excellent! Bullets—effective but loses power quickly. Explosions—NO!*'

I blinked. That '*NO!*' was very large and underscored. Nona had been speaking from personal experience.

I read and reread the notes that seemed to be either nona's copies from some other source, or her writing down someone's instructions.

It... seemed straightforward.

I would need a physical object which I w'd have to inscribe with symbols Lena had taken great care to draw very neatly. She was prone to start scribbling, and it was easy to see the times she'd realized this and slowed down, making her letters bigger and more legible.

Afterwards I was supposed to '*focus and fill the charm with energy.*' Apparently I would need to '*feel for the main symbol and open myself to it.*' I would know it's working because '*the energy will flow through the maker and into the charm. Once the charm is filled with energy, it will grow warm to the touch and remain so for as long as there is charge.*'

Under that was an addendum, '*If you focus you can feel it get colder as it's being depleted!*'

Alright. I got up and started looking through the various drawers and shelves in the impossible room and, after maybe twenty minutes of finding all kinds of things, again with a strong impression Lena didn't, in fact, have any kind of a filing system, I was back at the table.

In one of the smaller cupboards—among the ones placed against the wall, but not actually mounted on it—I had found a box full of cheap metal bracelets and rings. At first I thought they were Lena's or mementos, but then I realized there were dozens of identical copies of each kind, and they all had lots of flat, wide surfaces. Ideal for inscribing with a set of carving tools I'd found on one of the shelves, between bits of animal (I hoped) bones and a stack of old, dusty maps. The tools were in a leather cover, unrolled on the shelf, and they looked *fancy;* definitely handmade and well-maintained. Fortunately for me, I knew what I'd been looking for because the instructions contained images of the tools.

Walking back to the table, I passed by a cupboard I hadn't opened yet. Out of sheer curiosity, I cracked open its door for a peek. Then I opened it fully.

It was a tall and slim cupboard, the kind you'd expect to hold flour and rice and spices and pasta. An orange light flickered on inside, obviously triggered by the door opening. It was buzzing softly.

No flour or rice. No spices or pasta either. Steel and iron, though...

I remembered the padded room and the crate full of wooden replicas of all kinds of weapons.

Most of those weapons were here as well, only *these were not replicas.*

Knives and hand axes and daggers and—

"Swords," I said out loud to no one, staring at the contents of the cupboard.

"Lena loved blades," Bowie said. I looked down. He was standing next to me, so tiny as he gazed into the—well, into grandma's armory.

"Didn't like guns very much."

I was staring at the sizable collection of bladed weapons, trying to take it all in. Some were neatly laid out on the shelves, others hung on the inside walls of the cupboard, top to bottom. And there was a weapon on the inside of the cupboard door as well, I noticed now. It was the only one with a long strap attached to its scabbard—the kind of strap that could fit over your head and shoulders, so you could carry the weapon hanging by your side, but high—maybe so it wouldn't get tangled in your legs?

I took it off its peg. The scabbard was light—aluminum—but the blade inside was old. *Old.* At least it looked and felt that way when I drew the weapon. It was thin and strangely curved—no, bent was a more appropriate word for the way the top half was at an angle to its bottom half.

I looked at Bowie, the scabbard in one hand, the weapon in my other. "This was her favorite?" I asked. "Just guessing from the fact it looks ready to go."

Bowie nodded up at me. "First one she ever had," he said.

I glanced at the cupboard. "Not last, though."

"It's very old," Bowie said, looking at the blade. "Powerful."

I stared at it. "It's *magic*?"

"It won't shoot fire or cut rock," Bowie said. "But it's not like the ones you would see in a museum."

I looked at him for a moment, silent. "Did it use to be in a museum?"

Bowie made a very poor job of concealing a tiny grin. "It was needed for other things."

I felt slightly queasy because things a sword would be needed for, well...

"What is it? A scimitar?"

"Older," Bowie said. "It's a *sika*. Illyrians made it."

"Illyrians?" I blinked. *Very* old then. Illyrian tribes had lived along the Adriatic coast long before Romans ever came into existence—including here, where Rijeka would stand centuries after both civilizations were gone. This weapon *did* belong in a museum.

It felt hard, solid—no-nonsense. This thing was made for a specific purpose, and it was probably very good at fulfilling that purpose, in the right hands.

I turned back towards the table. The book was there, waiting, and so were the bracelet and the carving tools in their leather roll.

What was I doing?

237

No, I told myself, pushing that particular thought away, refusing to take a walk down the path it was beckoning me towards. *Later.* I'd think about it later—about what the fact I was holding a weapon in my hand actually implied. The fact I was apparently going to take it with me.

You found a weapon. That's one check mark. You didn't know you needed one, but with everything that's happened so far...

Now the next check mark. Make the protective charm.

I placed the sika, back in its scabbard, on the edge of the table opposite the book, walked around and sat down.

I took the bracelet in my hand as I bent down to have a closer look at the instructions and the drawings.

It definitely didn't look too complicated or hard.

Carving definitely hadn't been hard, even with only one really good hand.

I was worried my right hand might slip but the tools sat very well in it and they cut the metal with such smoothness and precision that I wondered if the tools were also magical in some way. Then again, even though my hand didn't slip and I didn't cut myself or ruin the work, the symbols were a far cry from their textbook counterparts.

They were ugly.

But you could still very clearly make out which one was which if you placed the bracelet next to the drawings.

And now came the part I was actually nervous about. Holding the bracelet, I looked at the symbols, focusing on what the instructions called the *main* one. The symbols themselves were like something from the history textbooks I read in high school: each was simple, all straight lines and right angles and the occasional dot. Perfect for carving.

Looking at the main symbol—a square with a large dot in the middle and another, smaller dot just above the top line—I... had no idea what to do.

I didn't know what I was expecting, to be honest.

Maybe it wasn't working? Maybe I'd carved something wrong and this was just a ruined piece of cheap jewelry and a waste of time.

I relaxed, pushing back the various thoughts that now crowded the forefront of my mind. The vilenica, the Vranja house, the half-built house I'd been held prisoner in, the psychotic Slav who kidnapped me, his zombies, Perdida and her dog-something-creature, Katrina's ghost network—all that and more (what I was doing and what I would be doing and why wasn't I on the flight back home and...) was shoved back behind what I decided was a shield wall with a bunch of angry Vikings shooting mean looks at each and every thought so they might give me just a moment's peace to just... *focus.*

And in that moment or two of peace and quiet—of me ignoring the distant murmur of thoughts demanding they be allowed back—I felt it.

It was a subtle sensation of something passing just above my skin, missing it by the breadth of a hair—the sound of something crystal gently cracking in my ears, at the very edge of hearing—the impression that the symbol I was staring at was changing, the lines becoming deeper and sharper to my eyes even as the rest of the bracelet went increasingly fuzzy.

Is this it?

I allowed it all to come forward, slowly, afraid I'd break this strange state I seemed to be in.

Not forcing it actually worked. The sensation on my skin grew stronger, the sound in my ears was clearer and the symbol was now so sharp I felt it might cut my eyes.

I pushed with my mind at the symbol, imagining I was touching it with my finger. I immediately felt something flow across that imaginary finger and into the symbol; the symbol now felt... heavier. Just a fraction, but even so—something had passed into it, using me as a conduit. I imagined touching the symbol again, and again something flowed, but I didn't feel a change in me—whatever was happening wasn't affecting me. I was just a tool here.

Touching the symbol in my mind for the third time, I imagined the flow increasing and I felt it happen. What had been a trickle was now a steady stream.

And then I simply knew it was done.

Then I became aware that the bracelet was warm in my hand—just like the instructions said it would.

Slowly, I pulled my imaginary finger and my mind back, returning to the impossible room. My thoughts and concerns came rushing back, the Vikings gone, but I didn't pay them no mind.

In my palm was a simple metal bracelet, carved with ugly but legible symbols. And it was full of energy.

It was *magical*. I have just *done magic*.

Yes, I'd brewed a potion and I'd done all kinds of stuff in the astral realm but *this*, this was different somehow.

It was warm in my hands and it was the most amazing thing I'd ever held in them, as far as I was concerned.

I was tired. I was hungry and thirsty and my bladder was about to burst.

I left the bracelet across the open pages of the book and went to take care of all that, buzzing from delight and excitement.

A few minutes later, as I was eating scrambled eggs and bacon, my phone rang.

"Yes?" I answered.

"*They found her!*" Katrina shouted over the line.

SUGAR IS A CRYSTAL

As I rushed through the apartment, getting ready, I stopped short. The dream monster the vilenica had mentioned. If I was going to fight it, I'd need to be asleep.

"Bowie?" I called, standing in the living room, the fresh T-shirt I was about to put on still in my hands.

"Master?" he asked, standing on the armrest of one of the leather recliners.

I frowned at him lightly.

"I'm sorry," he said. "It's hard not to call you that. You're the master of the house."

I am, aren't I? "That woman I mentioned I was going to help, we found her. But I think I'll have to go into the astral realm. Now, there's no way I'll fall asleep. And I seriously doubt nona was able to fall asleep on command either."

Bowie was deep in thought for a moment. Then he turned and pointed at one of the cupboards that held my grandma's—special ingredients. "In there," he said. "She used it often."

I opened the cupboard with the jars and tins and paper and plastic bags filled with all kinds of strange looking powders and roots and... *stuff*.

"A glass jar with red crystal shards, do you see it?" Bowie asked from behind my back.

I started rummaging through the stuff on the shelves, found said jar in the back.

I turned and saw Bowie had moved to the kitchen table.

"What is it?" I asked him.

"She would use it to put herself to sleep fast." He looked at me. "But I do not know how much you should take."

I left the jar on the table and went to my backpack, took the book out and started leafing through furiously, hoping to see a drawing of the red crystal. And, to my great relief, I did, in the bottom left corner of a page with several drawings of various crystal-looking objects.

There was just a short note and it said to break off a tiny piece and put it on your tongue. 'Guaranteed to work within minutes,' it added.

I was less than enthusiastic about putting strange stuff in my mouth.

But time was short and Katrina would be arriving by taxi any minute now.

I opened the jar and felt like I'd just been punched in the nose by someone clutching a crushed lemon in their fist.

I closed it and shoved the entire glass jar into the backpack, followed by the book.

The *sika* was also in there. I wondered what Lena used to carry stuff around. A messenger bag would be more practical, I guessed. Although, the *sika* had me concerned. If the police caught me with it, there would certainly be trouble. And I had zero experience fighting with any kind of weapon.

Why am I taking it with me anyway?

Who am I going to fight?

I shook my head at the thoughts. No one. It was an insane idea. And yet, if I'd had a weapon yesterday night...

What, exactly? It would've meant nothing against the zombies, with their speed, and they probably didn't even care if you stabbed them. Would I have used it against that crazy Slav?

And yet, when I held the blade in my hands, it felt... good. There was a firmness and solidity to the weapon that gave me a sort of self-assuredness.

Isn't that how people actually die, getting cocky because of a weapon?

Then again, I didn't really think I was going to have to fight anyone physically, *sika* or not. The vilenica's problem was a dream monster, wasn't it?

I remembered the mora and shivered. But I was smarter now. I'd given in to rage and overconfidence and paid the price, but I wouldn't make that mistake twice.

As I passed through the hallway, I glanced at the mirror on the wall, under the coat hooks. There I was, a krsnik with his magic book and weapon in a hiking backpack, about to come to someone's aid.

A sane person would have been terrified. I was. But I was still going to do it.

Bivio, the part of Rijeka where the vilenica had taken shelter— where Katrina's ghost network had found her—was as far as you could get from nona's apartment and still remain within Rijeka town limits. I'd been there a few times as a kid—my parents had friends there and we'd often go visit them—and what I could recall from those days was not that different from what I could see now: clumps of family houses and lots of trees. It was still a fairly wooded area, but I could also see large buildings had sprouted here and there in the many years that had passed.

As the taxi slowed down in front of the house the vilenica was supposed to be inside, my gut tensed. It was listed online as a short-term rental.

Katrina explained that the ghosts finding the vilenica so fast was mostly sheer luck on our part. The woman we were about to meet had sought out a remote location instead of trying to get lost in the crowd. Lots of local ghosts liked places in Rijeka where there were less living people. The vilenica was also new to the town, and, according to Katrina, her ghost network was mostly made up of ghosts who *love* it when something new is happening, when something changes, when someone new and unfamiliar to them appears.

Katrina's ghost network was, in essence, full of curious grannies, in spirit if not literally.

And the woman we were about to meet was not just new in Rijeka, but had, according to ghosts, surrounded herself with charms that—from the ghosts' description of the 'energy' they were giving off—Katrina believed were supposed to ward off evil incorporeal entities.Lights were on in the house, in all the rooms. Did she have company? Or maybe she just wanted to give off the impression she wasn't alone in there.

We got out of the taxi, and as we walked towards the house, I looked around. This particular area had obviously only recently started being developed as a housing area—all the houses were relatively new-looking and there was at least one empty lot with a for-sale sign. It was quiet. It seemed, to be honest, a nice place to live away from the noise and hubbub of the town center, provided you had a car.

"Paul," Katrina said as we were approaching the front door. A shadow was moving on the other side of the strip of glass stretching almost from top to bottom of the door.

Someone was in there, definitely.

We rang the bell. Katrina called to the person inside to open the door, saying we were here to help, that we'd read the email and had been trying to call her.

As the door opened, my gut tensed some more. Were we about to find out we'd been dead wrong?

I looked into the eyes of the young woman who had cracked open the door, both terrified and tired.

We were at the right place.

"Thank you for coming," she said for the third time since we'd come into the house, as she placed a cup of coffee in front of Katrina and a glass of water in front of me. I had no idea if the coffee would interfere with the sleeping crystal, but it was better not to risk it.

Katrina and I exchanged a quick glance, and I could see sympathy in her eyes, the same one I felt for the woman now sitting across the kitchen table from us.

I've seen exhausted people. I have, myself, felt exhausted more than once in my life. But this woman was beyond that. She was something I hoped to never have to experience.

Her eyes seemed to stay open by sheer force of will, the same one that was setting her limbs into motion. She *radiated* a bone-deep desire to not so much sleep as simply fall to the floor and spend the next two days borderline comatose. She seemed to be about my age, but at a glance you could have mistaken her for sixty.

That she'd thanked us three times in the span of five minutes was not just understandable but completely expected. I just hoped the coffee would give her a jolt, allow her to explain what's going on and what exactly she needs from us.

I looked at the kitchen counter next to the sink and saw that the coffee pack she was using was almost empty. And it was a big one. That much caffeine couldn't have been good for her on top of everything else.

"I'm sorry for your loss," she said again. I realized she was looking at me, her eyes either sad or tired, or both.

"Thank you," I repeated. Before we'd entered the house, we'd explained that Lena had passed away and that I was her grandson who'd come back from far away, and was ready to help her. If it had sounded unbelievable—and it had *to me* while I was saying it out loud—she hadn't seemed to notice it. It had also been the first time she'd expressed her condolences.

She gulped down her coffee, putting the empty cup aside so she could rest both her elbows on the table and massage her temples with her palms for a moment.

Katrina and I were both unsure how to proceed.

"What can I do for you?" I asked, deciding to take charge of the conversation. After all, it was my help she was hoping for.

"Help me finally get some sleep," she said, looking at me from under her eyebrows. She closed her eyes for a moment and mumbled something to herself, probably in Croatian, but too low for me to make out.

She put her hands down and her eyes seemed to clear. She was... focused, as much as that was possible in her state. When did she sleep last, for god's sake?

"If I fall asleep, the creature comes for me. It attacks me and it hurts. It hurts not just in dreams."

She pulled up the sleeves of her blouse. There were red marks on her forearms. Long and thin and red; as if something had clawed at her.

"It's not a mora, I was told it's not," she added and I felt a tinge of relief. "I have a friend, she did a reading." She looked at me, as if to see if I understood what she meant. "With tarot cards?" she added.

"Okay," I said, stealing a look at Katrina who just nodded barely perceptibly. So tarot readings were also real. Okay.

"She said it wasn't a mora. She said it was something specifically created and sent to attack me. Torture me."

It was working, I thought.

"Who sent it?" I asked. "Why are they doing this to you?"

She smiled weakly. "I help people. I don't hurt them."

"You're a vilenica, a healer," I said then.

"Yes." She shook her head. "I'm sorry. My mind... it's hard to think. I thought I'd already told you."

She took a deep breath, closed her eyes for a moment.

"There's a man who wanted me to work for him," she said, eyes once again open. "I refused. I have to be free to choose. I can't be someone's slave. He tried to make me a slave." She was looking at me and there was anger in her eyes. "I had to run." She let out a long breath. "He couldn't find me but he sent that demon to torture me in my sleep. Another friend gave me the charms. I put them throughout the house but they're not helping."

This man was trying to force her to become something she didn't want to be.

246

She looked straight at me. "Please help me."

Looking into those tortured eyes, the only thing I could say was, "Of course."

She let out a sigh and a weak spark of life returned to her eyes and movements.

"Why didn't you answer the phone?" I asked.

"When there was no reply to my email, I thought... I don't know, that I was given the wrong address." She took a gulp of coffee. From Katrina's cup. "My friend—the one who did the tarot reading—called me, said I should go to Germany. Said that man had been searching for me and that I shouldn't use my phone or computer any more, to get rid of them. So I did. There are people in Germany who could also help me if Mrs. Lena couldn't. My friend, she..." She shook her head, no doubt trying to clear it. "She said she'd come to Rijeka, bring me money—cash, I can't use an ATM. I've been waiting."

"How long have you been awake?" Katrina asked her.

She looked at us for a long moment, silent. "What day is it?" She glanced at the wall calendar before I could answer. "O bože. Six days."

How the hell...

"I have this tincture I once bought from a witch in Slavonija, it prevents you from falling asleep," she answered just as I was about to ask. "And I've been doing this... It's a kind of meditation. It gets me to the very edge of sleep but not over it. It helps. I would go insane with just the tincture."

She fell silent then and didn't seem far from going catatonic or just keeling over, dead from exhaustion.

"It's alright. We're here now," Katrina said. The woman seemed just about ready to cry hearing those words.

"Before we continue," I added, "can you tell us your name?" We'd both introduced ourselves to her at the door but she hadn't responded in kind. I didn't hold it against her. It was a miracle she was coherent at all.

247

She just stared at me blankly for a long moment. Then she smiled. "Mara," she said.

"Mara," I said. "How long before the tincture stops working?"

"I have to take it every night." She looked at the clock on the wall, just above the calendar. "It stops working in... an hour or so."

"Then in an hour or so you'll go to sleep. And when you dream, I'll be there."

"You're sure this isn't too big of a dose?" I asked Katrina in a low voice while the vilenica—while Mara was in the bathroom. Coffee gets your urinary tract going.

Katrina looked at the fingernail-sized piece of red crystal-that-smelled-of-lemon in my palm and nodded. "I had no idea Lena used it, but in retrospect, makes sense. But yes, that's enough." She'd used the sleeping crystal before, she told me when I showed her the jar. Viki had taken her into the astral realm to show her what it's like, and she'd had her take a sliver of the crystal to make her fall asleep.

"According to Viki, it's safe even if you take an entire chunk. It'll push you straight into the dreaming part of your sleep cycle. Oh, and the first time you go to pee after, don't be alarmed when it's dark red. And smells incredibly sour."

"Great."

"It's just that one time. The next time your pee will be back to normal."

"Good."

"I'm ready," Mara said from the living room doorway. God, she seemed to be barely holding on, walking to the couch like she wasn't even aware of her own body.

She lay down on the couch, and closed her eyes, the look on her face pained. She was very clearly anxious almost to the point of nausea at the prospect of falling asleep..

248

I sat down next to the couch, in a large leather armchair, one of those that could change shape into an almost-bed.

Katrina nodded as I looked at her. I nodded back. I put the tiny piece of red crystal in my mouth.

It fizzed lightly on my tongue. It wasn't crystal, it was sugar.

Well, sugar's a crystal.

Yes, but it looked like a crystal-crystal...

The hell is a crystal-crystal...

I was in a room, nondescript, white. There was the red door and nothing else.

And when I opened it, on the other side was my impossible room.

Fuck. I had really hoped I would appear in the astral version of the same place I fell asleep at.

I ran towards the glass wall and leapt through the opening, taking flight. Rijeka was on the other side in all its shades of gray and white. There was no carnival of colors now, though, only the occasional solitary blob here and there. It was too early for sleep for most people.

I pushed myself to go faster and faster, buildings zooming below me, the city an even bigger blur now.

I grinned.

I felt good.

Nothing hurt or ached, and I didn't feel tired at all. I was full of energy. The moments ahead of me seemed full of... *potential.*

The vilenica was in need of my help. Something was torturing her in her sleep. Well, as those rat-looking dreambugs had found out, you don't do that to sleeping people in my town.

Hell, even if you're a mora, you better beware.

Sure, the thing had given me a beatdown, but I was still alive, wasn't I? And I'd given it something to remember me by, didn't I?

I could recall the feeling of that horrible eye bursting under my fingertips.

Yeah, definitely a lesson learned, I thought as I pushed myself to go even faster.

Then I had to slow down, hard. I was over Bivio and all the houses looked goddamned the same.

Fuck.

No, wait.

I was being an idiot. I looked for the road we'd come up in the taxi, and then counted the houses. There.

There was no colored shape in the house, nor in the vicinity. I could see points of pale white light; the charms she'd placed around the house in the hopes it would keep the monster at bay. Their light was so weak I wondered how it was supposed to keep anything away. Then I reminded myself I actually didn't know the first about magical charms or how they're supposed to manifest in the astral realm.

I was early, I realized. Mara was obviously still going through the sleep cycle, wasn't yet at the dream stage.

Maybe I shouldn't be in the open like this.

I flew to the house across the road, floated down behind the top of its roof. I had an unobstructed view of the rental house, but unless the thing that was torturing Mara came directly from behind me, it wouldn't be able to see me when it arrives.

I waited for the colored outline of vilenica Mara to appear inside.

And finally it did. Dark blue and light green, with shades of red flashing deep inside. Even from this distance I could see all those colors because they were intense. She was a beacon.

And then there it was. It didn't fly in from any direction. It slowly appeared above the house, first a vague silhouette, then details fading in. A bald head, a body like a human's—and there the similarities stopped.

It had six arms. I had no idea how many legs it had because, while it was naked from the waist up, from the waist down there was some kind of fabric hanging loose around its body, in torn strips, like a dress that had had a nasty encounter with a very large cat.

It had its back to me as it floated down to ground level.

I left my cover and flew towards it.

It reached with several of its arms, the hands full of bony fingers. They were reaching forward as if beckoning to the prone figure inside the house.

Then it slowly glided closer to the house.

Yeah, that wasn't going to happen.

"Hey!" I shouted.

It turned.

Its head was just skin stretched taut over a round skull. There was no mouth. No nose. No ears. Just two large holes where the eyes should be.

Its torso was thin, bones outlined beneath skin that was, now that I had a moment to look closely, more like leather. Too many bones, and in wrong places.

Definitely no legs, unless those many strips of fabric trailing gently beneath the waist in a nonexistent breeze *were* its legs.

Six arms, each ending in a hand, and each hand with more than five fingers. Each finger with a bone protruding out of the skin at the fingertip, twisted and, I was willing to bet, sharp as fuck.

All this I noticed in that first second as it just floated there, facing me.

In the next it was upon me, swiping with two of its right hands, hard and fast.

This time, unlike with the mora, I was ready and I was paying attention. I ducked—well, lowered myself in the air—and felt limbs swoosh above my head.

I punched the creature in the stomach with all the strength I could muster.

The strike pushed it back and it bent in the waist just a little. That, and the feeling of something hard like a wooden board giving way just a bit under my fist, ignited in me a spark of satisfaction.

"Get the fuck out of here," I told the thing, staring at the leather-rimmed eye sockets as I roseup in the air to meet its empty gaze. "Leave her alone."

I wanted it to fly away, disappear, because it was, for all my outward calmness and hard man stance, *freaking me out*. It was just human-looking enough for each and every part that was decidedly nonhuman to look that much more disturbing.

But I also, deep down, hoped it wouldn't give up right away.

That Slavic zombie master flashed in my mind, screaming and kicking and punching me.

"Leave," I repeated, snarling now.

It just floated there, arms down by its sides.

Then it flew at me, arms outstretched, grabbing.

I tried to dodge, but six arms were too much to deal with. It caught me by the foot, pulled me back and stabbed my upper arms with all the fingers of two of its hands. I shouted as the twisted, sharp bones dug into me.

And then stopped digging.

Oh, it hurt like burning knitting needles—but the tips had, I realized, only penetrated to the very top of the flesh under my skin.

The creature was suddenly very still. It seemed confused, probably as much as I was.

I felt different than just a moment before: there was a power inside me resisting the attack. My body was pushing back against the creature's claws.

I grinned through the pain and headbutted the ugly fucker. It staggered backwards in the air, tearing its fingers out of me, my flesh burning. But I could feel it healing as well.

This one was weaker than the mora. Or maybe I was stronger now. Or maybe both.

It wasn't important.

I slammed into the still stunned creature, drove my shoulder into its sternum. As it flew backwards again, I grabbed two of its now flailing arms and pivoted hard in place, releasing my grip a moment later.

I grinned as I watched it arc across the street even as I was thrown backwards myself. A moment later I slammed into the house behind me and fell to the ground with pain shooting through me.

I could only pass through walls if I concentrated on it. Noted.

It was coming at me again, arms outstretched, and if it could have, it would have probably been shrieking furiously. I jumped into the air, sore but eager, flying headlong towards it. At the last moment, I pushed myself higher and the creature passed under me. I immediately dropped and grabbed it from behind, dragging myself up its back using its ribs for handholds, until I managed to put it into a headlock. It swung its arms, reaching for me, but I was willing to have parts of my flesh torn as I tried my best to snap its neck. It clawed at me and it burned, and if I could have bled, I would have, but I was focused on a single thing.

"Fuck... you..." I growled, pushing and squeezing. Its neck was sinewy and it was like trying to break a streetlight pole. Its arms did something unexpected—with a cracking of bone and a sickening, sinewy crunch, they *rotated* at the shoulders.

Now all six arms were facing *backwards*. I screamed as all of its claws sank into my skin—and then deeper, finally piercing the flesh under it, digging deeper. Going for the bone.

The pain made me let go of the creature's neck.

Panic clawed at me, but I was too furious for it to take a hold.

It managed to pin one of my arms to my body, but the other was still free. I suppressed the urge to grab the creature by the neck or tear the claws out of me—I focused inward instead. My astral body had reacted on instinct when the creature had first sunk its claw into me. Could I do the same now, but consciously?

And from within myself, I pushed out. There was resistance; there was pain—so much pain—but the good kind.

It worked, but only partly; some of its claws were still buried in me, and the others were about to try again.

With my free right hand, I tore the remaining few claws from my left arm. It felt as if I were taking chunks of flesh out with them, but I didn't care.

Both hands now free, I grabbed the creature's nearest arm and snapped it at the elbow. Then, as it clawed at me again, I gritted my teeth, focused on pushing the claws, putting aside for the moment what I had in mind for its now broken arm.

Claws pierced skin, dug into my flesh. My flesh resisted once again on its own.

I bent at the waist, pressing my feet against the small of the creature's back, still holding onto its broken arm as if my life depended on it.

With purchase for my feet found, I pushed myself backwards with all the strength I could drag from deep inside.

I tore all of its claws out of me, closing my eyes by reflex at the blinding pain.

But I didn't care, because I still had its arm in my hands.

And it wasn't attached to its body any longer.

Burning with pain and rage, I opened my eyes and the creature swam into focus.

It was facing me, pawing with two of its left hands at where its third left arm used to be, its right-hand three hanging by its side.

I grinned at it, waving its torn arm. Taunting it.

"Come on!" I shouted.

Everything hurt. Red puncture marks covered my body. My left arm throbbed.

It attacked. I dodged to the side, but too slow. It swiped at me, raked my belly with its claws.

I swung with all my might, holding the torn arm in both hands. The creature's limb flopped a little because of the broken elbow, it only provided an extra whipping motion for my makeshift weapon. The claws struck the creature's back.

The skin tore like tissue paper, revealing the twisted bones beneath and the emptiness behind them. The monster was hollow.

It flailed its claws at me in blind fury as I kept moving backwards, dodging some claws, accepting the pain from others, all the while beating it with its own arm, slashing deep cuts across its torso.

A claw caught me in the left side and it felt a torn a strip of flesh. I slashed at its neck, exposing the hollow on the other side of the leathery skin.

And then I wasn't holding onto the severed limb anymore because it had struck it from my hands.

It didn't matter. I launched myself at the monster, slammed into it and, through the pain, I grabbed its neck.

I hooked the fingers of both my hands into the gash on its sinewy neck.

I strained and pushed and screamed in rage, reaching deep down inside myself for every shred of strength and power I had left.

The skin tore under my fingers, my hands flying out to the sides as the monster's head fell off the neck I'd just torn to shreds.

Its body sagged in the air, its clawed arms flopping down to the sides.

And then the dream monster dissolved into smoke and shreds of skin and a moment later there was nothing.

No.

I glanced down at the movement. The head, still falling towards the gray-white ground, was disintegrating, but there was a weak yellow light inside. Something flew out of the remains of the skull just as it disappeared: something sickly yellow, maybe the size of my fist. It flickered weakly and flew away, fast, disappearing in the distance in just a few moments.

I wanted to give chase.

I knew it was impossible to catch it.

I flew down to the house.

Mara was still there, but now there were no red flashes, the fuzzy outline of her body just blue and green.

I smiled, relaxing even while in terrible pain.

Floating there, I felt the call of the waking world somewhere deep inside me.

I let go.

COLD PIZZA IS
THE BEST PIZZA

"Better now?" Katrina asked me as I started on the second pizza.

I stopped chewing, raised my head from the plate and nodded. I swallowed, felt my pulse racing and my stomach getting heavier.

Maybe I should slow down...

"Yes, thank you," I said as I leaned back in the chair, taking a deep breath through my nose, one of the very few parts of my body that didn't hurt or ache in any way.

"I was afraid you were going to choke on a bite. But I really don't like it when someone tells me to eat slower, so I didn't say anything."

I drank another full glass of water, and as I refilled it from the heavy pitcher, I said, "She's still asleep?"

Katrina leaned backwards, glancing through the open kitchen doorway towards the living room. "Yep."

I focused, eyes closed, and after a few moments I could hear Mara snore. I concentrated a little more and I could make out her heartbeat, barely.

I eased back my hearing to 'normal' and was surprised at how better and more natural it felt than yesterday in the playground.

Maybe I really was figuring out this krsnik thing.

I glanced at my arms, still feeling the strange, tingling sensation all over them—two separate tingling sensations, in my left arm, although the one from the healing wound was now almost gone and the arm itself was mostly back to fully operational.

I felt it across other parts of my body as well, at every spot the creature's claws had sunk into me. A pricking sensation, as if I'd received an electric shock—no stronger than when I'd once fiddled with the Christmas lights, and the contacts were loose and I got zapped. Now it was all just—*just*—a dull, low ache, but when I woke up last night it had been straight up pain. My left arm had been especially hurting, having now received a lot of punishment in both realms.

There were no more marks on my skin that had been there when I'd woken up—apart from my left arm being still slightly purple where the zombie had bit me—but I could still very vividly recall their color, bright red, as if I'd been beaten with a red hot poker.

I'd fallen asleep maybe half an hour after that, this time without the need for magical edible sugar crystals. Katrina had been freaked out after the fight, and it was completely understandable; there I was, in the fold out chair, lying stock still, with these red marks just popping up on my skin and my face looking increasingly pained with every moment.

And then, according to her, my face had gone slack and, for a moment there, she was certain I'd died.

And then I'd woken up, groggy and weak from pain.

But next to me, I'd seen through the haze, Mara had been sleeping and she looked so calm and relaxed and peaceful that all the pain was definitely worth it.

The second time I'd fallen asleep that night, I'd found myself again in front of the red door. The room behind was as silent as all the times before. I sat down at the table... then I took the chair, brought it to the glass wall, sat down and just took in the view for some undetermined amount of time. Dots of colors slowly sprang up all over the landscape as more and more people were dreaming.

I glanced behind me, saw the door—and I wondered.

When I opened it, there was just that white space on the other side. It was calm and quiet and empty.

I stepped into it. I closed the red door behind me.

Next thing I knew, my eyes were open and it was the middle of the morning, and Katrina was on her phone in the kitchen, cursing at some game she was playing on it.

We'd drunk coffee and I told her I was starving, and so we'd ordered pizzas.

We didn't want to wake Mara up. She had been in desperate need of rest. If, I'd decided, she didn't wake up by this evening, I'd have Katrina call Viki or Perdida and ask for advice. But for now, I treated her as someone who just needed a lot of good, uninterrupted sleep.

Katrina had to leave at around two in the afternoon. Business meetings again, with potential new clients.

"Are you sure you don't want me to call the girls?" she asked on her way to the door.

"Not yet, no."

"Are you feeling better?" Katrina asked again.

I nodded. I did. I was still aching all over, but I was functional.

She smiled. "I'll be checking in every hour or so."

I kept the television's volume down low, but I was pretty certain that it wouldn't have woken Mara up even if I'd put it on full blast. She was currently on her side, back to the living room, face snug against a pillow, covered in a veil of her black hair, snoring. I'd taken it as a good sign that she'd been turning in her sleep, switching back and forth between her back and sides.

And as the hours passed, as I was sitting in the fold out leather chair, occasionally glancing at her just to make sure she was still breathing, the change had become obvious.

The signs of exhaustion had slowly been sliding off her features since that morning. She was indeed around my age, I guessed,

258

although last night I could have been forgiven thinking she was about fifteen years older, and fifteen years of a bad life at that.

The bags under her eyes had become less dark. Her face had lost a lot of its previous puffiness, and now it was obvious her cheekbones were high and sharp. When she'd fallen asleep last night, her mouth had been tight, lips a thin, almost white line as if she were fighting through pain; now they were pale red and on the verge of a smile. Even her dark hair seemed to have a sheen that hadn't been there a day ago.

She looked... *serene*. Like she was having a really pleasant dream about something or someone. Almost made you hope you were that someone.

At one point late during the afternoon I heard a polite cough to my side. I looked and there she was, eyes open and smiling a little awkwardly as she was propping herself up on both elbows.

"Hello," I said, sitting forward and turning towards her.

"Hi," she said. "Is it..."

"Yes. It's gone. How did you sleep?"

She blinked and her eyes were the biggest mark of change: fear and exhaustion had, over the course of sleepless days, drained them not just of life but color. Now her dark green gaze was bright, sparkling with energy.

"Is there any food?" she asked.

"Cold pizza?" I offered, glancing at the kitchen table. The third cardboard box from this morning was there, still unopened.

"The best kind," she said, rising and stumbling.

I was on my feet next to her, hands on her upper arms. Thin but taut muscles under the thin sleeves, I couldn't help but notice— last night she really did seem like a stiff breeze would knock her over, but it wasn't like that, not really.

"I'm alright," she said, looking at me. She was my height, I realized to my surprise. She hadn't seemed so last night. The exhaustion and fear must have shrunk her down. "Now I'm alright. Just a little... dammit... light headed?"

I nodded, letting go of her gently, for a brief moment very aware of the warmth of her skin through the fabric. "Sleeping for almost twenty four hours will do that to you sometimes."

Her eyes went wide. "That long?"

"Yep."

"Where's your friend?" she asked, glancing around.

"Katrina had work to do."

Mara smiled lightly, obviously glad. "And you stayed to keep watch over me?"

I shrugged, doing my best to play the consummate professional. "I couldn't just leave you. But, if you hadn't woken up soon, I'd have called someone to take a look."

"Understandable." She yawned softly and stretched like a cat. Then she froze for just the briefest of moments, aware that she was doing so in front of someone who was not exactly, but still very close to, a stranger. And then she smiled again. "Sorry. I forgot my manners."

My mouth started saying that it didn't mind, but my brain managed to push out an, "It's okay."

Was there an amused glint in her eye? Did she read my mind—well, my eyes, really—and knew what I had almost said?

"Oh god, I need a shower," she said suddenly. After the briefest of pauses, she added, "No. Food."

At the kitchen table, I opened up the pizza box and pushed it towards Mara as she produced a scrunchie from the breast pocket of her pajamas and tied back her shoulder-length hair.

"I apologize in advance," she said, and then proceeded to not so much eat as attack the pizza. It was like looking in a mirror.

After a few slices, I felt it was okay to ask her something that had been bothering me for a while now. "Mara, wasn't there someone in Zagreb to help you against the dream monster?"

Zagreb was the capital of Croatia, and a city significantly bigger than Rijeka. Surely they had a bigger supernatural community there. They must have their own krsnik. Do they? These were all good questions, I realized.

How would I get in touch with other krsniks, while we were on the subject?

No, not now.

"I was afraid to ask," Mara said, visibly anxious again. "The man who wants me to work for him... his people have a lot of power and influence in Zagreb. I was afraid people would be afraid to help me." She took a deep breath, calming herself down a little. "My friend—the card reader—she told me about Lena. So I sent her an email." She looked at me. "I don't know if I told you this, but I'm sorry for your loss."

"You did," I smiled at her. "But thank you again."

"So, um, if it's okay for me to ask," she said after another two slices, "how come you're Rijeka's krsnik and you're not Croatian?" She stopped then, frowning. "No, wait, you told me this last night, didn't you. I'm sorry, it's... the last few days are a blur."

I shook my head lightly. "It's no problem," I said. "I'm Croatian, but my family moved out in the mid-nineties."

"Oh?"

I gave her a very short and heavily redacted version of my life's story, just the basics of me moving and coming back for the funeral and discovering I'd inherited nona's powers. I'd skipped Barba and the crazy Slavic zombie master, but I did tell her about the mora, even though I omitted the part about almost getting killed because I was a reckless idiot.

It was a thing that was worrying me more than a little, now that I had some time to think about it. When in the astral realm, I would... change. It would draw some parts of me to the fore, push others in the background. But I was still me, just—as I'd explained it to myself while thinking about it this afternoon—it was like my personality was a song controlled by an equalizer, and being in the astral realm apparently pushed the bassline and drums all the way up.

"Your week was maybe even worse than mine," Mara said, after a few moments of silence.

I chuckled. "The way you looked last night, I'd say I was better off, actually."

"I look better now?" she asked, with genuine concern. "Honestly, I'm afraid to look in the mirror. I felt so... drained, for days."

"You look fine. Great, actually," I said. "A good sleep does wonders."

A smile tugged at a corner of her lips as she looked at me. "You're not just saying that to be nice?"

"I'm forbidden from lying by the ancient krsnik code," I said.

She raised her eyebrows. "And what would happen if you broke the code?"

"All my hair would fall out," I said the first thing that came to my mind, and immediately regretted it because it sounded so incredibly stupid.

Her eyes went wide just a bit as she said, "Goodness."

I shrugged.

"Then I hope you're not lying, because that would be a damn shame."

Okay, so maybe it wasn't as stupid as I'd feared.

She shook her head then, putting down the second to last slice of pizza with a sigh. "I can't really describe the last few days. Yesterday was the worst, after you came. I was... I was afraid something would go horribly wrong at the last minute."

I thought about my fight with the dream monster. "Well, it all turned out for the best in the end."

She smiled at me. It was warm and full of nothing but honesty, and a string thrummed somewhere deep inside me. "I can't thank you enough." Then, after a moment, she said, "What... what do I owe you?"

Oh. Was I supposed to charge for my service? Had Lena been charging? And what exactly do I charge? She must have somehow earned all that money she left Katrina and me. Unfortunately, I hadn't come across any handy list of standard rates in the book.

"I'm new to this. So I have no idea," I said.

"I usually don't charge for healing either," Mara said. "In our world, it's better if you ask someone to return you a favor."

"Well," I said, "in that case I'll take a return favor."

She smiled back. "I'll be more than happy to return it." Was there also a glimmer of teasing in her eyes, or was I just seeing things?

"Oh," I said to avoid an uncomfortable silence and reached into my pocket. "I've got something for you."

She looked at me expectantly.

"I wanted to come prepared. I'm glad we didn't need it in the end, but still, here."

I slid the cheap bracelet across the table towards her. She picked it up carefully, her slim fingers sprinkled with charred flour.

"It's protective," I said. "Well, it should be. It's the first one I've ever made, but the instructions were very clear and, well, if it's warm, it's a sign it's working."

Both her eyebrows were raised now. Then she smiled as widely and as warmly as she was probably able to, and something thrummed deep inside me again. "Thank you," she said. She tried to put it on but kept fumbling.

"Sorry, could you?" she asked. "My fingers are still shaking a bit *and* they're greasy."

I leaned forward as she stretched her arm towards me. Her fingers looked perfectly fine to me. Her skin was smooth and warm where my fingertips brushed against it. Mercifully, my own fine motor skills were good enough to attach the ends of the bracelet on the first try. And they didn't shake either, which my masculinity was extremely pleased with.

"Wait," she said as she looked closer at the bracelet now. "You said 'it should be'. You didn't test it out?"

"I didn't have time," I said.

"Oh," she said. "I'll carry it as a memento for now. I'll have someone test it."

"I mean, I could throw something at you, if you want?" I said, smirking.

"Surely a gentleman would put the bracelet on himself and offer me to throw something *at him*?" she said, feigning displeasure.

"I'm just a krsnik, not a gentleman," I shot back without thinking.

"I'm starting to think so, yes," she replied, a smile once again tugging at the corner of her lips. She returned to her pizza then, letting the silence stretch, tense with... something.

"So," I asked as she continued eating, "what will you do now? You mentioned Germany?"

Mara paused mid-chew, concern lining her face. "My... I guess you could call him my teacher, he lives in Germany now. I'll go to him as soon as my friend comes here with the money."

"Is this a usual thing?" I asked. "Threatening someone with supernatural powers unless they decide to work for you?"

She breathed out. "Sometimes, yes. Someone I know has already gone missing because he wouldn't work for..." She made a disgusted face. "They're basically criminals, thugs. Some use supernatural powers, others are supernatural, but they're first and foremost basic, human scum."

There was so much anger in those words, but even more of something else—she *despised* those people in a way I've rarely seen anyone express. "So this man, he wanted his own personal healer?"

"Yes," she said but it wasn't just that. Was there something else?

She opened her mouth to say more but just then I turned in my chair. I thought I'd heard something. I focused, and yes—tires were crunching over the gravel in front of the house. Then car doors opened and closed. No, slammed, in quick succession. One. Two. Three. Four.

"What is it?" Mara asked, noticing I'd gone tense.

"Living room, now," I said. "Stay close to me," I added as I rushed to my backpack.

It was then that the front door of the house burst open, banged hard against the wall, and a man appeared in the doorway. He was of medium height, but built like a brick shithouse, as they say in the movies. His green tracksuit bulged in places all over his torso,

264

arms and legs, the body of a man who basically lived in his local gym.

His head was clean-shaven and it just added to the menace. But it was his face that was the worst: a huge, disturbing grin was plastered over it. His eyes promised violence.

He said something that I didn't understand.

Mara stumbled backwards in panic.

He stepped into the house.

"Mara, back door. Get out and run," I said, pushing my phone in her hands while still facing the man. "Call Katrina."

She didn't fumble with the phone, didn't try to convince me to come with her. I had been pretty certain this man was here for her, that this wasn't just a random home invasion, and her actions confirmed it.

As for me... I had no idea what I was going to do.

The man wasn't taller than me, in fact, he was a bit shorter, but he had muscles for two of me and a bit to spare.

I don't have to fight him. I just have to distract him.

He grinned even wider as he made another step towards me.

Sheer, unadulterated fear slammed straight into my gut, spread through me in a flash. I wanted to run. I wanted to curl into a ball and cry. I wanted to beg.

I was paralyzed where I stood.

But my heart kept beating despite the horror I felt and my insides pushed against the fear.

This isn't natural.

He's scary but not that scary.

The feeling inside me, my body resisting the fear... It was familiar. It wasn't exactly the same as when my astral form resisted the dream monster's claws—but it was obviously coming from the same place.

I reached for that feeling and pushed, forcing it outwards.

The terror that threatened to consume me fell back. Oh, it was still there, beating at me, but further away from my core now.

And becoming aware I could push it back helped me focus. This man was using some kind of magic to terrify me into submission—and it wasn't working as intended.

All this took maybe a couple of heartbeats.

I heard Mara shout.

I turned and saw her move backwards into the living room, tense with fear. There was another man in front of her, similar in size and build to the one I'd turned my back on now. Similar fashion style. Same hairdresser.

And also... same magic. I felt waves of terror emanating from him, powerful pulses slamming into me, overlapping with his friend's.

I heard the man behind me step closer. My instincts told me he was about to attack.

I have to fight.

And inside, I felt something respond to this thought, a well of power beckoning to me.

I reached for it, fast, borderline panicked.

The man who'd prevented Mara from escaping was focused on me now, grinning, fists clenched in gleeful anticipation of violence to come.

The two of them were throwing their magic at me now in full force.

I tensed, pulling at that strange well of power inside me.

And then I pushed out, hard, shoving all that dread back at the men. The tide of terror stopped washing over me.

I was still afraid, but now it was... the normal amount of fear for this situation. Still a lot, though.

The man in front of me almost fell on his ass. The thud behind me told me his friend didn't manage to stay on his feet.

I grabbed Mara's hand, pulled her towards the seating area.

One of the men was rushing us now; I could hear him closing in on my back. I let go of Mara and leapt forward, rolling onto the couch, over its back, grabbing for my backpack even as my head slammed into the pillows and, for a moment, I couldn't see anything.

But I felt the rush of air, the thumping of the man's feet on the floor, vibrating up the couch legs.

I shoved my hand into the open backpack. My fingers slid over the top of the book, found the handle.

I pulled.

The *sika* came out of the backpack, sliding out of its sheath smooth like water as I turned on my back, slashing at the air.

I struck something.

On my back now, looking up with eyes probably the size of saucers, I stared at the face of the thug. He was staring back. Pale. His gaze switched from me to his hand.

The *sika* was stuck in the forearm; the bone must have stopped the blade.

Blood was flowing down the blade, down my wrist, dripping onto my chest.

He screamed, more shocked and confused than in pain, just as a loud crash of glass came from somewhere.

Holding my weapon firmly, I rolled onto the floor. I felt something splash against the back of my head.

It's blood spurting from the open wound.

Rising to my feet, I searched the room for Mara. She had just broken open a window with a chair.

The other thug rushed into view, shouting, almost snarling. There was something in his hand, thin and long—one of those collapsible metal sticks you see on TV.

He lashed at her hard as she raised her arm instinctively. I could already hear the bone break from the savage attack.

Except…

…the air glimmered as if from intense heat, and the stick simply stopped in its violent downward arc as if it had hit something hard and solid, but also invisible.

It works! The bracelet works!

267

The thug was confused. Mara wasn't, and she kicked him in the groin as hard as she could.

I ran towards them.

The man was in pain, but he was also *furious*, and the rage must have kept him upright instead of doubled over as he turned towards me and charged.

I had the best intention to step to the side and avoid his stick.

I did step to the side.

But the stick caught me on my hip, and for a moment I could literally see stars.

I stumbled, dropped the *sika* and then fell to my knees because, as I was trying to pick it up, the metal stick caught me in the shoulder, and then across my back.

I was on my side, and the searing pain convinced my bones had just been pulverized.

But... it didn't hurt as much as it should have.

I could still fight. I could.

I pawed at the *sika's* handle, too far away, until it slid into my hand because Mara kicked it towards me.

I held the weapon tight and I slashed, rolling onto my back. I slashed again, wildly, and this time the blade connected.

The thug had parried my blind attack with his stick. With a look of utter contempt on his face, he kicked me in the stomach.

Forcing my eyes to stay open through the pain, I saw him swing with all his might, stick aimed at the wrist of the my *sika* hand.

I instinctively reached for that well of power deep inside—power still constrained by something I couldn't break it free of, something that I was certain limited me to just scraps of power available.

But it would be enough.

I hoped.

I pulled my arm back, faster than I thought I would, and the metal stick slammed into the parquet floor.

I stabbed upwards, awkwardly, since I was still on my side. I missed the man's belly—*holy fuck I almost spilled his guts what the fuck am I doing I can't kill someone what the fuck what*—but the tip did make contact with something.

That something was his upper arm, and as he recoiled in pain, he made the wound even worse, raking a ragged line in his flesh.

Then water splashed my face and there was once again the crashing sound of broken glass.

The water was from the vase that now lay shattered on the floor where it had fallen after—after it had hit the thug squarely in the face. It was one of those old, heavy vases, made of thick glass.

The thug stumbled backwards and I pushed myself up to my feet. It wasn't working.

Then hands grabbed me under the armpits and helped me up.

Mara was next to me now as I—my vision blurry but still clearer than it should have been; my body hurting but pushing through far better than it should have—surveyed the living room.

The first thug was on his knees close to the front door, wailing and holding onto his arm. He was pale and there was blood *everywhere* around him, a long trail leading back to the couch.

The second thug had his back against the wall next to the broken window Mara had tried to escape through, pressing the palm of his good hand against the long gash on his other upper arm, blood welling between his fingers as he frantically squeezed the wound. His face was a mess as well, bruised, nose very obviously broken by the vase's impact. He wasn't looking at me at all, just the wound, and there was sheer horror on his face.

Not used to getting as good as you give, are you?

His stick was on the floor, forgotten.

"Let's go," Mara said, pulling me by the hand.

I felt better than just moments ago. My vision was clear and all the aches were dull, as if from an injury now healed.

Oh. Of course. She was holding my hand. She was healing me.

It really works that way? Just like that?

We ran towards the back door.

There was something there, just inside the doorway. The floor was covered in a thick and black substance resembling tar: a glossy black surface reflecting the light from the living room in an otherwise dark, short corridor connecting to the back door.

I had no idea what that was, I just knew that it probably wasn't tar because there was no stench.

The surface of the liquid moved. A—a—a *tentacle* made of that black, viscous stuff shot out towards Mara. It struck an invisible wall just a few centimeters from her face.

The bracelet definitely worked.

Then another tentacle shot out.

Mara shouted, horrified.

The bracelet was on the floor, shattered into charred, smoldering pieces.

A black tentacle was around Mara's left ankle, coiling tightly. I squeezed tight the *sika's* handle, ready to slash.

It pulled and she dropped on her back. More tentacles now reached for her, tying her legs together, wrapping themselves around her, immobilizing her arms and pinning them against her sides as she screamed and thrashed as I hacked and hacked with the *sika*, but even though each tentacle that I cut would turn into loose tar and slop onto the floor, two more would appear from that puddle and take its place.

Then something hit me in the back, and as I stumbled, I turned around.

There was a man there. Not one of the thugs—he was my height, slim, and dressed in a fine suit.

He punched me, hard.

Gloves, I thought in a haze. *Who wears leather gloves in early summer?*

I hit the wall of the corridor with my back as I lashed out with the *sika* blindly, just trying to keep him away from me.

My wrists were—something was holding both of them.

I looked down, saw ropes of black tar. They were tight, like a vise grip.

I pulled, trying to break free.

The man in the suit—he was young, I noticed as he stepped into my view again, maybe a few years younger than me—smiled. Then the smile turned into an ugly grin.

He had more teeth than a human being should. They were all dark and stained and sharp and crooked.

His breath was horrible even from a distance.

Mara was fully bound by the black tentacles now, pressed against the other wall, abject fear in her eyes.

The man in the suit stepped closer to me and punched me in the face. And again. And again.

I fell to my knees, the black oozy tentacles still holding my arms upright. I felt the man's nails dig into my fingers as he pried the sika out of my hand. The weapon clattered on the floor.

He turned to Mara. He took a handful of something out of his suit's jacket pocket and threw it at her.

As the objects landed on the floor I saw what they were. Tarot cards. Some were crumpled and torn. All were bloody.

Mara screamed at the sight of the cards, a shriek of pure despair, and a black tendril of tar wrapped itself around her head, cutting her off mid-scream.

Can she breathe?

The man was speaking to her, and even though I couldn't make out the words—my head was ringing—there was such viciousness in his voice I knew he was gloating.

Then he turned to me.

He grabbed me by the front of my shirt, and as the tentacles suddenly released me, the young man lifted me off the floor like I was nothing and threw me across the apartment.

I landed on the floor next to the couch and pain shot through me like lightning.

He was next to me then. My vision was swimming, blurry.

I saw someone else at the back door now. A shape was rising from the tar. Then there was no tar on the floor any more.

Mara was still bound by the black, viscous ropes, but they extended from the body of a slim woman who now stepped fully into the light of the living room.

The young man in the suit knelt next to me.

He punched me again, and then once more.

He said something.

"Fuck... you..." I muttered, staring at him, but only with one eye. The other was closed, I realized.

He frowned. Said something again, but it was just sounds.

"Not Croatian?" he said, enunciating as if he were talking to someone he considered slow.

"Fuck... you..." I repeated because, at that moment, defiance was all I could muster.

No. That power deep inside me. I reached for it, but it was so far away.

I had to reach it.

I felt it so close.

There... there...

The young man smiled as if he'd just thought of something very interesting.

Then he lifted my shirt and tore my belly open with his teeth.

All the pain I'd ever felt was nothing compared to this. The zombie bite had been a wood splinter.

He raised his head, grinning at me with a huge chunk of bloody flesh and skin and fat between his teeth.

He spat it out, laughed with a throaty, wet sound.

"You'll live," he said, as the light in the room dimmed and with my one open eye I could see him turn to the woman who was also a tar monster and—

272

REAL LIFE IS DIFFERENT

Hours passed. Maybe days.

They took me somewhere, tied me to a chair and left me there.

There were more of them than just the young man in the suit and the woman who had pale skin and dark hair and could turn into a puddle of tar.

Voices, muffled...

Lights, blurry...

One of my eyes was closed, the other couldn't see all that well...

My stomach... my stomach was numb... and it burned... a cold fire in my gut...

I tried to speak, several times...

My fingers moved, at least I thought they did...

As time flowed slowly, thick as molasses, I tried to reach out... I could hear but couldn't make out what... my eye saw just fuzzy outlines... I had no idea if I was somewhere cold or if it was just the ice that was burning me up from inside...

I reached inside... that dam was still there... the power behind it... so near...

I couldn't...

I strained...

...

Someone was slapping me, gently, to wake me up.

I opened my eye. My eyes; the swelling had gone down a bit. It didn't do me much good though, because all I could see out of those eyes was a blurry blob of light.

There was a chair across from me. The person who had just slapped me now leaned back, relaxed.

"You and me," the young man said. "Krsnik and štrigun. Mortal enemies." He was grinning theatrically. The grin then turned into a frown. "Well, I don't like stories. In stories you beat me." He shrugged. "Real life is different."

I was silent.

If my swollen eye had gotten better, maybe other parts had as well.

The parts of me that were sore from the beating were... less sore, definitely.

But it didn't matter, because the wound in my belly.... it was as if my body were falling apart there, rot chewing its way through me, spreading...

"It hurts, yes?" he asked, leaning forward. There was a gleam in his eyes. "You would be dead if you were..." He smiled. "Normal, is that a good word? No. *Ordinary. Simple.*" He reached with his hand.

Pain burned through me, a white-hot agony searing my insides...

He pulled back, gazing at his hand. Blood dripped from it, but also something dark and sludgy.

I looked down. The shirt had been torn in the fight and my stomach was exposed. It was terrifying. A chunk of my body was just gone, a ragged hole caked in dried blood and dark slime that oozed from the open wound.

That's... that's not good...

"I was told krsniks had amazing powers." He frowned, wiping his fingers on his trousers. "I thought you would be healed by now. And that you would be free already." He was shaking his head lightly. "Why aren't you fighting me?"

While he was talking, I was focusing through the ebbing waves of pain, trying to hear Mara. Maybe she was near...

"Where is she?" I asked finally, just to take my mind off the pain.

"Mara?" he asked. "She is here. She is not hurt."

"Why... what do you want?"

He took a deep breath, smiled at me with his horrible teeth. "From her? Or from you?" He leaned forward again. "From her, I want... well, her. Powerful people want her, told me to get her for them. I thought she was somehow special, but it seems she is not. She is a vilenica, which *is* special enough. And now I am going to sell her to one of them." He inclined his head. "And you... I don't know. If you are still alive tonight, maybe I will sell you too. Or just your stuff. Your book, I can't read it. You took precautions." He smiled. "So maybe I'll burn it." He smiled wider. "But that sword..." He sucked in an excited breath. "Now that is something. Those two idiots, if that was just a normal knife, they would be here, beating you up. But you had a *magic* sword. And if I hadn't been there..." He leaned back. "I had to punish them for being idiots."

They were still alive...

I didn't kill them...

The young man—what did he call himself, a *strigun*—it was something from the stories I was told as a kid, wasn't it—not a *striga*, a *striga* is a witch, but a *strigun*... a *strigun* was... Lena had...

"I was told a krsnik is also a warrior who can enter people's dreams," he said. "And you did... you were amazing, I have to say."

"You... *you* sent that thing."

I wanted to keep him talking but... but this wasn't the same as with the crazy Slav. Keeping this man occupied served no purpose.

It keeps me alive longer. That's enough for now.

He nodded. "To make her submit. When you killed it, you didn't destroy its essence, you let it escape. It showed me bits of your fight when it came back to me."

That yellow light... I should have reacted faster, should have caught it...

I failed... again...

275

"And as to how I found you," he said, waving it off with his hand. "Mara has a dear friend. A nice girl. Tarot reader. A little beneath Mara, but not everybody is aware of their worth. I found her and made her tell me where Mara is." He shook his head then. "Well, Mara *had* a friend." His face suddenly went grim, his eyes dead and monstrous. "I tore that girl to pieces. She is now a lesson to everyone."

The bloodied tarot cards...

"Bet you wish you could get some rest, ha?" he asked, smiling pleasantly once again. He reached and touched my neck. I flinched despite myself. He chuckled.

I could feel he was playing with something around my neck. A necklace? A collar?

"This stops you from sleeping deep enough to dream. I can't have you asking for help." He tsked. "It also prevents tracking spells, so if you left someone something of yours to use to track you, tough luck. So," he said, palms pressed together and against his mouth. "Tonight you are either dead or someone buys a krsnik. A shitty one, or maybe just inexperienced. I have no idea, but... it doesn't matter.

"She will be there too, so you can say goodbye," he said after getting up.

He glanced down at my stomach. He then looked me in the eyes. He must have noticed the daggers I was staring at him. He smiled.

SOMETIMES A PLEA IS ALL YOU'RE LEFT WITH

I was fading in and out of consciousness... the wound in my belly was growing, I was certain... all my strength was draining out of it... dripping on the floor...

Time didn't pass or maybe it did. I had no way to measure it. The strigun had said 'tonight' so at least one day had passed between the attack at the rental house.

Katrina. And Viki and Perdida. And Bowie. Were they looking for me? Katrina would have sent me a message asking how Mara was doing. Then she would have called when I didn't reply. Then she would have come to the rental when I didn't answer.

And then... what? Would she have called the girls for help? And how would they be able to find me?

The same way we found Mara.

"Hey," I said.

I had literally nothing to lose. Not even my dignity, because I was the only one in this empty and poorly lit room with bare concrete walls and floor.

"If... if there is someone here... if you're a ghost..."

This is ridiculous.

"If you know... Katrina... Katrina... tell her.... tell her Paul needs help... Mara needs help... tell her where we are...

"Please..."

Someone was standing in front of me. I squinted in the dim light. A woman.

That woman.

She looked so... so normal. Average face. Average build. You could see her a dozen times in a single day and forget her each time the moment she went out of your view.

Apart from the eyes: cold and black. Dark pools with an abyss for a bottom.

I was ready for... I had no idea what. Maybe she'd come to kill me.

But she stepped behind me and everything tilted.

She was pulling me backwards, still tied to the chair.

We passed through an open doorway, and as we did a chair leg struck the frame and my wound screamed or maybe I did...

HOW MUCH FOR
THE KRSNIK?

The light in *this* room was very bright.

And it wasn't really a room. It was the main floor of a small warehouse, with metal and wooden crates, as well as stacks of barrels scattered around. The main double door was open, and on the other side was darkness.

The air here was cold, but a pleasant cold. Fresh air. I could smell something. Nature?

The tar woman had dragged me to a spot in the middle of that space, turned me towards the main door and left me there.

There were people moving about. People in tracksuits and jeans and combat fatigues, built like MMA fighters. Other people in fine suits. Men and women, old and young.

Thugs and their masters, I guessed.

The fresh air and the cold were doing me good. My mind felt a little clearer.

And then I heard the scraping sound of a chair being dragged across concrete and I turned my head left and saw her.

Mara was tied to a chair just like me. Her eyes went wide as she took in my appearance.

I smiled. At least I thought I did.

"That bad, eh?" I said. Maybe.

Someone clapped, once, sharply. I turned, saw the štrigun standing in the center of a kind of half-circle formed by all the people in the warehouse.

He spoke then, in English, which made me think his audience was international. I caught only bits from the fuzz in my head, but the gist of it was clear: these were the potential buyers, originally here just for Mara, and now I was also to be a lot at this auction. He was also presenting himself as the amazing mastermind who had not only caught the escaped vilenica but also brought down her protector.

He *had* done all that. But he was still an arrogant little shit.

He approached me, grinning widely, horribly.

He turned back to the room with flair and shouted, "So, how much for the krsnik?" Then he bellowed, "Or maybe just his balls?"

They laughed. Of course. Hilarious.

"I don't expect to get much for you. You're alive but I don't think you'll last long," he said, leaning close to my face.

He seemed flabbergasted. Spittle dripped from his left eyebrow.

I... did I just spit on him?

I guess I did.

That face *was* human, but the creature under it wasn't. I'd seen a glimpse or two of it before, but now it came out in full.

My head lolled left and right, back and forth with his punches and savage slaps.

Someone shouted.

He roared back, over his shoulder.

There was commotion, people raising their voices.

He looked back at me, horrible teeth bared. "*Koji je kurac ta buka?*" the štrigun then shouted angrily, looking around for the source of the noise.

The noise which, I now realized, wasn't just a pounding inside my head.

The noise... noise I'd actually heard once before.

He was glaring at me now, equal measures confused, disgusted and angry. And he had every right to be because, instead of pleading for my life or screaming in horrible pain—which I was just about to start, before he'd drawn my attention to the noise—I was laughing. Cackling, to be precise, as much as you can cackle with a hole in your belly and what felt like a face turned to mush. Hysterically, like a complete and utter lunatic.

The noise was real, alright. A pounding, deep and resonant, the kind you feel in your chest, all the way down to your bones.

"That," I said, "is the bass dropping."

The main doors of the warehouse were already open, so there was no dramatic entrance with wood splintering as both sides of the door flew off their hinges.

They simply stepped into view, majestic.

Blinding sparks of rainbow dust flashing, shrieking and clicking of claws and screams and shouts as the witches let loose. Tentacles of light and glitter flashed, striking and grabbing. There was hissing and screeching as creatures from nightmares threw themselves at the thugs. The thugs and their employers returned fire with both magic and guns. Some shots went wide, into the roof and floor and walls. Others hit invisible barriers. But some found their targets and people screamed.

And there was Katrina as well. Katrina didn't have magic, but she didn't need it. Katrina had a rifle.

She was shooting left and right, fast and grim-faced. *It's an odd rifle*, I thought, my mind increasingly numb. She would shoot and then move the hand on the trigger down and up and shoot again. More lights flashed. There were screams and shouts and gunshots and buzzing and hissing and thuds and thumps.

I smiled to myself. Mara would be saved.

I was sliding away from it all.

And then I wasn't.

I was at the precipice, but standing firmly with both feet planted at the edge. Just a moment earlier I was about to go over but...

Someone had pulled me back.

Aware of the chaos of the witches and Katrina fighting everyone who wasn't tied to a chair, I was also aware that my stomach didn't hurt as much as before. Oh, it was still a cold fire but it was a different pain now, as if that rat I could feel making the wound grow was now being burned away. A sweet pain, definitely, as sweet as when Viki had burned the zombie bite.

There was energy in my limbs and body that hadn't been there bare moments before. I was still in pain—hell, it hurt to breathe—but it all hurt less. If I wasn't tied, I was pretty certain I could actually get up, move about.

I looked to the left. Mara was looking at me, her mouth gagged, and there was a momentary flash of relief in her eyes when she saw me look at her.

Then there was an intensity in them as she nodded, confirming.

I was conscious and feeling much better because of her.

And it all clicked into place. My fight against those thugs in the rental house. Still fighting when I shouldn't have been. I'd thought it was maybe my krsnik powers, my body healing itself, but... but when she'd held my hand and healed me, it felt the same. I just hadn't had the time to put it all together.

I thought she was somehow special but it seems she is not, the štri-gun had said. Her silence when I'd asked her if they wanted her just because they wanted a personal healer.

Mara could heal *at a distance*.

So, I was better. Now if only I could get myself free.

No one was near me who could have helped me. I strained against the ropes, but these had been tied by a living person. I shook through the pain, thinking that, if I couldn't break the ropes, maybe, if the chair fell apart—and it was a little creaky, a little wobbly...

Something exploded to the right of me in a flash of bright light and glitter and something else slammed into me.

I blinked, in pain and on my side, with a man atop of me. A dead man, I was certain, heavy as a fallen tree.

I was still tied. But the chair was in pieces now, so while my arms remained bound to the armrests, the armrests themselves were not attached to anything anymore.

I groaned, pushing, trying to get the dead man off me. Adrena-line pounded through me now and pain from the beatings and the bite were at war with the pain of my wounds healing *fast*, a brutal sensation in itself as I felt my flesh stitching itself back together.

As I strained to be free of the corpse, I caught sight of Mara. She was staring at me, intensely, and she was pale and her forehead was drenched in sweat. It must have been taking a lot out of her to heal me, and it was all coming atop days and days of fear and stress and lack of sleep and being captured and desperate—

The dead thug finally slid off me. I rose to my knees, stumbled to my feet. Violence was in full swing all through the warehouse: gunshots and flashes of light, thunderclaps, screams and screeches. I turned, rushed to Mara—and then I bent over double, air suddenly gone from my lungs.

"The fuck are you *doing?*" a mocking voice said. I looked up, all the pain in my body somehow concentrating in my solar plexus. The štrigun's fist was still tight, his grin demonic. He punched me and I fell to my knees.

I pushed myself up. Another punch, and this time I almost fell on my side.

Back again on my knees, I glanced at Mara. She was crying now, her eyes full of apology.

The healing pain had stopped, I realized. The cold fire had been almost doused, but there were all kinds of other pains still there.

She's spent.

"*Ma ubit ću te, pička ti materina,*" the štrigun said, angry and derisive. *I'll fucking kill you*—funny, just what I had been thinking. Behind him someone's magic hit another someone's invisible barrier and for a moment the štrigun's face was just white and black lines and surfaces.

I wished for a weapon of any kind, just to let the bastard remember me for the rest of his life.

My hands would have to do. I drew on all the strength I had left, ready to grab him, beat and tear and gouge at anything I can, before he kills me.

I felt it then, rising from deep inside me, reaching frantically for the surface, slamming into me.

283

It was like a dam bursting—wasn't that what Lena had told Katrina?

That is how it felt: a torrent breaking through a levee. I let it, then grabbed it and felt it give in, submit to me almost desperately. I enveloped it and was enveloped by it.

And I felt the change.

It was just a flicker. One moment I was on my knees, bleeding and bruised and beaten to within an inch of my life. The next I was on all fours, loping over concrete, snarling.

I had been wondering what it would feel like if it ever happened. And the word I'd never thought I'd use was the word that now fit all of it so perfectly: clarity. My mind was as clear as a mountain stream. Things in that warehouse were so, so simple. There were my friends and I. And there were the bad guys.

I pounced, slammed into the thug standing next to Mara, unsure what to do and where to go, and I tore his throat out while he was falling on his back. Blood filled my mouth as I landed atop him, and I thought I should be gagging, but I wasn't. I didn't break my stride as I rounded on the next nearest thug, grabbing his leg with my teeth, tripping him and dragging my claws across his back, ripping shirt, skin and flesh as if they were tissue paper.

I tore Mara's ropes with my teeth. She slumped forward, removed the gag from her mouth. She looked at me, amazed and thankful.

I turned around, searching with my gaze. There he was, far away. He'd run, I remembered. He'd run the moment the wolf came out.

The strigun was standing there, looking at me, fury burning in his eyes. Then he shrieked defiantly and leapt in a long, swinging arc. He landed just next to the open warehouse door and then he was out, disappearing into the night.

I gave chase, weaving through the chaos, jumping over corpses.

That night and that terrain and that forest would have been insurmountable obstacles to me as a human.

But to my wolf, the night wasn't uniform darkness; it was shades of lighter and darker black, outlining shapes. Patterns completely invisible to the human eye were as plain as day to me. The ground was rough, tall grass and thick shrub and rocks and stones everywhere—and I crossed over all that, jumping over some, simply breaking through others, the crack of sticks and branches the only sound of my pursuit.

Paul the man could never have kept pace with him. My prey was up in the trees, leaping from branch to branch, tree to tree.

The wind picked up, stirring the leaves and the grass around me—and high above he was crashing through canopy after canopy with the sound of a thousand explosions.

I could smell him. His stench was overpowering, retch-inducing: he was something rotting, but still alive.

He was moving up the forested slope, faster and faster, and I pursued, my body bursting with energy and rage, but most of all with the *desire* of the hunt. Muscles burned as I clawed up the steep ground, every rock and every root just another step leading me towards my prey.

I was gaining on him. I could hear him growl with every leap, grunt every time he crashed through branches, catching, grabbing. He was still ahead, but I was closing the distance.

And then I broke out of the tree line and onto a clearing, under the light of an almost full moon. It was colder here in the open and the wind was stronger.

And there he was, just a few steps ahead of me. Facing me.

Lights shone in the distance. There was another light, closer and to the left of me: a chapel.

I know where we are, a distant part of me said. Veli vrh. We were at a hilltop at the very edge of Rijeka. And the wind was stronger here because, just a few steps behind the štrigun, was the edge of a tall cliff. We were above the Rječina canyon and it was a *long* way down a sheer cliff face with rocks and trees at the bottom.

The wolf didn't care about any of that, apart from the single important thing: my prey had nowhere to go. The only way to escape was the way we'd come, or down a road to the right that he couldn't get to without passing close enough for me to sink my teeth into him.

He was trapped.

"Come on!" he shouted, taunting me.

He was ready for it. He *wanted* me to attack.

I obliged.

I was on him, clawing and trying to bite and he was punching and kicking and keeping my fangs from tearing out his throat.

We were rolling and snarling and he was strong and sinewy, muscles like steel cords. I felt grass and rocks under my back. The cold and the wind were even stronger now.

Careful.

I was in a murderous rage, but the edge of the cliff was just there. I would be just a broken mass of blood and bone at the bottom if I fell.

If he threw me off.

I pawed and found purchase and pushed, breaking the grapple, rolling away.

He jumped to his feet as I lay on the ground, waiting, ready. I could smell confusion on him. That had been his plan: take the bites and the torn flesh, protect his throat and face and get me close enough to the edge to push me or throw me to my death.

He was strong. I was strong.

He wanted me dead. I wanted him dead.

He was fast. I was too.

He was crazy.

I had to be crazier.

I charged. He readied himself, laughing gleefully.

I leapt.

Over him.

There was still maybe a meter or so of ground between his back and the cliff's edge. I was very new to this shape, this body.

I'd misjudged.

I landed at the very edge, slipped, slid.

My front paws clawed at the rocks and soil. My back paws scrambled against the cliff face. One paw found purchase, slight but enough. I pushed myself up and a front paw caught a piece of rock with its claws and I pulled and I was up, back on firm ground and the štrigun was turning and he would now charge and push—

—but I was already slamming into him.

He was on his back.

My teeth sank into his flesh.

I tore his guts out.

I retched as some of his entrails slid down my throat, swallowed by pure reflex.

He was screaming.

He was slashing at me with a pocket knife.

I caught his hand at the wrist, clamped down hard and tugged just as much as was needed. Bone cracked, blood flowed and the entire limb went limp.

I stepped back.

I threw up bile and pieces of my enemy's insides.

When I looked up, he was on his feet.

He shrieked at me, defiantly, his face distorted, his eyes insane.

I leapt, teeth catching his throat, tearing it out.

As my paws once again hit the ground, the štrigun was stumbling, his face turning towards me.

Under the moonlight I could see the light go out of his eyes.

He fell over the edge, limp and lifeless.

I ran to the edge. By the light of the almost full moon, I could make out his pale body tumbling down the cliff face like a discarded rag doll, hitting one outcropping and then another and another and finally vanishing among the trees and rocks far below.

I was alone.

I was alive.

I'd won.

The crack of a twig stopped me mid-howl. I rounded on the source of the sound.

287

It was Viki. Mara was next to her. She ran up to me, knelt in front of me.

"Paul, you can come back now."

Come back?

There was... there was something there, yes. The wolf was here, clear, but just behind him was... two hands, two feet, an upright body...

But this is good. The cold air, the call of the woods and the night. The power and the speed and...

No. I needed to go back.

The wolf retreated, reluctantly. The man stepped forward.

And then I was stark naked on the ground, shivering in the cold night.

So fucking cold.

I felt Mara's hand on my cheek. I looked up. I could make out most of her face in the moonlight.

Someone was crouching next to me.

"Paul, can you get up?" Viki asked.

"Yes," I said.

And then I did. I stumbled right after, but I stayed on my feet.

A GOODBYE

We were in my nona's apartment's hallway, just Mara and I.

I felt better. I was better. A full night's and half a day's sleep will do wonders for you. Well, after your vilenica friend has had enough rest and recuperation to magically, fully heal a štrigun's bite and remove all the other—the *many* other—pains.

We'd spent the time since Veli vrh mostly asleep or resting on our backs. I'd been the gentleman after all and given Mara the use of nona's double bed while I slept on the couch. Katrina had volunteered to stay with us because, after all we'd been through, we needed to be looked after—especially if my wound started festering or Mara needed help before recovering enough to heal herself.

Scars remained, though, both on my stomach and left arm. Apparently it's not the štrigun's bite itself that will kill you, as much as your body going magically gangrenous from it. Very similar—but not the same, as Mara had pointed out to me—to a revenant bite.

That fucker.

She'd offered to remove the scars. I've refused. They were my reminders that this was a dangerous life.

"You're sure you don't want to stay?" I asked.

Mara shook her head, but she was smiling. "You've helped me enough. And my teacher says it would be good for me to leave Croatia for a while. Some people may still be looking for me." Her eyes betrayed genuine concern when she added, flippantly, "I think you'll have enough trouble without me attracting more."

"Once again, I'm sorry about the bracelet."

She glanced at her wrist. There were no burn marks there, because she'd removed them. Apparently I'd botched the engraving masterfully, so not only did the bracelet stop working after just a few hits, but it also—well, the way Viki had explained was that it had basically shorted out and, in the process, seared Mara's wrist.

I had to take Mara's word for it because, when she'd showed me her hand, the skin had been as smooth as when I'd first tied the bracelet there, that evening in the rental house.

"So, Germany," I said.

"Yes," she said.

"Send me a postcard?"

"I will."

Her wristwatch beeped. "The bus is leaving in fifteen minutes," she said.

"Alright. You've got everything?

She glanced at the backpack she carried by the shoulder straps. My backpack. Her own had been retrieved by Katrina when she'd gone to the rental house to find out why the hell I wasn't answering my phone. But it was also ruined because Mara had kept it in the living room and one of the goons had bled all over it.

So I'd given her mine, because I obviously wasn't going anywhere soon, and besides, Rijeka had sporting goods stores, which meant all my backpack needs would be easily met.

"I have no idea what to say to someone in a situation like this," I said, chuckling.

"The ancient krsnik code doesn't have a chapter on this?"

"To be honest, I just skimmed it."

She sniffed, shaking her head. "I don't know what to say either."

"Vilenica Mara, take care of yourself."

"You too, krsnik Paul."

She leaned forward and kissed me on the cheek.

And then she left and I closed the apartment door.

Katrina stood in the kitchen doorway.

"Don't," I said in response to her raised eyebrow, the same one that I'd seen rising occasionally the past few days, mostly when Katrina thought I wasn't looking.

"I have no idea what you're talking about," she said, letting me pass into the kitchen.

"Ancient krsnik code?" she whispered at my back, with heaps of smirk in her voice. I ignored her.

It was almost noon. I was hungry. I wanted to eat, because then I wouldn't be thinking about... things.

"I just texted with Perdida." Katrina was serious now. "She searched the woods under Veli vrh again. Nothing."

"Maybe someone's removed his body?" I asked. There was no way that fucker was alive, that he had limped, crawled or even dragged himself away. No way.

"She just said she wants to talk to you later today about it."

I sighed inwardly, because I guessed I wouldn't like the conversation. "But he's dead. He has to be. I tore him open. I tore out his throat. He fell a hundred plus meters, straight onto rocks."

Katrina nodded. "She said that he's definitely dead. As to who might have taken the body..."

That tar woman...

Very few people had actually died that night in that old warehouse, in a usually very quiet and mostly abandoned part of Drenova, Rijeka's quarter right next to the hill atop which Veli vrh is situated.

For all the magic and shooting that went on when Katrina, Viki, and Perdida had come to my rescue, there had been scant few corpses to show for it, and the ones that had not been removed the same night by their still living comrades had ended up in Perdida's care.

As for how the girls had found me in the first place...

If there had been a ghost in that room listening to me, they hadn't gone and found Katrina.

The girls had found me using a tracking spell.

Yes, the štrigun had said that the collar-thing he'd put on me, the one that had burst apart when I transformed into a wolf—

—fuck me I could turn into a wolf—

—a big, dirty white one, Katrina had told me—

—that collar really did prevent tracking spells. *The standard* tracking spells, as Viki had pointed out to me yesterday when she'd come to the apartment so both Mara and I could get the full story of our rescue.

As Viki had explained, usually you'd use a piece of someone's hair or a fingernail—or a drop of their spit or some *other* bodily fluid—but the collar had been made by someone who knew their stuff and had crafted it to block that kind of connection.

But... if you had something more than just a single hair or a tiny fingernail... if you, for example, had a *large chunk of someone's flesh, a chunk big enough to fill a monster's maw* and all the blood that accompanied it, well then, then you could break through that block.

The štrigun had obviously been smart, but not too smart. Just smart enough to make a stupid mistake or two, courtesy of also being cocky and arrogant.

Sounds familiar.

Shut up.

"Katrina, what's with the rifle?" It had been on my mind the last day or so, once more pressing questions had been answered.

"Oh." She smiled sheepishly. "Lena's gift."

"But, I mean, Croatian laws, I mean, European laws in general..."

"It's not like I carry it around while shopping," she said. "Lena knew I liked westerns. And a few times we'd found ourselves in situations where it would've been handy to have a firearm. So she gave me one."

"A Winchester rifle," I said. I'd finally remembered what the weapon was called. It was a staple of westerns, I remembered that as well.

"Look, you want to give a girl who likes westerns something nice, you give her a Winchester repeater." Katrina shrugged. "That's gunslinger 101."

I nodded. "Well, in that case, *pardner...*"

She stuck her tongue out at me.

"So, what's next?" she asked then. "You've had your first case. Helped someone. Twice, actually," she added after a pause. "Mrs. Remac and then Mara."

And I've also heavily wounded two men and torn a third one to shreds.

They would have killed you if you hadn't. And he only looked human.

"Well... I have no idea," I replied honestly. "But it's... worked out so far. I guess."

She nodded slightly.

"Actually," I said, "there's the Vranja house. And that water in the basement."

And the house where that crazy asshole had kept me hostage.

And the asshole himself, while we're at it—I owe him a... pleasant chat.

"But in the meantime, I know exactly what's next for the two of us."

She smiled, reading it on my face before I said it.

"I think we both deserve a *burek*."

"That," Katrina said, "is the best thing I've heard today." She looked at me curiously then, tilting her head a little. "You have gray hairs. I didn't notice that until now."

"In my beard? Yeah, they've been popping up at random these last few years."

"No, in your hair," she said. "At your temples."

"Er... are you sure?"

She turned on her phone's camera to selfie mode and held the screen up to me like a mirror. And there they were.

"They aren't gray," I said, turning to catch better light from the window.

Just a couple of hairs, but definitely not that shade of dark gray I was used to discovering in my beard. These were also a little

coarser and a little thicker than the dark brown hairs that surrounded them. And they were dirty white.

Epilogue:

SOME LESSONS NEED REPEATING

He's asleep and again it's come for him.
Dark wings swallow the light.
It's at his window again.
It's perched on the windowsill.
He can't move.
He can't breathe.
It's reaching for him.
A single eye, terrifying, gleaming. That eye is all there is. That terrible eye.
And then the claws release him. It looks away.
Someone is out there. He can see him.
There's a man in the air, outside his window.
The monster is looking at the man now. That terrible eye is glowing with hatred.
"You just don't listen, do you?" the man says.
And then the man—incredible—insane—attacks the winged monster.

ACKNOWLEDGEMENTS

Well, there it is. You've just read my first published novel. Hope you liked it, and that you're not glancing at the acknowledgements to find out the entire roster of people to be blamed for wasting your time and money.

First off, all my thanks and huge props to my publishers and editors at Shtriga Books. Antonija and Vesna, without you this would be in a file somewhere on my drive, very likely unfinished. Here's to you both and the many successes you are sure to enjoy.

If you've been thinking, That's a sweet cover, it should be framed as a poster, you're not alone. Korina Hunjak knocked it out of the park and into outer space. One day, when she's as sought after as she deserves to be, I'll be able to say, Yes, well, she drew my covers before you heard of her.

Thanks also go to my beta readers. It's not easy to find good ones, so when you do, thank them, preferably with food and do your best to keep them interested in staying your beta readers. Irena, Tamara, Koviljka and Ivana, your input was invaluable. An extra thanks goes to Tamara for putting my words in the shape of the physical book you are reading.

And I also must thank several established authors. If I hadn't been—in my capacity as head of hospitality for Rijeka's Rikon SF convention—taking you guys on tours of my lovely town, I don't think I'd have ever written this. But after repeating several times that Rijeka means river in Croatian, the title "A Town Called River" appeared in my head and it was just too good to ignore. Also, your general delight with your stay in Rijeka was an inspiration as well. So, in chronological order my thanks go to: Thomas O. H., Emma and Peter N., Aliette D., and Gareth P.

A few words about the Spotify playlist

https://sptfy.com/ATCR

The idea was to create a sort of a musical soundscape of songs that are mentioned in the novel or that would serve as soundtrack if this were a film. The playlist is presented online without an explanation, but for all of you who finished the novel, here's a little behind the scenes extra.

Walking On Sunshine by Katrina and The Waves is, you guessed it, here because it's the song that gave Katrina her name both in ATCR's universe and my head as well.

Jutro donosi kraj by Vesna Pisarović is the song Paul wakes up to after a night out with Viki and Perdida. I needed a Croatian song and at the time that chapter was being written I'd been hearing that early 2000s hit a lot so I put it in.

Changes by the one and only David Bowie is what plays when Paul has his first interaction with Lena's record collection. I also mention that his nona was a fan of Zappa and Blue Oyster Cult, so I've chosen two songs that I decided she liked as examples of what she was into apart from David Bowie: *Astronomy* by BOC is simply an amazing song, and Zappa's *Joe's Garage* is here because Lena was a fan of concept albums, especially those dealing with dystopian futures.

The Good, The Bad and the Ugly is Katrina's ringtone. Ennio Morricone is a legend.

And now two songs that aren't actually mentioned in the novel but that I've had in my mind when writing particular scenes.

When Paul is recalling his night out with the witches, I imagined it as a montage set to Oh The Larceny's banger *Turn It Up*. They're not nearly as popular as I think they should be so go listen to more of their stuff if you liked this one.

And if you need a general idea what kind of music Viki plays when in her glitter witch asskicking mode, the last track of this playlist is a good approximation of the, heh, bangers she makes on the side. While I'm personally not a fan of dubstep, she is and you can't deny that when the beat drops in *Bangarang* (this particular version especially, I find that the female vocal elevates the original), you can imagine bodies being flung all over the place.

ABOUT THE AUTHOR

Igor is a lot of things. A writer, a translator, a voracious reader, a cinephile, a podcast addict, a puzzle aficionado, a hiker and a lover of all things geeky.

His fiction in Croatian won several genre awards, his translations include over a dozen novels and hundred plus short stories and novellas. His work as a copywriter has so far appeared in everything from tourist agency pamphlets and lifestyle webpages to fashion and financial magazines. He makes a pretty good pizza and can be found (semi-successfully) burning off the calories hiking one of many local hills.

You can check out Igor's Goodreads page or follow him on his Instagram (@irendic) and his website (igorrendic.com).

ABOUT SHTRIGA

Hidden Stories In Your Pocket.

Scifi, fantasy and horror on the go.
Publishing your daily dose of speculative fiction
since 2020.

Visit shtriga.com for more information.

Follow us @shtrigabooks
on Twitter, Instagram and Facebook.